About the Author

John Steinberg spent many years in business before becoming a writer in 2007. Since then, he has co-written and produced comedies for the stage and has created a series of books for children. *Blue Skies Over Berlin* is his second novel. He is married with three children and lives in North London.

By the same author

Shimon
Nadine

BLUE SKIES OVER BERLIN

John Steinberg

2QT Limited (Publishing)

This revised edition published 2019 by
2QT Limited (Publishing)
Settle, North Yorkshire BD24 9BZ _www.2qt.co.uk_
Copyright © 2019 John Steinberg
The right of John Steinberg to be identified as the author of this work has been
asserted by him in accordance with the Copyright, Designs
and Patents Act 1988.

Cover concept & illustration by Balcony Art & Design Studio

Printed in Great Britain by IngramSparks UK

All characters in this book other than those clearly in the public domain
are fictitious, and any resemblance to real persons, living or dead,
is purely coincidental.

A CIP catalogue record for this book is available
from the British Library
ISBN 978-1-913071-38-7 Paperback
ISBN 978-1-913071-40-0 eBook

To Ben Barrie,

a very special man whose guidance I shall always cherish.

A single act of kindness can transform darkness into light.

David Goldstein

1

London, 1956

On a cold, drizzly April morning, a young woman got out of a taxi at the exclusive Mirabelle restaurant on Curzon Street, where she was greeted by a man in a uniform and swiftly ushered into the noisy, smoke-filled establishment. Once inside, she immediately felt out of her depth, for she had not been in such opulent surroundings for a very long time - and certainly not since she came to live in London. Charlotte Brown had been looking forward to this lunch and in fact had spent a week's wages on her new, navy-blue belted dress. She had thought she looked smart, but as she saw other women wearing chic little hats, tight-fitting pencil skirts and dark red lipstick, she began to wish she had refused the invitation.

The head waiter gestured for one of his underlings to take Charlotte's coat and scarf then led the way through the full restaurant to a quiet corner table, where a stocky man in an olive-green sports jacket sat chatting to one of the waiters.

'Mr Morris, your guest has arrived,' the man announced, and then left to resume his position at centre stage of the establishment.

'Hello, my dear,' Bernard said, getting up from the table and extending a thick paw to her. 'I'm very glad to see you.'

Bernard Morris was in his mid-forties with a round, friendly face, and he was solidly built, like a boxer. His accent was rough cockney and, all in all, he was unlike anyone Charlotte had met before. She wasn't quite sure what to make of him. The waiter pulled out her chair and in a single movement expertly unfolded the linen napkin, placing it on Charlotte's lap.

'The Chablis is excellent,' Bernard confided. He signalled to the sommelier, hovering a few feet away, to take the bottle from the ice bucket and begin pouring the wine. 'And I'd recommend the smoked salmon, followed by the coronet chicken. Ain't that right, Alfonso?'

'As you wish, sir,' the waiter replied, bowing obsequiously.

'After all, it's not every day that we have a new Queen on the throne, is it?' Bernard added cheerily.

'That sounds delicious. Thank you.' Charlotte was hungry, and also aware that time was limited. She only had an hour for lunch.

'Anyway, good health,' Bernard said, raising his glass to her. 'I'm so pleased that you agreed to come. There's nothing like a nice lunch in the company of a young woman, especially one as pretty as Vivien Leigh, to make an old bloke like me feel a bit special,' he remarked with a glint in his eye. 'So, have you had a chance to consider my offer?'

'Mr Morris, I'm most—'

'Please, call me Bernard since we shall be working together. We can do away with all that formal rubbish.'

Charlotte had carefully prepared her reply to his offer,

made a week ago at his club in St James. She'd been working long hours, putting the finishing touches to an exhibition of Dutch Old Masters, and at first was far too busy to take much notice of the man who visited the gallery where she worked on several occasions, each time armed with a different list of well-informed questions. But then, during a lull in the activity, the man introduced himself, confiding in her his desire to open his own gallery specialising in modern art, and saying that he needed an expert to give him advice. Charlotte politely suggested that he seek out someone better qualified, possibly from one of the big auction houses. But she soon learned that Bernard Morris was not a man to take no for an answer.

'I was intending to say that your offer is most generous,' she told him now, 'but I don't have the experience required to run a gallery. I'm only an assistant curator, and my specialist modern knowledge is limited to the Pre-Raphaelite period. I am not sufficiently familiar with any other twentieth-century artists.'

Bernard smiled. 'So what about those two paintings of yours that you let me show to that friend of mine? I'm no expert, but they don't look like any of the stuff you spend all day staring at.'

'They are just what I do in my spare time,' Charlotte replied, blushing, still wondering why this man had been so insistent on seeing her work when he had delivered her back to her flat.

'Well, young lady, I have a surprise for you.' Bernard produced a cheque from the inside pocket of his sports jacket and passed it across the table.

'Fifty pounds!' Charlotte exclaimed, looking bemused. 'But what is it for?'

'I thought you'd be pleased. Those pictures were sold the day after they were hung up.'

Charlotte stared at the cheque. 'I don't know what to say.'

'You're obviously a better judge than you think. I'm offering you twenty quid a week to start straight away. The war's been over for more than ten years now, and people have had enough of being miserable. All you have to do is fill the place with colourful modern pieces, none of that old drab stuff. Once the punters get a taste for it, there'll be no holding 'em back.'

To her surprise, Charlotte found herself reconsidering her earlier decision to decline his offer. She wasn't enjoying her current job, and this man had presented her with an opportunity as unexpected as it was exciting. It could be wonderful, she thought to herself. Should she take a chance and go for it?

'I'll have to give in my notice,' she said, finishing the last morsels of chicken on her plate with a sigh of pleasure. 'I don't know whether they will give me a reference, Mr M— Bernard. I have only been there three years.'

'I don't need a reference,' Bernard snorted. 'I go by my gut instinct, and it tells me that you have an eye for what people want.'

'Where is this gallery?' Charlotte wanted to know. 'Which part of London?'

'Mayfair. Where else?' Bernard shrugged.

'That's expensive for a new venture.'

He smiled. 'I'll look after the business side. We won't have to worry about the landlord trying it on.'

Charlotte looked confused. 'I don't understand.'

'A pal of mine who owns the gaff told me that the people

4

who rented the shop from him have just gone *mechuleh*,' and at her look of incomprehension, 'their business went bust. And since he's lost his tenant and wants to get rid of the place for good, I reckon I can pick it up for a song before it goes to auction. The building is Georgian, and it's in remarkably good nick considering what the Jerries threw at us.'

Charlotte sat pensively while the waiter cleared away the plates, wondering whether she had been too hasty in accepting employment from someone she barely knew. And yet she found herself strangely drawn to Bernard's warmth, sensing that here was a kind man.

She looked down just as the waiter was pouring hot chocolate sauce onto a pyramid of choux pastry balls on a dish in front of her.

'You've got to taste these profiteroles. I'm telling you, they're the best in London.' Bernard had scooped up two large spoonfuls even before his guest had picked up her spoon. 'Just as well the government put an end to those bloody food coupons,' he mumbled, licking his lips.

The taste of chocolate, pastry and cream combined made his lunch companion almost swoon with delight.

'So, are we on?' he asked, wiping his mouth.

'Mr M— I mean Bernard, I would very much like to accept.'

'Good, so that's settled. I'll start you off at twenty-five quid a week.'

'But you just said twenty pounds!'

'Did I? I must have forgotten. It's what happens when you get to my age,' he grinned.

Charlotte felt embarrassed at the amount he was offering. 'Isn't it too much?' she said.

'Look at it as an investment in the future.' Bernard lifted his arm, trying to attract the waiter's attention. 'Alfonso! Bring me the bill, will you, son? This young lady and I have to get back to work.'

'Yes, Mr Morris, straight away,' the man responded.

Bernard held up his glass. 'To success! *L'chaim*,' he toasted, clinking glasses with Charlotte, who was already feeling tipsy, and as she took a small sip of what remained of her Chablis, she wondered where she had heard that word before. She thought it would be rude to ask.

'Now, my dear, William should be waiting,' her host announced, finishing the last of his drink. 'He will have you back at work by two, so no one will get the hump with you for being late.'

Together, they proceeded to the front of the restaurant where the cloakroom attendant was already holding their coats open for them. The doorman gently pushed the revolving doors for Charlotte. Bernard followed behind after placing two five-pound notes in the head waiter's hand.

Catching sight of his boss, the chauffeur dropped his *Daily Mirror*, leaped out and opened the rear passenger door.

'I shan't be coming,' his boss said. 'I need to walk off my lunch.' And off he went.

Settling back in her seat, Charlotte started to panic. Mr Morris hadn't mentioned when he needed her to start. Nor did she have the address. How could she give in her notice, when she hadn't even received a firm proposal? Then just as the car was about to draw away, Bernard gestured to Charlotte to wind down her window.

'It'll take another couple of weeks to finish doing up

the place. Can't have you moving into *dreck*, so why don't we say we'll meet up three weeks today? I'll get William to pick you up at your place. Midday all right? Look after yourself!' He grinned and walked off.

As the Rolls glided away from the kerb, Charlotte let out a sigh of relief. She had worried for nothing. She rummaged around in her handbag, trying to find her packet of du Maurier cigarettes. The chauffeur, watching her in his rear mirror, pushed in the cigarette lighter and then passed it to her over his shoulder.

'Thank you.' Charlotte lit up and inhaled deeply. Ignoring the slight wheeze in her chest, she decided she would hand in her notice that same afternoon.

2

A week later, Charlotte left her flat in West Hampstead and headed towards the underground station, a small leather suitcase in one hand. She had lived in this area of north London for four years now, moving here shortly after she arrived from Zurich in 1952. Her obvious expertise, coupled with excellent references from her professor at Basel University, were enough to impress the staff at the National Gallery, and she was taken on as an assistant curator at ten pounds a week. The employment enabled her to move out of a grimy hotel near Euston station and into the pleasant rented flat here in Hampstead that she had made into a home.

Now she was facing a new challenge, working for Bernard Morris, and wasn't at all sure she was qualified to make a success of it. While she related easily to painters like Picasso, Seurat and Matisse, more recent works by the likes of Jackson Pollock and Mark Rothko left her cold – but this was the kind of art Bernard wanted in his gallery. She would do her best, Charlotte decided as the *Night Ferry*, the boat-train, set off from Victoria station; if she failed, it would not be from lack of effort.

The job was due to begin in two weeks. In the meantime, Charlotte was bound for Paris, and then on to the Swiss mountains. She was drained from the long winter and equally long hours spent working at the National Gallery.

Her asthma had got worse and she badly needed a break. However, this trip wasn't just a holiday. The letter from the bank in Zurich had arrived at her flat a week ago. There had been a major change in her family's financial affairs, it stated, so would she please attend their offices as soon as possible? Charlotte telephoned them and made an appointment immediately. She was convinced that the bank was chasing her for money, and as her train rolled through northern France, this did nothing to help her feel better.

At the Gare du Nord, Charlotte changed on to the Orient Express to Budapest, stopping at Zurich. At this point in the journey, her mind turned to Johann. She hadn't seen her first and only lover in almost two years and wondered whether his feelings for her were still the same. She had written to tell him that she was coming, and hoped that he would be able to free himself from his wife and family so they could spend time alone again together.

They first met in 1940 in Berlin, when the girl was just fourteen. Her father was a decorated officer in the Luftwaffe and Johann a handsome, newly qualified doctor who had been conscripted to serve in the medical corps, the Sanitatdienst. The two men quickly became friends despite the difference in their ages, having established that both came from aristocratic families in southern Germany, although unlike her father's family, Johann's people had lost their fortune in the Depression of 1929.

With war raging in Europe and the wider world, the lonely fourteen-year-old escaped from the violence into her passion for art. The disruption of millions of lives to her seemed as surreal as some of her own paintings. And the longer the dread dark war years lasted, the further she retreated into a world of glorious landscapes and sunshine.

She couldn't hide from reality for ever. She was nineteen when hostilities finally ended, a young woman faced with a broken and disgraced homeland and the painful realisation that she was on her own. Her father, to whom she was always devoted, had died after being injured in the war, while her mother had suffered a breakdown and was committed to a mental institution soon after being notified that her beloved son Hans – the girl's only sibling – had been killed on the Russian front.

Berlin was thus a miserable place for her, and the young woman decided to take herself away from the city and the traumatic memories it held. By a lucky chance, her mother had been born in Switzerland, which entitled the girl to change her nationality to Swiss. To complete the reinvention of herself, she changed her name at the same time. Eva Schlessinger, the girl born under the blue skies of Berlin, became Miss Charlotte Brown. And then she left Berlin for good.

Unlike Charlotte's father, Johann survived the war unscathed and moved to Switzerland to resume his career in psychiatry. He and Charlotte had, however, established a bond and for a while remained in close contact. She remembered how disappointed she had felt when he wrote that he was getting married. She had hoped that she might one day become his wife.

Their affair started soon after she arrived at the University of Basel, where she had come to study for a History of Arts degree. Even though she was over a hundred miles away, Johann would send for her each time his wife left to visit her parents in Geneva. He would install her in his private apartment on the top floor of the sanatorium, where he had been appointed as director. Here, Johann introduced her to sex. Charlotte was attractive but she was also tall and had a slightly boyish figure and as a result had been plagued by self-consciousness through her adolescence. But thanks to Johann this was replaced by an appreciation of her own body. For the first time, she began to experience pleasures that she had always felt were reserved for everyone else.

When difficulties started to surface within his marriage, Johann suggested that Charlotte should further her career in London. His father-in-law owned the sanatorium where he worked, and he knew that one day it could be his; this was the reason why he was prepared to marry the man's only daughter. Albeit deeply in love with Johann, Charlotte was realistic: she knew that he would never leave his wife and endanger or abandon his future prospects. And so reluctantly, she accepted her destiny.

As Charlotte Brown, a Swiss citizen, she was able to travel to Britain as a completely new person, her German past concealed from one and all.

The train arrived at Zurich just after midnight. Charlotte booked herself into the Hotel Schweizerhof opposite the station and was shown to a large room with a view over the city. Although she had managed to sleep most of the way, she needed a hot bath and was looking forward to a comfortable bed and fresh clean sheets.

The next day, after breakfast in her room, she put on her new beige suit and left the hotel. It was a glorious May morning so she took the opportunity to walk to the private bank in Bahnhofstrasse, ten minutes away. Fritz –

or Uncle Fritz as he was always known to her – had been her father's personal banker for thirty years. She thought that the two men had probably been the same age. 'Fritz knows what has to be done,' she remembered her father saying in the more lucid moments of his final days. He was always so secretive about his affairs. She knew he just wanted to help and protect her, and he was right: she didn't have much aptitude for financial matters. It might have been different if he'd had a son to leave to run things, but Hans was dead now.

Charlotte took a deep breath and rang the bell outside the bank's inconspicuous stone building. She was let in by a doorman, who led her through the entrance hall to the receptionist.

'Good morning, my name is Charlotte Brown and I have an appointment with Herr Grossman at ten,' Charlotte announced in a perfect Swiss accent to the well-groomed young woman.

'The director is expecting you.'

Charlotte was escorted up the stairs to the first floor. She hoped there would still be enough money left in the account to pay for her holiday and to tide her over until the start of her new job. Taking the paperwork out of her handbag with the details of the numbered account that had been opened for her by her father, she was shown into a simple room containing a heavy oak table with six high-backed dining chairs. Underneath the window, which looked out onto a well at the back of a neighbouring building, was a sideboard on which sat a telephone and a plain wooden tray with a jug of water and two glasses.

After a few moments, a small silver-haired man appeared, carrying a black leather document holder.

'Eva, my dear! Or should I say Charlotte? It must be at least five years since we last met,' the banker said, shaking her hand. He took a seat opposite her and placed his folder down in front of him. 'How is life in London these days?'

'I think I have adjusted quite well,' Charlotte replied. 'The work is interesting. I have had a good position at the National Gallery.'

'So, as they say in England, you have fallen on your feet.'

The young woman smiled weakly, apprehensive about what was coming next.

'Let me come straight to the point,' Herr Grossman continued. 'Your father entrusted our bank with his family affairs and made me the executor of his estate. I should inform you that there have been some recent developments in this regard. By the terms of his last will and testament, he left everything to your mother with the provision that she was of sound mind, and thereafter to you, once you reached thirty years of age. I was notified three weeks ago that your mother's condition has deteriorated. I immediately had her independently assessed, which confirmed the diagnosis.'

He handed Charlotte a copy of the medical report.

Charlotte pretended to read it. She had always found the prospect of visiting her mother in the psychiatric hospital too traumatic. She wanted to remember her as the glamorous woman whose beauty turned the heads of men and women alike, and for whose approval she still yearned.

'Now you have reached your thirtieth birthday,' the banker explained, 'I have to complete my obligations as executor and transfer the remainder of the estate into your name.'

'You mean that there's nothing for me to pay?' Charlotte asked, starting to believe that she had worried unnecessarily.

'On the contrary,' Herr Grossman replied smoothly. 'The sum that has been settled on you amounts to a little under five million Swiss francs.'

'Herr Grossman, I should only like to draw three thousand francs from my own account,' Charlotte announced, completely oblivious to the full meaning of the banker's words. Her train to Davos was due to leave at midday and she still had to pack and pay her bill at the hotel.

With no change of expression, the manager picked up his pen and started to fill in a withdrawal application. He then passed it across to Charlotte for her signature.

'Please excuse me for a few moments while I go and draw your funds,' he said politely, then took the slip of paper, got up from the table and left the room.

Ten minutes later, Herr Grossman returned.

'This is the receipt for the three thousand francs.' He passed it to Charlotte for her to sign and then she was handed a stiff envelope containing the currency.

'That will still leave a balance of a little under four million nine hundred and ninety-five thousand Swiss francs,' the banker calculated on his notepad. 'What is your instruction for the balance, may I ask?'

'I have no other immediate requirements,' Charlotte answered, shrugging her shoulders. She didn't give any thought as to what to do with such a vast sum of money. Uncle Fritz would take care of everything.

'Then be assured, my dear Fraulein, that we shall continue to look after your interests,' Herr Grossman responded tactfully.

Charlotte got up from her seat and followed the banker out of the small office. He accompanied her down the stairs to the entrance.

'Remember, do contact me whenever you should need us again,' he said, reaching for Charlotte's hand and shaking it. He then bowed, turned around and went back to his office.

With a great sense of relief, Charlotte arrived back at the hotel as the clock-tower struck a quarter past eleven. She went up to her room, gathered her things and called for the bellboy to carry her case downstairs. She paid for her night's stay in cash and walked the short distance to the railway station, her heart light and a smile on her face.

3

It had rained all morning and puddles had formed in small craters on the uneven roads. The East End of London still carried the scars of the Blitz, which had left wide areas devastated and local communities bereft of so many of their loved ones.

Dressed in a long gabardine raincoat and matching beige fedora, Bernard nimbly sidestepped the puddles as he turned into the narrow street that was already bustling with people. He grinned at the haggling – punters pitting their wits against the stallholders, trying to get the best bargains. Comments like, 'You've already taken out my *kishkes*. What more do you want!' Or, 'Where else can you find such quality?' echoed around Petticoat Lane in a variety of accents. From rolls of multi-coloured materials, shirts and boots and trousers in all sizes, and metal pots and pans, to leather trunks and nylon stockings, as well as new or second-hand pieces of furniture, there was nothing that couldn't be found in Petticoat Lane, known to one and all as 'the Lane'. Bernard knew the place like the back of his hand. The smell of fresh bread, warm from the oven, wafted through the air and made his mouth water. It was three weeks since he'd been back and he'd missed it.

'Morning, Berel. Bit early for you, ain't it?' the short man with a kind face called out from the doorway of his shop. He was brandishing a long knife with thin strands of smoked salmon still clinging to its sides. Sam Marks was the second-generation owner of Marks, the most famous Jewish deli in the whole of the East End.

'How are you, Sam?' Bernard replied, going up to shake the man's greasy hand. Entering the small establishment, he suddenly felt ravenous as the aroma from the food counter filled his nostrils.

'My leg's playing up again, Esther's not as young as she was and we never get to see the grandchildren. Other than that, I mustn't grumble,' Sam said good-humouredly. He placed a heap of smoked salmon expertly between two slices of fresh rye bread and passed the sandwich over to his childhood friend.

'Still got that Roller?' he added. 'What my missus wouldn't do for a ride in that. Still, you worked hard enough for it.'

'Yeah, still got it. How's your Harry?' Harry was Sam's older brother.

'Still complaining that he's got stuck with most of that Army clobber you lumbered him with,' Sam chuckled.

Bernard bit a huge chunk out of the sandwich as he thought about the fortune he'd made from Army surplus after the war. All the factories in the area had closed down and he'd purchased the stock from the receivers for a few pence in the pound. To start with, he recalled that Harry and his mates couldn't get enough of the gear - but it was the character of the Lane to always have something to *kvetch* about.

'Help yourself to cucumbers, they're fresh in this morning,' Sam said, pointing to three large barrels filled with brine by the side of the counter. 'I'll do your mum's now. You don't have to tell me - I'll make sure it's nice and tender; her teeth been playing her up again, have they?'

Bernard gave a nod, his mouth full of food. He had grown up in the next street to Sam. He knew everyone and everyone knew him - Berel, eldest son of Annie and Lazar Moscovitch. For the first thirty years of his life, this was the only world he had known.

Bernard had left the Jews' Free School at fifteen. Unlike his two brothers, who'd followed their father into the family tailoring business, he got a job in a local estate agent. With the influx of Russian and Polish Jews into the East End that had started in the 1890s, there was a constant demand for housing to accommodate their large families - and they were prepared to pay considerable amounts of key money to get in. He recalled several occasions where more than one family were fighting over a couple of small rooms in his own buildings just so they could be next to their kinsmen. This taught him a lesson that those with wealth got what they wanted. And Bernard was determined always to have money in his pocket.

When his father suddenly just dropped down dead, exhausted from years of eighteen-hour days of hard labour, Bernard being the eldest son had to take over as the family's main provider. He began travelling all over the country buying small job lots of goods that he knew could be sold in the Lane. By putting down no more than a deposit, this well-dressed young man - he borrowed the suit from a friend - persuaded the factories that he was good for the credit. Most of them took a chance and trusted him to pay them back. He didn't let them down, and it wasn't long before he established a reputation for himself.

Bernard made up his mind that as soon as he had

enough money, he would move away from the squalor that thousands of others had accepted as the best that life could offer them.

Then the war came. Like all of his friends, he was in a hurry to join up and fight for his country. But the recruitment centre in Whitehall had different ideas. Bernard was too old for the first group of conscripts. He was unceremoniously dismissed by a bad-tempered sergeant with a loud voice and a bushy moustache, who told him to go back home and wait to be notified. He eventually received his papers a year later, but his fighting ambitions were put paid to once again - this time by the Medical Examiner discovering that the willing conscript had a heart murmur.

Bernard quickly overcame his disappointment and spent the following few years building up his business. He soon generated so much money that he was able to afford a place of his own. First, was a modest home in Euston Square for which he paid a thousand pounds, and then a few years later, intent on becoming part of the 'rich set', he changed his name from Berel Moscovitch to Bernard Morris and moved to a white stucco Georgian house in Mayfair. At forty, he was well on the way to his first million.

'How much do I owe you?' Bernard asked.

'Eightpence for the two sandwiches and I'll throw in the cucumbers,' the proprietor replied.

Bernard rattled a few coins in his pocket, producing a florin, which he put in Sam's hand. 'Keep the change. Go and buy Esther something. It might help cheer her up,' he said, taking his mother's lunch.

'See you next Sunday?' Sam asked.

'Nah, I got a site meeting in the West End with my

architect,' Bernard replied, chewing the last mouthful of his sandwich. The prospect of a freehold building in Mayfair was too good an opportunity to turn down. The gallery on the ground floor with his name on it would be a bonus, giving him the respectability that he craved.

'And I thought it was a young lady,' the man behind the counter winked. 'Send my regards to Mrs Moss!' he called out, but his friend had already stepped out of the shop.

Bernard adroitly negotiated his way through the crowds, acknowledging several familiar faces. He knew from experience that the serious punters never showed till later in the afternoon, when they could smell a bargain. It felt good to be back. For a moment, he missed the buzz of dealing at the sharp end, his pockets weighed down by the day's takings. But he had moved on to bigger and better things.

Turning right down Wentworth Street, he quickened his pace past the bomb-site opposite but it was no good. He could still see the pert, innocent little face and hear the sound of her voice.

Miriam Taffler was the prettiest and most sought-after girl in the neighbourhood - and was his girl, despite being a good ten years younger than him. After a brief courtship consisting of Sunday afternoons in the back row of the Empire Cinema with a box of Black Magic chocolates, they became engaged.

Then one cold winter evening in 1940, the sirens were heard and the whole street rushed out of their beds to take shelter on the platform at Aldgate East tube station. Miriam stayed behind, however, first making sure that her three younger sisters got out of their fourth-floor flat safely. She was too late. The Buildings where she lived suffered a direct hit. In one brief instant, a whole family were wiped out.

Of course, there had been plenty of other women since then, but no relationship had lasted more than a couple of weeks. The truth was, the night Miriam died, a part of Bernard died with her.

Two hundred yards further down the road, he stopped and looked up at the plaque on the Peabody Buildings where he was born. He passed through a narrow arch that led to a series of five-storey dwellings and began climbing the stairs to the second floor.

Nothing had changed, not the smell of bleach from the communal wash-room nor the intrusive aromas of cooking from the poorly ventilated flats that had at one time been home to more than 200 mainly Jewish families. However had the seven of them managed to survive such squalid conditions! he thought to himself. And there used to be eight, except his eldest sister Malka had never recovered from the cholera that had consumed the area in an epidemic, soon after war broke out.

Bernard knocked on the outside of the shabby front door.

'Who is it?' a peevish voice called out.

'Mother - it's me, Berel,' her son answered.

There was the sound of a key turning in the lock. A few seconds later, a stooped old woman wearing a threadbare green house-coat and woollen slippers appeared through the partially open door.

'You're late!' she said harshly. 'You're always here at a quarter to and it's twelve o'clock already! You had something more important perhaps?'

'*Mame*, you're not getting dressed today?' Bernard

asked, making his way into the two-room flat. He went over to the tiny kitchen area and filled the kettle at the sink, then took out a match and lit the stove.

'I brought your lunch,' he said, wheeling a small gold trolley over to where his mother was sitting.

'About time,' the old woman snapped. She sat back in her tatty fireside chair and reached for her packet of cigarettes.

'How many have you had today?' asked her son.

'It's only my second,' the old lady lied, starting to cough. 'Anyway, what's it got to do with you? I don't ask you about your business.' There was a short pause as Annie Moscovitch inhaled deeply.

Then: 'I see you've got another new coat,' she commented, a look of disapproval on her face. 'Must have cost plenty. Well, that's your affair, good luck to you.' She coughed again, clasping her chest with a badly arthritic hand. 'I don't even know where you live - my own son,' she wheezed. 'It's a disgrace! None of the others come. I could be dead, as if they should care.'

'*Mame*, we've been through this a hundred times before. I live in town, up West.'

'And I'm supposed to know where that is? You've never offered to take me there.' The old woman looked hurt. 'It's not right that I have to depend on neighbours to take me to the washhouse and get my shopping.'

'I've offered to buy you your own place,' Bernard said wearily. 'There are some smashing new flats in town that are being done up.'

'It's the daughters' job to look after their mother,' Annie complained, ignoring her son's proposal.

'It's only because you always upset them. Anyway, Rose

22

has got her own family and a sick husband to look after.'

'That lazy bastard, never done a proper day's work in his life! I told her not to marry him. It was only because he put her in the family way. A beautiful girl, she could have had her pick of the whole of London.'

'*Mame*, if I remember, weren't you always drumming into her how plain she was and should be grateful for the first man that showed any interest?'

'And her sister? I suppose *she* also has an excuse?' Mrs Moscovitch snarled.

'Millie would come but she daren't go against Phil. He's always out on his tally rounds. He's even taken Joe on. More often than not he makes her go with him. He doesn't want to take the chance of leaving her at home on her own.'

'What, he thinks a prince is going to sweep her off her feet? Don't make me laugh. And that other no-good, he's still running around with that *shikse*?'

'Lenny's Lenny, what can you do?' Bernard shrugged, reflecting on his youngest brother.

'Thinks he's too good for the rest of us, with his Robert Taylor looks. Couldn't keep it in his trousers for five minutes, the bastard!' The old lady cackled and began coughing again. 'All no bloody good, the whole lot of you,' she sighed, put her head back in the chair and shut her eyes.

The church bell at Whitechapel struck one. He still had half an hour until William brought the car round. Bernard took off his coat, poured himself a cup of tea and sat down next to his mother, who was sleeping peacefully.

*

23

'Where to, guv?' the chauffeur asked.

'A hundred and ten Whitechapel High Street. I've got to see a bloke about some paintings,' Bernard replied, and took a stack of postcards from the inside pocket of his coat.

The Rolls made its way slowly down the narrow street, avoiding the noisy crowds of people laden with their purchases from the market. Ten minutes later, they stopped outside a grim Victorian building that had fallen into disrepair. Bernard got out of the car and rang Max Freedland's bell. A scruffy unshaven man peered out through a small aperture just below the roof.

'Fourth floor, second door on the left!' a gruff voice shouted. There was the sound of a window being slammed shut.

Bernard stepped through a broken door that had been left hanging off its hinges and carefully made his way up the stairs of the old building. Max and he had been in the same class at school, but Max had never had any ambitions other than to become an artist. Apart from just about getting by as freelance cartoonist for two of the morning newspapers, he was also a highly accomplished oil painter and was able to supplement his income from the sale of copies of famous works: these were frequently on display in the market. They were so good that only a forensic expert could detect that they weren't the originals.

Bernard was convinced that Max was a genius. But like many other gifted people, Max had a self-destructive streak, not helped by a serious injury he had suffered at Dunkirk and which had left him with half a leg and a tin prosthesis.

Bernard knocked on the door, and Max appeared at the entrance, dressed only in pyjama bottoms and a stained vest.

'Berel! So, what brings you back here? Come in and take your coat off. I'll put the kettle on unless you don't plan on staying.'

Bernard followed the man into the dingy abode where damp patches had penetrated the walls. The smell of gas pervaded the place. Entering into the living room, he saw reams of paper with half-finished drawings and artists' pens strewn all over the floor. In one corner was a rickety easel held together by string. On it sat a large canvas depicting a group of semi-clad dark-skinned women plaiting each other's hair amidst an exotic greenery of tropical ferns.

'Very nice,' Bernard remarked. He moved up to take a closer look at the painting. 'Who's it by?'

'Nah! It's one of me own,' the artist replied, not showing much enthusiasm. 'Anyway, son, you didn't come here to talk about my work. What you got in mind?'

'I've got a job for you, but I need it in a hurry.' Bernard took out the postcards and handed them to his friend.

'Big demand for Impressionists these days,' Max commented, taking his time looking through the illustrations. 'Christ knows why. Can't compare them to the real masters.' He singled out two of the cards and announced, 'You can have these by the end of next week.'

'That'll do. How much?' Bernard asked.

'Including canvases and paints, call it thirty quid for the pair.'

'Done! Oh, and by the way, throw in your nudes over there and a few more besides, and there's an extra ton in it for you,' Bernard said.

'How many do you want?' Max asked.

'How many have you got?' came the reply.

'Hold your horses.' The artist scurried awkwardly over to a tall cupboard in the corner of the room. It was jammed full of paintings. He methodically took out each one and held it up to gauge his customer's reaction.

After the first few, Bernard lost interest.

'And they're all yours?' he asked.

'Yes, all done by my own fair hand. There's a few that I forgot to sign though,' Max said casually.

'Hmm, well, they'll have to have a name on,' Bernard told him. 'No one will touch 'em otherwise.'

'Say they're by Daniel Petrovitch. That's a good Russian name,' the artist suggested.

'Wait a minute!' Bernard exclaimed. 'That was Danny Peters from the Buildings and he's dead.'

'So there's no proof that he didn't do them, is there?' Max said, grinning.

'You've got a point. Say I'm prepared to take the lot?'

'What are you going to do - open a bleedin' gallery?' the painter joked.

'Something like that,' Bernard muttered under his breath.

'Two hundred and fifty and they're all yours.'

'You're on.' Here was something to be getting on with. Bernard peeled off a wad of five-pound notes. 'My chap will pay you the balance when he picks the stuff up,' he told Max. 'Though with this lot, he'll probably have to make two visits.'

Convinced that he'd just done a cracking deal, Bernard left his friend's flat, calling back, 'Look after yourself, Max. Don't worry, I'll let myself out.'

As he began making his way down the four flights of uneven stairs, he was grateful he'd been able to escape the awful dump and would soon be returning to the considerable comforts of his own home in Park Street, near Mayfair's Grosvenor Square.

4

The train pulled into Davos Platz station on time, at precisely one minute before six in the evening. Apart from a very old man who slept for the entire journey with a blanket pulled up tight under his chin and a young cadet in smart blue uniform who sat concentrating on his army manual, Charlotte had the second-class compartment to herself. As they drew slowly into the station, she opened the window a little and could feel the pureness of the cool mountain air against her face. The train came to an abrupt halt, jostling the old man out of his stupor and sending the young flaxen-haired recruit opposite into a fit of giggles. Charlotte hid a smile then yawned and straightened her back. She had become stiff from sitting too long in one position.

She had got up to remove her suitcase from the luggage hold when the young cadet intercepted her.

'Please, Fraulein, permit me to help you,' he said in a distinctive Swiss-Deutsch accent.

Charlotte gazed at the young recruit, who stood a good head above her, and immediately saw her brother Hans. This youth had the same athletic build and strong jawline, and the same piercing blue eyes. The similarity was uncanny. She tried to put the image out of her mind. She didn't want to think about the past.

'Thank you,' she replied quietly.

The young cadet, slinging his army satchel across his shoulder, picked up the suitcase and then with his other hand opened the door onto the platform. Trying to keep up with him as he strode ahead, Charlotte presented her ticket, which was stamped by the guard on duty. She then hurried through the arrivals barrier, whereupon the recruit put down her case at the station exit.

'I wish you a pleasant stay in Davos,' were his parting words. He saluted, turned on his heel and marched briskly off towards the town.

Charlotte hailed one of the open horse-drawn carriages that were waiting in line outside the terminal and instructed the driver to take her to the Blauerberg Sanatorium. The sun had disappeared behind the snow-capped mountaintops, creating an immediate chill. She pulled the thick fur rug up to her waist and sat back on the padded leather seat. A soft crack of the whip and they were off, beginning their ascent up the mountain on a winding road that took them through a series of thick pine forests. Charlotte's heart was beating fast in the expectation of seeing Johann again. His tersely worded telegram, devoid of any warmth or affection, and simply confirming her two weeks of treatment had been the sole contact between them.

Before she had left to live in England, he had assured her that he still cared for her and that they would eventually be together. They were reunited briefly for ten wonderful days when his wife was taken into hospital for an appendix operation, but that was ages ago. Even then, Charlotte found it strange that Johann hadn't found the same need to be equally discreet while she was at the university in Basel.

She had had plenty of opportunities to meet other men in London; introductions through a few girls at work to make up a foursome for an evening, for instance, but nothing came of them. In the coffee bars that had sprung up all around Central London, she was always more interested in the paintings that decorated the walls than in jiving to live rock 'n' roll bands with friends from the gallery or listening to the jukebox playing hits like Elvis Presley's 'Heartbreak Hotel'.

Now, as the carriage rattled over the mountain road, she was forced to admit the truth to herself. Things could never be the same. Johann was married with a family. What right did she have to expect that they could just pick up where they had left off, as if they had never been apart? But if that was the case, why hadn't he told her not to come?

Charlotte began to see that coming to Davos was a huge mistake. Her chest felt tight with tension; her breathing became laboured. She tried to calm herself by deciding that, even if it was over between them, the fact remained that she badly needed the rest. An exciting new challenge lay before her, working for Bernard Morris. He had given her the unique opportunity of running her own gallery in one of the most prestigious streets in London. Instead of an ill-fated love affair, she would concentrate on her career, she vowed.

Night fell. An hour passed before the carriage drew up at the entrance of the sanatorium. The driver negotiated his buggy expertly between two tall, eagle-mounted pillars, bearing left on a gravel driveway that took them around to the front of the main house. Spotlights were strategically placed at equal distances along the edge of a green verge, revealing a large four-storey building of smooth grey stone, with olive-green shutters that gave it the appearance of an elegant country house. Humming to himself, the driver jumped down from his cab, opened the door of the carriage to help Charlotte alight, then collected her case from the rack at the rear of the buggy.

The arrival of a visitor stirred the attention of an elderly retainer who, disturbed from his nap and attempting to button his open uniform, shuffled over to the carriage to pick up the solitary piece of luggage. Charlotte opened her handbag and paid the driver, then entered through the arched front door. Although she had been here many times before, she was struck anew by the stark interior with its institutional lighting and plain painted walls, as if it were merely a façade to cover up a grander past. Worse, her eyes started smarting from the odour of disinfectant that pervaded the place. She walked slowly across the shiny linoleum floor, whereupon the face of a bespectacled man suddenly peered at her through the two glass sliding doors of the reception desk.

'Fraulein Brown, you were expected at seven. There is some reason perhaps that your journey took longer than anticipated?' was his only greeting. Without waiting for a response, he commenced writing in the register. 'It appears that we have your medical records from two years ago, dated August 1954. I assume that you have brought the latest reports with you?' he asked without looking up.

Charlotte opened her suitcase and took out a large brown envelope containing a copy of her chest X-rays and a letter from her doctor. She passed them through the opening to the supercilious administrator.

'Your stay will be for two weeks,' the man informed her,

squinting over a second open journal on his desk. 'The cost of your accommodation and treatments will be forty-five francs per day, and we should appreciate settlement at the end of each week.'

Charlotte, already aware of the procedure, just nodded politely.

He picked up the telephone, uttered a few words in German and replaced the receiver.

'A nurse will show you to your room and the doctor on duty will assess you in exactly thirty minutes.'

Again, without waiting for any acknowledgement, he closed the sliding glass doors and returned to his clerical work.

After a few moments, Charlotte saw a shapely young blonde-haired woman in a tight-fitting nurse's uniform moving confidently towards her.

'Fraulein Brown, I am Nurse Weiss. If you would please follow me,' she requested. She began leading Charlotte in the direction of the main staircase. They made their way up past the first floor, which housed a large dining room and kitchen, together with two smaller, comfortably decorated recreation rooms for the guests' quiet enjoyment.

Meals, she recalled, were taken promptly three times a day. Breakfast commenced at six thirty, lunch was at midday and dinner was served at seven. Visitors were only allowed at weekends. Every guest had to sign out and in again on their return, if they wanted to take advantage of the mountain air on a walk through the extensive grounds. Some more daring patients ventured to the next village forty minutes away to surreptitiously buy cigarettes and chocolate, smuggling this contraband back in their pockets.

'Dr Metz is on duty this evening and will carry out your examination. He's very nice, so there's no need to be nervous,' the young woman said, attempting to put the new patient at ease.

After a few minutes, they arrived at the second floor, where a series of rooms were laid out on both sides of a narrow corridor. This, together with the floor above, provided the entire accommodation for the forty guests.

'When you're ready, just go back the way we came and follow the stairs down from the ground floor to the basement, where the doctor will be waiting for you,' Nurse Weiss added. They stopped outside a door that had been left ajar.

'At the end of the corridor are two bathrooms with separate lavatory facilities. I do hope that you will find your stay beneficial. Please ask for Nurse Weiss. I'm in charge on this floor if you need my assistance.' The woman then went off to resume her duties.

Charlotte entered the bleak, chilly room. Apart from the narrow bed, it was furnished only with a single wardrobe and a small chest of drawers. A wood-framed fireside chair sat on the grey carpet facing the window. There was also a small sink for basic ablutions. The rooms at the front of the house faced several levels of perfectly manicured lawns that led down to an artificial lake, at the far end of which was a raised, cone-shaped bandstand. From a previous stay, Charlotte knew that the rooms at the back offered a stunning view of the snow-capped mountain peaks, and the sheer drop of the valley 1500 metres below.

Feeling weary from her journey, she stripped down to her underwear and put on the white linen robe that was hanging on the inside of the door. She then put on the towelling slippers that were still in their wrappers and hurried off to the lower-ground floor, where the treatment rooms and X-ray facilities were situated. Not having eaten a thing since the morning, she could have done with a proper meal and was tempted to pick up something from the dining room on the way. However, she knew better than to be late for her appointment. Johann had often boasted that his hospital ran on a strict routine that couldn't be altered.

After a thorough examination from the fresh-faced young doctor, she returned to her room armed with charts detailing her diet for the period of her stay and the timetable of her treatments. It had been a long day and she was soon fast asleep.

The next morning, Charlotte woke early. Feeling ravenous, she put on her robe and slippers, permitted only at breakfast, and hastily descended to the dining room on the floor below. A handful of guests were already scattered around the half-dozen or so tables that had been laid for breakfast. Charlotte sat down opposite a woman of indeterminate age with a pale complexion and long black straggly hair, who was looking at her suspiciously from behind her cup of hot chocolate.

'No waiter service here, dearie,' the wide-eyed woman remarked, gesturing at the breakfast buffet. 'Have to go and help yourself.'

Laid out at one end of the long refectory table were large bowls containing fresh fruit and yoghurt. There was also a choice of finely sliced cheeses and cold meats on silver platters, whole brown breads, traditional baked plaited loaves, jams and cereals. At the other end, in aluminium heat-proof cooking containers were slices of omelette, and poached and scrambled eggs.

Knowing what to expect from her previous visit, Charlotte reached over and poured herself a cup of black coffee from a tall metal pot. She then got up and, taking her plate with her, went across to the buffet and helped herself to a few slithers of white cheese and pieces of ham. Then, taking two crusty rolls from the bread-basket, she scooped out a generous amount of butter on to a side plate with a large dollop of apricot jam and returned to her seat.

'They are trying to kill me, you know,' the woman whispered, leaning across the table. Charlotte, concentrating on eating her breakfast, just smiled politely. By the wild gaze in the woman's eyes, she suspected that she was not quite right in the head.

'You see, they don't realise it, but I know what they're up to,' the woman went on, sounding proud of herself.

At that moment, the pretty nurse who had shown Charlotte to her room appeared carrying a small plastic cup containing three coloured capsules.

'Frau Goldstein, your medication,' the nurse announced and placed the cup on the table in front of the patient.

'I don't want it. The pills make me sick,' the woman replied petulantly. She pushed the cup aside with a swipe of her elegant hand.

'They're the same ones that you always have. So please take them now!' the nurse ordered briskly.

The woman, her large dark eyes pleading for someone to intervene on her behalf, finally resigned herself to her fate, put the tablets in her mouth and swallowed them.

The nurse marched off, leaving her patient looking listless and withdrawn. Twenty minutes later, the same woman, miraculously transformed, got up from her chair and with head held high, emphasising her exceptionally fine posture, she walked regally out of the dining room.

Charlotte took her time finishing her meal. There was no hurry; her first treatment wasn't until nine. She would go and collect the results of her tests beforehand, although she didn't need to be told what they would say. As a child, she had always suffered with her chest. Every cold put her to bed with heavy blankets wrapped around her by an over-protective mother, only concerned that having a sick child at home might jeopardise her social life.

As suspected, the results of her tests showed severe inflammation in her bronchial passages and an infection in her left lung. A thermometer was stuck in her mouth, recording a temperature of 38.5. She was immediately put on a course of antibiotics and instructed to inhale a decongestant three times daily. She was also prescribed a series of infra-red treatments and told to take two hours of fresh air per day.

For the next week, Charlotte felt drained from the effects of the medication. She had lost her appetite, and apart from her treatments and the regular afternoon exercise that she took strolling around the grounds of the sanatorium, she spent the rest of her time sleeping, determined to get well. She had, moreover, decided to stop smoking.

Charlotte gradually gave up hope that Johann would suddenly appear and summon her to his apartment. She had accepted that their relationship was over.

During the second week of her stay, her temperature returned to normal and she found that she had more energy. On her last afternoon, returning from an extended walk to the village tearoom where she had treated herself to a cup of hot cinnamon tea and a piece of Sachertorte, she passed the dark-haired woman she had encountered on that first morning. She was sitting upright on a bench facing the lake, warmly dressed and with a round fur hat on her head. From a short distance away, she appeared to be in a trance.

Then: 'Hello!' she called out, seeing Charlotte walk past her. 'You're the one from breakfast. Come and sit down next to me.' She tapped the bench with the palm of her hand. 'It gets lonely spending all day with no one to talk to.'

Charlotte went over and took up a place at the other end of the bench.

'You meet all different types in here. But they never stay more than a month or six weeks. Then they return to their busy lives in Zurich or Geneva.'

'Do you mean that you live here permanently?' Charlotte asked, wondering how that could be possible.

'It was my home until it got taken from me.'

'I don't understand,' Charlotte said, sure that the patient sat next to her was suffering from delusion.

'We even had our own Goldstein family crest,' the strange woman announced. She began drawing the shape in the air with her gloved hand.

'So, you come from Germany originally?' Charlotte asked.

'Yes. My family is from Frankfurt.'

'What happened to them?' Charlotte asked innocently.

'When the Nazis came to power, our bank was closed down – and yet my father had fought for Germany in the First War! But it made no difference, since we were Jews.

37

My parents and my two younger brothers were thrown out of their apartment and they were sent to Poland. I never saw them again.' She bowed her head. 'Ach, such dreadful times.'

Charlotte was shocked. She suddenly recalled the Trupp family, her neighbours in Berlin. They lived in the apartment on the floor above hers. Ben, their thirteen-year-old son, was her best friend.

A memory came to her fleetingly. Ben had just had his Barmitzvah, his religious confirmation, and she had been invited to their family celebrations. She remembered his parents beaming with pride at their boy's achievement in their synagogue the previous day, and the sight, strange to her, of men dancing with men, women with women. In her mind now, she could still hear the clinking of glasses and the shouts as the guests toasted each other in what Ben told her was Yiddish. For those few hours, they were somehow able to forget their precarious situation and enjoy themselves.

The next morning her mother had told her that she should stay away from Ben because his family were Jews. One day, not long afterwards, the Trupps just disappeared. When she asked her parents what had happened to them, they just said that the family had been resettled somewhere where they could be with 'their own kind'.

She was forbidden to mention their name again.

Charlotte sat looking at the lake, her heart heavy. It was years since she had thought about the family in the upstairs apartment. Never knowing for sure what had happened to them, for a long time she had waited for Ben to just turn up so she could give him the painting she had done of him. But he never did. Then gradually, as she immersed herself in her studies, intent on establishing herself as an artist, little by little she forgot about him.

'How did you manage to get to Switzerland?' she asked, clearing her throat.

'I was a cabaret artiste. Look - I still have great legs,' the other woman pronounced with pride. Pushing the rug away from her knees, she raised the hem of her woollen dress, exposing shapely legs. 'You wouldn't believe it now, but I was a real looker in those days – "a white Josephine Baker", that's what they called me. I worked in the most famous cabaret venues all over Europe. Paris, Vienna, Berlin - you name it. I lived to sing and dance.'

She began murmuring the words of a tune and moving her arms and legs to the rhythm of the music that only she could hear.

'Gustav was our manager. He was the most handsome man I'd ever seen,' she said. 'Even though he was married, all the girls were mad about him but he chose me - Margot Goldstein - to be his mistress. That didn't go down at all well with the others.' She startled to chuckle.

'The girls tried all sorts of ways to discredit me. One time they even set me up. They arranged for this tall streak of nothing to appear at a rehearsal and say he was my fiancé.'

'That's hilarious!' Charlotte burst out laughing. She found herself liking this eccentric but charming woman, who was prepared to divulge so much about herself.

'Of course, Gustav saw through it immediately. It was only their idea of a bit of fun.'

'Then what happened?' Charlotte asked, drawn into the story that no one could have invented.

'The Nazis started pushing their weight around in

Frankfurt. They began asking whether the venue employed Jews. Gustav, bless him, saw that it was going to be too dangerous for me to stay in Germany.'

Charlotte shuddered. As a child asleep in bed, she recalled being woken up by the sound of angry voices shouting outside her window. On one occasion, she got up and peered fearfully through the curtain, to see a small crowd of people, still dressed in their nightclothes, being escorted down the street by men in uniform. The next time she heard the same kind of disturbance, she pulled the bedsheets over her head and lay there quaking.

'Do you know what he did, the clever bugger?' the woman continued. 'He only organised for our troupe to perform in Zurich. It was before there was a restriction on leaving the country. He then arranged with his friend, Émile, to fix me up with a cabaret slot in his club. After I had the baby, that's where I spent the rest of the war.'

'You were pregnant?' Charlotte blurted out, shocked by this latest revelation.

'Yes, with Gustav's son. Unfortunately, living in a one-room flat above the club, I was in no position to care for a child - not with the hours I was working.'

'What did you decide to do?'

'It was agreed that Gustav would take him back to Germany.'

'But what about his wife?' Charlotte asked.

'Apparently she had difficulty conceiving and they were thinking of adopting. Gustav fed her the story that one of his dancers was looking to give up her baby so she could get back to work. It wasn't unusual. Those girls were always getting themselves into trouble - and now I was one of them.' Margot shrugged philosophically. Then her smile faded. 'They gave my David a suitable Aryan name. They called him Axel. I knew that Gustav and his wife would look after him, but it broke my heart to give him away.'

'It must have been a terrible ordeal for you,' Charlotte said gently.

'Then after the war,' the woman continued, not offering a response, 'I assumed they would have had children of their own so I could go back to Germany and they would return my boy to me.'

'And did you?' Charlotte whispered, completely absorbed in the tale.

'Gustav was shot by the Nazis, caught smuggling weapons to the German resistance. So the letter from his wife said.'

'She knew about you, then?'

'Only that I was the mother of her adopted son.'

'And the child - your David?' Charlotte asked

There was no reply. Only tears. A terrible grief.

The sun had started to drop behind the mountains, causing a brief shimmering effect on the lake before dusk descended.

'It's getting cold. We could walk back together,' Frau Goldstein sighed eventually, and holding onto each other's arms, the two women made their way up the steep path, intent on reaching the house before it got dark.

'I was the only one of my family to survive,' Margot Goldstein said suddenly, continuing with her story. 'At the end of the war I returned to Germany, desperate to see my son. When I finally located the address and introduced myself to Gustav's wife, I was full of excitement at the thought of being reunited with David after so many years . . . but it wasn't to be.'

Sensing that something awful had befallen the child, Charlotte tightened her grip on her companion's arm.

'My son had died in an outbreak of tuberculosis that had swept through the town,' Margot said brokenly, then somehow she found the courage to finish her story. 'My light, my David – he had contracted the disease and died. My soul cried out for him.' She pulled at her long black hair. 'If only I had been able to care for him! He would still be alive. Hi death will haunt me for ever.'

Charlotte could only imagine the terrible torment that this woman had been forced to endure. She wondered whether she herself would have been able to survive in similar circumstances.

'So what did you do?' she breathed.

'I ran away from Germany as fast as I could. We still had this place. It had been unoccupied during the war, so I came to live here.'

'On your own? How did you manage?'

'There wasn't anybody else around to help. My family had all been taken, murdered in Poland. At first I somehow got by, but eventually I couldn't afford the upkeep. You see, I stopped working when I had a nervous breakdown.'

'Couldn't you have moved somewhere smaller?' Charlotte asked.

'Dr Fischer, who was treating me in Zurich, bought the house from me. He'd been looking for a place that could be turned into a sanatorium. Part of the agreement was that I could continue to live here. Three lovely rooms on the top floor - it was like having my own apartment.' She gazed nostalgically up at the two gabled dormer windows of her former family home. Then her expression darkened.

'But when he retired and his son-in-law took over - that

vile man Dr Weber - everything changed. Weber told me that I wasn't entitled to such "extravagant accommodation" as he put it. Can you imagine how degrading that felt? Margot Goldstein, once the toast of Berlin,' she twirled her arms dramatically above her head, 'forced from an apartment in her own family residence into one dingy room. It was only because he wanted a place to entertain all his women friends,' she added bitterly.

'Surely you were entitled to remain in the apartment?' Charlotte said, incensed by the injustice that her companion had suffered, and taken aback by the revelation about the women.

'Not being well, I was hardly in a position to make a fuss,' the woman answered. 'That swine can't wait for me to do myself in so he can get a paying guest into my room. It wouldn't surprise me if the pills they keep plying me with are doing the job for him.' A contorted expression appeared on her face.

Some people, Charlotte thought, had been given too much loss and suffering to endure.

It was six o'clock by the time the two women entered through the main front door and went up to the administration office to sign themselves back into the sanatorium. Charlotte accompanied her new acquaintance back to her room on the same floor. She had found Frau Goldstein's account of her experiences deeply disturbing, even if her reports of Johann's philandering sounded far-fetched. However, it was clear that the woman had suffered emotional trauma, and that this had taken its toll on her mental stability.

Until that afternoon, Charlotte hadn't thought about her

own pre-war years in Berlin. After all, she had only been a girl of thirteen when war started. Surely she couldn't have been expected to disobey her parents? Feeling unsettled, she passed along the corridor towards her room. She needed to pack since she was leaving the next day and catching the 10 a.m. train from Davos Platz to Zurich.

As she entered, she saw that a message had been put under her door. She took off her coat and sat on the bed to read it. It was from Johann, asking her to come to his apartment on the top floor at eight that evening. How convenient, she thought, since he knew very well that it was her last day. Even so, she might still have gone up to meet him, had she not been made aware of his callous actions and the way he had taken advantage of the vulnerable Margot Goldstein - purely for financial gain.

Charlotte put the note back in the envelope and quickly changed for dinner. She consumed a meal of grilled sole and vegetables and a glass of sparkling white wine alone at her normal table. Every so often, she looked up to see if Margot had appeared, but her companion of the afternoon had remained in her room.

Charlotte finished her main course and, declining the offer of dessert, she left the dining room and went up to bed.

Unbeknownst to her, Margot's crumpled body, fallen from the window-ledge two floors above, was discovered at daybreak by the old retainer outside his lodge. Her face had been carefully made-up and she was dressed in her cabaret costume. By the time the guests arrived for breakfast, the corpse had already been taken away. It was as if Margot Goldstein had never existed.

*

The next morning, still unaware of the tragic demise of the woman whose story had played on her conscience, Charlotte settled her account and ordered a taxi to take her to the railway station. Johann's envelope remained in her room. She knew that she would never again be returning to the Blauerberg Sanatorium.

5

It was raining heavily when Charlotte stepped out at Victoria station the next day. On the long stretch from Zurich to Paris, she had not slept, unable to stop thinking about the tragic woman who had tried to befriend her. Certain that Frau Goldstein could only have been a few years older than herself, she now felt guilty about not telling the woman that she was leaving. At least she should have looked in on her when Margot didn't appear at dinner. And maybe, if she had accepted Johann's invitation to his apartment, she might have been able to get him to act more benevolently towards the lady who had experienced such adversity. She would never know now, Charlotte thought.

Nor would she ever know about the note incriminating the Director, Herr Johann Weber, of cruelty towards his patients that was left by Margot and found by the cleaner in Frau Goldstein's room beside an empty bottle of tranquillisers. The woman diligently handed the note to the person in charge of the floor, the buxom Nurse Weiss, who put it in a safe place, knowing exactly how to make use of it, if ever the time came.

The overnight train to England from Paris had been delayed. A heavy storm had prolonged the crossing by two hours, so that when Charlotte arrived at Victoria, nearly half the day had gone. She decided to return home immediately, drop off her luggage then use the afternoon before starting work the next day to come back into Central London and visit the exhibition of modern art that had just opened at the Royal Academy in Piccadilly. Feeling travel-weary, Charlotte treated herself to a taxi, and in a short while was on her way back to West Hampstead. The thought then entered her mind: what if the job had fallen through? After all, she hadn't had any contact with Bernard Morris for almost three weeks. He might have changed his mind and found someone else. Once more she berated herself for being too hasty in accepting his offer. Surely it would have been more sensible to have waited until the gallery was up and running before giving in her notice?

'What number did you say, love?' the driver called out as he turned into Gladys Road. 'Ninety-six, wasn't it?'

He pulled up outside the tranquil terrace of Victorian houses, and Charlotte paid him and retrieved her suitcase. Just as she was walking towards her front door, she saw the familiar figure of a man in a grey uniform standing on the pavement outside his car, a black Rolls-Royce. When she recognised that it was William, Bernard Morris's chauffeur, her heart sank. She had obviously made a mistake with the day and he was waiting to take her to the meeting with her new employer.

'Hello, miss, let me help you with that,' he called out, moving briskly towards her.

'I must have got my days muddled,' Charlotte said. Flushed with embarrassment, she began fumbling in her handbag for her front-door keys.

'Been somewhere nice, miss?'

'I'm so sorry. I just need a few minutes to get myself ready,' Charlotte said apologetically.

'Don't worry. It's only just twelve and the opening isn't

until one thirty,' William replied, helping her through the main front door with her case.

'Opening?' Charlotte echoed apprehensively.

'That's what the invitations said. Very nice they looked too. Picked them up from the printers meself.'

'But I didn't know! I mean, I didn't realise that it was so soon!' Panicking, Charlotte began running up the stairs to her first-floor flat.

'Just take your time and I'll wait for you outside,' the chauffeur called. He then moseyed back to the Rolls, got in and picked up his copy of the *Mirror*.

Only minutes passed before Charlotte, freshened up and in a change of clothes, her black hair brushed and shining, hurried out of the front door and over to the waiting car, thinking that she'd have to apply her make-up on the way. Suddenly, the back window was slowly wound down and a man's smiling face appeared.

'Come on, get in,' Bernard Morris said.

'I didn't expect you to be here,' Charlotte blurted out.

'Full of surprises, ain't I?' the man replied as she climbed in. 'And I've got another one waiting for you shortly. Isn't that right, William?' The chauffeur agreed as he started the Rolls.

'So, how was your trip?' Bernard asked. 'Where was it that you went again?'

'I was in Switzerland,' Charlotte answered, trying to remain calm.

'Very secretive, the Swiss, that's why they're so good in business. Never know what they're thinking. Anyway, you look good on it. The South of France is my favourite place for a holiday. Ever been there?'

'Actually, I went for treatment to the mountains,'

Charlotte responded, feeling that she had to justify herself.

'To clear your bronchioles and all that?'

'Yes, but how did you know?'

Bernard smiled and placed his hand affectionately on her arm. 'You had me worried, I can tell you, girl. Thought that when I couldn't get hold of you, I'd frightened you off.'

'We made an agreement, Mr Morris - I mean Bernard.'

'Oh, I forgot the Swiss sense of honour. Anyway, you're going to be in for a treat. We've had a few mishaps on the way, delays in getting the stuff delivered and so on, and then not finding anyone to hang the blighters. I've become quite nifty with a hammer and nails.'

Charlotte gasped, horrified at what she had just heard.

'I'm only pulling your leg,' the man laughed. 'All in all, I think you'll be quite pleased.'

'But I didn't think the opening would be today,' Charlotte said, panicking all over again.

'Don't look so worried, it's only the Private View. I've just invited a few business contacts of mine. We don't open officially till the day after tomorrow. Should give us enough time to sort out any last-minute hitches. Oh, by the way, this is for you.' He handed her an envelope.

'What is this?' Charlotte asked. She wondered what other surprises her new employer had in store for her.

'Your first month's salary.'

'But I haven't started work yet,' she protested.

'Hope you don't mind cash for the first month or two? The bank hasn't sorted out the new company chequebooks yet. Perhaps I should change from Martins to one of the Swiss ones, what do you think?'

'Bernard, it really is very generous of you. Thank you.' Charlotte placed the envelope in her bag next to the quantity of Swiss francs remaining from her visit to Zurich. She felt nervous, carrying around so much money with her.

The car turned into Bond Street and soon came to a halt outside a pristine shop-front adorned by a sign reading *Bernard Morris Gallery* printed in large bold black letters.

'Rather tasteful, wouldn't you say?' Bernard remarked, genuinely proud of the premises bearing his name. Not waiting for the chauffeur to do his job, he let himself out of the car and gestured for Charlotte to follow him, saying, 'Let me show you around.'

As Charlotte moved from the main entrance into the ground-floor gallery, she felt immediately uplifted by the lightness of the place. Benefiting from a large bow window at the front, its space and exceptionally high ceilings gave it a feeling of airiness. The interior was painted brilliant white and the walls were already lined with paintings, lit by wall-mounted spotlights. The prices and a description of the work were typed on neat white cards mounted by their side.

A crowd of people had already arrived and were admiring the paintings. A cluster of guests were focusing their attention on a Parisian picnic scene by Renoir just inside the door, next to which an older couple were discussing a landscape by Cezanne. The centrepiece, which was attracting most of the attention, was a striking Polynesian scene of scantily-clothed young women, painted by Max Freedland.

'Bernard, old chap, I think congratulations are in order. Damn fine show if I may say so,' bellowed a huge ruddy-faced man in a dark grey pinstriped suit, standing a few feet away. 'From the comments I've been hearing,

I think you may be on to a winner.' He helped himself to another glass of champagne from the waitress hired for the occasion.

'Good of you to come, Rupert. How's Lucinda, by the way?' Bernard asked, going up to the merchant banker.

'Sorry the old girl couldn't make it, something about a reunion with some of her school-friends from Roedean. Just turned up out of the blue at the house in Chester Square. Bloody inconvenient, that's what I say. Like a load of blasted starlings chattering away. Now who is this?' the man called Rupert asked, moving in on Charlotte. 'Aren't you going to introduce me, Bernard?'

'Sorry, I must have forgotten my manners. This is Charlotte Brown,' Bernard replied. 'She's joined us from the National Gallery, so she knows her stuff. She'll be running the place, under my direction, of course. Charlotte,' he said, turning to her, 'meet my good friend Rupert Meredith. His family own one of the oldest merchant banks in London.'

'I'm pleased to meet you, my dear,' the banker remarked and extended his massive hand to the young woman over whom he was now towering.

'Word of warning,' he went on, whispering in her ear. 'Bernard's a sly old fox. Better make sure you've got a cast-iron agreement. Can never be too careful with his sort.'

Then, consulting the gold pocket-watch from his waistcoat, he said aloud to Bernard, 'Have to be going, old chap,' putting his arm around the shorter man's shoulders in a false display of camaraderie. 'Got a shareholders' meeting in the City at three.'

He handed his empty glass to the waitress and, giving Charlotte a last lingering look, he strode out of the gallery to hail a taxi.

Unable to fathom the man's warning, which she put down to her inadequate knowledge of English, Charlotte proceeded slowly through the gallery trying to work out how Bernard had managed to obtain works of such undoubted quality. Suddenly she looked up and gasped. There, on the wall, were the two paintings that she had given to Bernard. They were priced at seventy-five pounds each.

'What are *they* doing here?' she said to herself, a little too loudly.

'Thought you'd be pleased, seeing your work up,' Bernard replied, appearing by her side. 'Look good, don't they?'

'But you said they were sold. You paid me fifty pounds for them!'

'They were sold to me,' Bernard explained.

'I don't understand.' Charlotte was beginning to feel uncomfortable. What was the banker trying to infer about Bernard? she wondered.

'I can tell by the look on that pretty face of yours, that you think I've pulled a fast one, don't you? Come with me, I want to show you something.'

Bernard took hold of her arm and led her over the newly laid oak floor to a recessed area at the back of the gallery, where a plump woman with too much make-up sat behind a simple wooden desk. She was busy with paperwork, which she had separated into well-organised piles.

'Charlotte, this is Joan Harding. Joan, this is the young lady who I've been going on about: Miss Charlotte Brown, formerly of the National Gallery. Show her the visitor's book with the paintings the punters expressed interest in, will you?' He turned to Charlotte. 'Joan's been with me for years. Knows more about my affairs than I do myself. Ain't that right, Joanie?'

'Mr Bernard,' the older woman protested, peering over her glasses, 'I assume you are referring to your *business* affairs.' Grinning mischievously, she handed her boss a brown leather-bound book.

'Now take a gander at this,' Bernard said, running his thick finger down the two full pages of visitors. 'There must be half a dozen of them interested in those landscapes of yours. Looks like we've already found our first new artist.' He glanced at his secretary. He didn't mention that Max's paintings had proven even more popular.

'You mean you want to feature my work?' Charlotte asked incredulously.

'Only if the Bernard Morris Gallery has exclusivity. Wouldn't want you flogging your gear anywhere else.'

'I don't know what to say.' Charlotte wondered guiltily if she had underestimated this man who, in addition to being her employer, was prepared to become her benefactor. Charlotte moved up to Bernard and kissed him on both cheeks. She couldn't remember ever feeling so happy.

'I think a toast is in order, don't you?' he proposed, looking around and seeing that the last of the guests had gone. 'Over here, love.' Bernard summoned the waitress. 'I'll take three of those off you.' He handed one to Charlotte and the other to the secretary, who was tidying up her desk.

'Obviously, we're going to need a few others as well,' he told Charlotte. 'So you'll need to get your skates on and see if you can identify some up-and-coming Rembrandts.'

'I thought we were specialising in modern paintings,'

Charlotte said innocently.

'Just an expression, love,' the owner laughed.

Charlotte smiled awkwardly at her misunderstanding.

'Come on, Joan!' Bernard bellowed out to the secretary.

Defying her size, the plump woman moved daintily over to join the other two in the middle of the room.

'To the success of the Bernard Morris Gallery!' he toasted, clinking glasses with his two female employees. 'And to our first exclusive artist,' he added, looking at Charlotte affectionately. 'Right then, if you two don't mind, I'll leave you to get to know each other. I've got a meeting with a bloke about a property that's come up. So I'll see you both, bright and early on Wednesday morning.' He turned to Joan, noticing her concern. 'Don't worry, the bank will give us the money. We're their largest customer. Oh, and Charlotte?' He beckoned her over. Sensing that it was something of a private nature, she made her way to the front of the gallery, unaware of the jealous look on the secretary's face as she passed.

'I'm having a dinner party at my house Saturday week, just a few friends. If you're not doing anything, I'd like you to come,' Bernard told her. 'Rupert and his missus might turn up if they're not in Sussex for the weekend. He's got a bit of a thing for the ladies, so don't be surprised if he tries it on with the charm.'

'Excuse me, Bernard, but didn't you say that his wife will be with him?' Charlotte commented.

'He's only after a bit of fun; Lucinda doesn't mind. She knows that she's got him where she wants him. He may be worth a few million but she could buy him out ten times over. Her family, the Lasalles, only own half of bloody Sussex!'

'If you're sure I won't be out of place, I should be happy to accept,' Charlotte said politely. Exhausted from her journey, she was trying her hardest to stop herself from yawning.

'Joan!' he called out to the secretary, who had returned to her desk. 'William should be here soon. Ask him to give you a lift home and to drop Charlotte at West Hampstead on the way. I won't be needing him again today.'

'I'm not skiving off yet! It's only three o'clock and I've still got work to do,' the woman answered, getting to her feet indignantly.

'There's always tomorrow,' Bernard said. 'Anyway, it'll be a nice surprise for your old man, you being home before him for once. What time does he knock off?'

'The factory's been on overtime and you know Reg, he's always the last to leave,' the secretary explained, displaying a distinct lack of enthusiasm for her boss's offer.

Just then, the Rolls drew up outside the gallery. Bernard went out to meet his chauffeur.

'Everything all right?' he mouthed to the man sat behind the wheel.

'All kosher, guv,' William answered, winding down his window. 'I gave Max the envelope as you told me. He said any time you want him you know where to find him.'

'Right, I'm off. See you in the morning. The girls are just locking up. I assume you don't mind taking them home,' Bernard said, before marching off down the road and disappearing round the next corner.

William smirked as he ran around to open the back door of the car for the two women approaching the kerb. The Rolls then moved noiselessly away down Cork Street, turning down several side roads before increasing in speed as it headed up to north-west London. Charlotte felt her eyes closing. The combination of three glasses of champagne on an empty stomach proved too much, and she was soon fast asleep on the back seat.

'Looks like she's out for the count,' William said, looking in his rear mirror.

'Seems he's gone soft on this one,' Joan whispered.

'Can't say I blame him. I mean, she's a nice looker,' the chauffeur responded.

'But he's only known her five minutes,' Joan bridled. 'He's too kind-hearted, that's his problem.'

'More than I can say for you,' the driver murmured under his breath.

'What did you just say?' Joan demanded.

'Only that it sounds to me like you're a bit jealous,' William answered, slowing down to avoid a delivery boy on a bicycle.

'Don't be ridiculous. I'm a married woman,' she hissed.

'Ahem.' William cleared his throat meaningfully

'That's different!' Joan was indignant. 'Anyway, I told you after last time, it has to stop.'

'Look, Joanie, we both know what we've got ourselves involved in. Everybody's at it, so where's the harm?'

A period of silence followed while the chauffeur negotiated his way through the back doubles that brought him a short time later into West End Lane. After a few hundred yards, the car drew to a halt outside Charlotte's flat.

'I wonder who's paid for this little love nest?' Joan commented sarcastically. She began prodding the younger woman to try and wake her. 'Come on, dearie, you're home,' she trilled. There was no response. 'William, you'll need to give her a hand.'

'That's no hardship,' the driver replied, grinning. He got out of the car and went round to open the rear passenger door.

'Just make sure you keep those hands of yours to yourself, and hurry up, if you know what's good for you,' Joan Harding warned him.

William reached over to Charlotte and gently helped her out of her seat. Taking her handbag, he carefully led her by the arm to the front door.

'Do you want me to come up with you?' he asked attentively.

Still half-asleep, Charlotte rummaged inside her handbag for the keys.

'You can leave me here,' she yawned. 'I'll be fine. Thanks very much for the lift, William. It was really kind of you. Goodbye, Joan.' She waved at the other woman.

'If you're sure,' William replied.

Feeling rather groggy, Charlotte walked up the stairs and let herself into her flat. She went through the small hallway into the bedroom where, still in her coat, she kicked off her shoes and collapsed exhausted onto the bed.

'Where do you think she comes from?' Joan was asking as the Rolls headed towards the North Circular Road.

'She's Swiss, or so the guv'nor says. Anyway, what's it to you?' William asked.

'There's something fishy about her,' the large woman remarked perceptively. 'She won't last, not if I've got anything to do with it,' she muttered to herself and began sucking on a Polo mint that she'd taken out of her bag.

Half an hour later, the Rolls pulled up in a deserted

lorry park on an industrial estate. William took off his cap and made his way round to the back seat of the car.

'You'll have to make it quick. By the looks of it, Reg and his mates have already gone home,' the secretary said. Then, undoing her coat, she welcomed him into her chubby arms.

6

It was still light when Charlotte arrived at the four-storey Georgian house in a fashionable street off Grosvenor Square. The front door had been left ajar and the chatter of other guests filtered through to the pavement outside. The young woman breathed a sigh of relief that she wasn't the first. She took a small hand mirror from her evening bag and examined herself in it. Adjusting her unruly black hair, which she had pulled back in a low bun, a touch of eye make-up was her only concession to liven a complexion which had already lost its glow from the visit to the Swiss mountains. It wasn't as though she hadn't made an effort; she had spent the entire afternoon trying to find a suitable outfit for the occasion, eventually settling on a smart dress and jacket from Selfridges which complimented her slim figure. She had then gone across to the gift department and purchased a set of wine coasters as a gift for her host.

Feeling self-conscious about her appearance, Charlotte entered the house still worried that she would look as out of place amongst Bernard's friends as she felt in her new working environment. After the euphoria of the gallery's opening, Charlotte had spent the first two weeks trying to apply her mind to cataloguing the twenty-four paintings on display into some sort of coherent order. The interest in Max Freedland's bright scenes of exotic young women had taken her by surprise. Sold stickers in the form of red dots had been applied to all but three of the labels accompanying his paintings. She had spent hours researching the artist but could find nothing on him other than the sparse details that Bernard had given her.

Even more mysterious were the six works by Daniel Petrovitch, who was apparently a contemporary of Max Freedland. Although no less accomplished, his style was completely different. One of the images, aptly named *Blight,* of a poor family in their heavy winter coats queuing in the snow to buy food, lodged itself in her mind. The gaunt faces of the children came to her at night. One of them was her friend Ben. She wanted to be able to help, to offer him a loaf of bread and a slab of cheese, but when she reached out to him, he just disappeared, swept away by a strong wind.

When she arrived at the gallery the next morning, the painting was there, searching her out. It was as if it had attached itself to her.

Being frequently left on her own, as if it were some test of her ingenuity, wouldn't normally have bothered her - but she was seriously worried that the gallery was running out of works to sell. She had to meet Max Freedland, Charlotte decided, and she had to do it soon.

'Charlotte, I'm so pleased that you decided to come,' Bernard said now, walking across the marble floor towards her. 'I see you found it all right.' He kissed her on the cheek.

As if on cue, a butler in full uniform appeared from around the corner and plucked her coat from her arm with his white-gloved hand.

'This is for you,' Charlotte said nervously. She passed Bernard the small carrier bag.

'What's that for?' the host asked, sounding genuinely

surprised.

'It's nothing much. I hope you like it.'

'I'm not used to being given presents by young ladies.' He put the gift down on a Victorian hall chair. 'Now follow me and I'll introduce you to the others.'

Bernard led the way through double doors into a vast drawing room. Three other couples had congregated in small groups. Charlotte looked around the room and for a brief moment of déjà vu, she thought, *I have been here before*. Somewhere, she had seen these same arched windows reaching upwards to the fine stuccoed ceiling, and the French doors that opened out onto the terrace. Then it came to her. She was with her parents and brother Hans at a reception in a grand residence in Berlin near to where they lived. The men were in full military dress and their wives wore their best evening gowns. She had gazed up at the huge crystal chandelier above her, seemingly suspended in mid-air. She remembered she'd been crying but her sobs were drowned out by the music and laughter that filled the room. Then she ran over to her father, who picked her up and kissed her forehead. She felt safe in his arms.

'Charlotte, come and meet Lucinda,' Bernard said, stirring her back to reality. He led her over to a blonde woman in a lime-green chiffon dress, perched on the arm of a sofa. She was smoking and looking bored.

'This is Rupert's other half,' Bernard said, making the introduction. 'Remember, he was the one who chatted you up at the opening?'

'Sounds like him. Incorrigible rascal!' his wife retorted. Tilting back her head, she drained the last dregs of her champagne. 'Bernard, be a love and get me a refill, would you, and perhaps whatshername here would like one too?' The host was shooed away with a wave of the woman's hand, which was adorned by a large sapphire ring encrusted with diamonds.

'So how long have you two known each other?' the banker's wife asked, taking another drag from her cigarette. 'Come on, do tell.'

'Mr Morris and I . . .' Charlotte began hesitantly. 'I mean that I manage the gallery for Bernard.'

'How positively charming. And I suppose it's purely a business relationship?' The other woman was being deliberately provocative.

Just then, the giant figure of Rupert Meredith came parading over to their part of the room.

'Ah, Charlotte. It's good to see you again!' the banker exclaimed. 'Couldn't wait to get away from those property chappies. Bunch of spivs if you ask me. Probably never done a proper day's work in their lives,' he muttered under his breath.

'Now, now, Rupert,' his wife chided him. 'Don't mind him,' she said, turning to Charlotte. 'It's just his public-school fagging coming out again; probably the result of too much buggery.'

'I'm sorry, I'm not sure what you mean,' Charlotte said nervously.

'Just a thing the English are rather good at.'

'Best public schools in the world, no doubt about that,' the banker enthused.

'Actually, I meant buggery,' Lucinda corrected him, slurring her words.

'Steady on the champers, old girl,' her husband answered back. Giving his wife a filthy look, he went off in a huff.

Charlotte felt uncomfortable. She did her best to attract Bernard's attention but saw that he was embroiled in a heated conversation with two of the male guests. Behind them were two women, presumably the men's wives. The older one of the two was drawing the other woman's attention to the two paintings by Renoir and Cezanne that had been returned to Bernard after the opening. Charlotte wondered whether she should go over and introduce herself but felt that she would be intruding.

At that moment, the butler appeared and announced that dinner was about to be served. Charlotte got up from the sofa and followed the other guests out of the salon and into a candle-lit dining room with dark wood-panelled walls and draped maroon velvet curtains. She found a place-card with her name on at the head of the table, which had been elaborately set for a dinner of several courses. Bernard was sitting directly opposite her at the far end. To her right, and much to his obvious delight, sat Rupert and on her other side was a dapper thin-faced man of a similar age. By his wooden expression, it was clear that he was there under sufferance.

Two waitresses dressed in black and wearing white headbands began to serve the guests with cream of leek soup from an elegant tureen. Armed with two bottles wrapped in linen napkins, the butler passed around the table pouring white wine to go with the first course.

'You must be Charlotte,' the man to her left remarked in a mild Scottish accent. Charlotte gripped his bony hand, surprised that he already knew her name.

'I'm James Robson, Bernard's solicitor. And that's my wife Susana,' he said, glancing across the table at the woman whom Charlotte had noticed before dinner.

Dressed in a crimson strapless evening gown which set off her coffee-coloured skin, his wife was extremely beautiful. Her raven-black hair flowed freely onto her bare shoulders and she was wearing a large emerald around her neck. The woman looked back at her husband, pouting her sensuous lips at him. Charlotte wondered what country she came from and what circumstances had attracted her to this much older man. Susana, she noted, was openly flirting with the fresh-faced young man next to her, who was thoroughly enjoying the attention.

'Seems like young Bertie Chesterfield has caught her eye,' the solicitor remarked. 'That's Bertie's fiancée, sitting next to Bernard – Lady Davina Ambleforth. By all accounts, theirs is going to be the society wedding of the year.'

Charlotte glanced at the doll-like young woman seated beside Bernard and thought how uncomfortable she appeared in her surroundings compared to her future husband.

'Davina is a distant relation of our new Queen through her mother's line, and his family are the owners of one of the largest estates in Central London,' the lawyer said, trying to impress Charlotte. 'It's well known that since his father's death, the Chesterfield family are having to sell off a large number of properties to pay for death duties. No surprise that Bernard is trying to get in his good books,' he added cynically.

Charlotte smiled politely, but the coldness in the eyes of the man next to her made her feel uneasy.

'Bernard tells me that you're going to be running that new gallery of his. You should talk to my wife,' the solicitor continued, taking another mouthful of soup. 'She's

Brockets' expert on nineteenth- and twentieth-century art. You'd probably have a lot in common.'

'That would be most kind,' Charlotte replied. Now she understood why the woman on the opposite side of the table had been paying such close attention to the paintings before dinner. Perhaps she was interested in purchasing them, she thought to herself. Taking a large gulp of wine, she made a conscious effort to try to relax and enjoy the evening.

'Listen, old boy, it's a bit off, keeping Charlotte all to yourself,' the banker interjected at that moment. 'You professional types are all the same when you can sniff the possibility of a new client.' He turned to Charlotte. 'So has Bernard been treating you all right?'

'I think a toast is in order,' Bernard interrupted. He tapped the table to get everyone's attention. 'Once our glasses have been refilled, that is,' he added, addressing his comments to the butler, who had been lax in his duties. 'Rupert, would you mind doing the Queen?'

'Pleasure, old boy.' Manoeuvring his huge frame out of the chair, the banker stood. 'The toast is Her Majesty Queen Elizabeth!' he bellowed, raising his glass high above his head.

The whole table got to its feet and rallied together in repeating, 'The Queen!'

'Now to all you lovely people, thank you for being here. Good health, and God bless!' the host toasted his guests, who had already sat down again and were busy attacking the succulent slices of roast lamb that had been served up as the main course.

'The Swiss don't have a royal family, do they?' Rupert remarked, teasing Charlotte.

Before she could respond, Bernard quipped with a mouth full of food, 'I dunno, the banks come a pretty close second.' The remark produced a sniggering around the table.

'Cedric, hurry up with some more of that red, will you!' Bernard called out. Looking harassed, the butler quickly refilled each of the guests' claret glasses, after which, failing to hide his displeasure at being reminded how to do his job, he promptly marched out of the room.

'We have not had a King or Queen in Argentina since 1816,' Susana announced.

'What do you think about the merits of the monarchy, Bertie?' the solicitor asked, attempting to embarrass his wife's dinner companion.

'I think the Coronation, which Davina and I had the privilege of attending, is proof enough of what most people in the country think of the Royal Family,' the young man replied calmly.

'Can't possibly expect a Scot to understand that,' the banker muttered, a little too loudly.

'Bertie was at Sandhurst. He received the Queen's Medal for his achievements,' Davina said shyly.

'My biggest regret is that I was too young to fight to defend King and country in the war,' Bertie said. 'But I'll tell you this, without the pride that the monarchy instilled in every one of us, Germany might well have prevailed.'

The table broke out into spontaneous applause.

'Hear, hear! Well said, young man,' Rupert and the solicitor shouted, united in their support.

Bernard thumped on the table, while of the women, only Davina and Lucinda clapped. Susana and Charlotte remained silent.

Charlotte, convinced that everyone was staring at her, felt herself blushing. What was she supposed to do? The truth was that she had buried her past and only thought of herself as one of the Swiss, who were proud to stand by their neutrality. And yet by not joining in, she was displaying disrespect to the country where she was attempting to make a life for herself.

She was saved from a most unlikely source. The attention was not focused on her as she feared but on Susana, who sat back with her arms folded and a look of defiance on her beautiful face.

All of a sudden, Lucinda, suffering the effects of too much wine, staggered to her feet.

'Something you might like to share with us?' she slurred, sneering at the woman seated on the other side of the table.

'I am half-German and I don't feel that I should have to share in your celebrations,' Susana told her.

'My wife's father was an agricultural engineer,' the solicitor interjected. 'He moved to South America in the twenties. Showed them how to improve the yield of soya beans.'

'Bloody efficient – that's one thing you can say about the Krauts - I mean the Germans,' the banker said, quick to correct himself.

The comment provoked an immediate exchange of glances between those at the table.

'I don't suppose there's a drop more claret about, by any chance?' Rupert Meredith asked, holding up his empty glass in Bernard's direction.

'So, Charlotte, you came to London when you completed your studies?' Susana enquired, turning her attention to the woman at the end of the table.

'After obtaining my degree at Basel University,' Charlotte replied.

'You studied Art?'

'My dissertation was on the Pre-Raphaelite period. I was then fortunate to obtain a position at the National Gallery,' the young woman said, blushing at the woman's sudden interest in her.

'So how did you come to meet Bernard? I mean, you can tell by all this,' Susana opened her hands out wide and looked around the room, 'that as a businessman he may be extremely successful, but art is not exactly his passion.'

Not for the first time that evening, Charlotte had been caught off-guard and felt that she had to justify herself.

'In the short time that I have known Bernard, I have found that he has a genuine interest in art. Otherwise I doubt he would have opened the gallery.'

'Really? I think that he has rather succeeded in fooling you.'

'What do you mean?' Charlotte answered, sounding as shocked as she felt.

'Susana, please can we talk about something else,' the solicitor said firmly, seeing that his wife was intent on embarrassing the young woman next to him and, even worse, discrediting their host.

'I would also be interested in hearing what she has to say,' Lucinda interjected. 'What dirt have you got on Bernard?'

The young woman next to Bernard suddenly stood up, looking distinctly unwell.

'Bertie, I think we should leave. I seem to have developed a migraine. Bernard, please would you excuse us?'

'But you haven't had dessert! Please stay,' Bernard Morris pleaded.

Ignoring their host's objections, Bertie got up from the table, any emotions hidden by his impeccable breeding. Acknowledging the other guests at the table, he left the room accompanied by his fiancée, Lady Diana Ambleforth.

Bernard followed them into the hall, where Cedric was already on hand with the young couple's outer apparel.

The room went quiet. Charlotte just picked at her food. She wished that she too could be permitted to leave. Bernard had made such an effort. Apart from the two who had just left, the rest of his friends had treated him deplorably. And yet for a reason she didn't understand, he seemed willing to demean himself, as if desperate to gain their acceptance.

Then the solicitor abruptly got up from the table, his face crimson with rage, and began berating his wife in full view of the other guests; the evening was descending into havoc. At the same time, Charlotte suddenly felt Rupert's hand on her knee; he had moved next to her, taking full advantage while his wife had fallen asleep at the table. She wished Bernard would reappear.

Out in the hall, Bernard was saying, 'I must apologise for Susana. It's just that she likes to speak her mind,' as he helped Lady Davina on with her shawl.

'Bernard, a brief word,' Bertie requested. Putting on his white evening scarf, he took his host aside.

'I'm aware of your interest in the Berkeley Square portfolio and personally I don't see why you shouldn't have the same opportunity as anyone else. But there are many I could name who think you're beginning to have too much of a presence around here. So just be careful, and watch your back. Anyway, good night, and thanks again.'

With that, the couple, their arms entwined, passed through the hall and out of the front door to where their chauffeur had been on hand all evening to take them back to their home in Belgravia.

The host stood for a moment, pondering on what Bertie had said to him. Then, letting out a deep sigh, he turned around and went back into the dining room. He had already decided to dismiss the young man's warning.

'Bernard, I should like to apologise,' Susana said, devoid of any sincerity. 'I certainly didn't mean to imply that you have been involved in any impropriety.'

'Forget it. I never take these things personally,' he said cheerfully, taking back his place at the top of the table. 'I hope Charlotte has been playing hostess while I was seeing those two lovebirds out.' He looked fondly at her for the first time that evening.

One of the waitresses had begun spooning out generous portions of strawberries onto the dessert plates while the other was carrying small jugs of cream.

'You know, we see it all the time at Brockets,' Susana continued.

Bernard looked confused.

'Susana, haven't you said enough for one night?' The solicitor was frustrated that his warning had failed to stop his wife from continuing with her vendetta.

'No – let her continue. She's obviously got something that she needs to get off her chest,' their host answered back, putting a heaped spoon of strawberries in his mouth.

'Does anyone know what's going on?' the banker asked, moving back to his own place.

There was a moment of silence.

'I have to inform you that your Renoir and Cezanne are fakes,' Susanna stated. 'I wasn't sure at first because there's no question that they have been painted by an accomplished artist. But we sold the original Renoir at auction two years ago, and the Cezanne autumn landscape has never come on to the market. It's held privately in New York.'

Charlotte gasped. She was horrified. She looked across the table at Bernard who seemed strangely calm and carried on finishing his dessert.

'Forgery's a serious crime, old boy,' the solicitor intervened wearily.

'Looks like you're going to find yourself in a bit of bother,' the banker joined in.

'Before you start accusing me of whatever you're accusing me of, perhaps you'd all like to come with me.' Bernard got up from the table and made his way over to the door. He winked at Charlotte as he passed. She noticed that he had a mischievous look on his face. How could she have allowed herself to be deceived? At the end of the evening, she would have to tell her employer that she had made a terrible mistake. She had left the National Gallery on good terms; perhaps they would agree to give her back her job? She got up, and for a reason that she couldn't explain, went over to Bernard in an instinctive show of support. He smiled at her and tenderly took her hand in his.

One by one, the other guests followed. First the solicitor with a perverse expression that suggested that he would be quite happy for his wife to have found her comeuppance. Then the banker, finding the whole episode highly entertaining and quite prepared to abandon Lucinda, who had nodded off again in her chair. And finally, Susana with her air of superiority, who appeared in no hurry to justify herself.

The party followed their host back into the drawing room and over to the far end.

'Susana, I would love to know how you're so certain that these two charming paintings of mine are forgeries,' Bernard said, pointing to the Renoir and Cezanne that were hung above the marble fireplace. 'That is what you called them, isn't it?'

'Bernard, I've already told you that that is *exactly* what they are,' the woman replied, irritated that her judgement was being questioned. 'But I'm sure that you are not to blame and that you purchased them in good faith. It's understandable that you must be very upset, finding out that you've wasted your money.'

'You've made your point, woman, now for God's sake drop it!' the solicitor admonished her.

The woman gave her husband a disdainful look, indicating that she was far from finished.

'After the Private View at your gallery, my research confirmed what I already knew,' she continued. 'Two such valuable pieces couldn't possibly find their way onto the market without my knowledge.'

'Or what you really mean is, how could an ordinary bloke like me have enough money to lay his hands on them,' Bernard smiled.

'I didn't say that!' Susana snapped.

There was a moment of silence as it now transpired that Susana had at first thought the paintings were authentic.

'Didn't you notice that there wasn't a price tag on them at the opening?' Bernard asked her.

'If you were familiar with the business, you would know that where valuable works of art are concerned, the price is a matter of negotiation between the gallery and their client,' she replied sarcastically.

'The reason why they didn't have a price on them was because they're not for sale. A bit of decoration to fill out the place, that's all,' the host remarked, appearing to enjoy the confrontation. 'But it's nice to know that you think they could have been worth a mint.'

Bernard then went across to a tall wooden church chair by the side of the alcove. 'Here, Rupert, gives us a hand with this,' he requested. 'It's bloody heavy.'

The rest of the party looked on bemused as the two men grabbed a side each, and carried the chair over to the fireplace.

'Charlotte, you've got the height, love, would you mind doing the honours? That one will do,' Bernard said, pointing to the Renoir picnic scene.

Feeling slightly woozy from too much wine, Charlotte kicked off her high-heeled shoes and was helped up onto the chair by the banker. She carefully removed the painting from the wall and passed it to Bernard, before being eased down again.

Susana remained aloof and began fidgeting with her emerald while her husband, seeming impatient to get away, remained in the distance.

'Right - now look at what's written on the back,' Bernard instructed. He turned the painting around so they all could see.

'*Scene at Versailles,* signed by Max Freedland, twenty-fifth of May 1955,' he read out, pointing at the inscription. 'So Susana, if I were you, I'd go back and make extra sure that those paintings that you have no doubt sold for a fortune, aren't signed on the back by some unknown artist.'

The room fell silent. All eyes were focused on the solicitor's wife; the air of superiority present just a short time before now replaced with a face flushed with anger. After a short pause and showing remarkable restraint, she approached her adversary.

'Thank you for your invitation, Bernard,' she said, extending her hand to her host.

'But surely you'll stay for coffee and brandy?' Bernard said pleasantly.

'Forgive me; I could do with some fresh air. James will collect the coats,' the woman replied without acknowledging her husband.

'Good night, Rupert, say goodbye to Lucinda,' she said to the banker. 'And Charlotte, it was a pleasure to make your acquaintance.'

Susana walked over to her. Standing so close that their bodies were almost touching, she kissed her on both cheeks.

'We should have lunch since we are only around the corner from each other. It would be an opportunity for us to converse – in *German*,' she announced, giving Charlotte a lingering look.

Did this woman have some secret insight into her past? This 'convivial meeting of friends' as Bernard had described it, had proved nothing more than an excuse to belittle him by his ungrateful guests. And now, when it hadn't succeeded, the main instigator merely detracted attention away from herself by directing suspicion towards someone else.

More complicated were Charlotte's feelings towards

Bernard. Not for the first time she had been ready to accept his accuser's words. What was it that prevented her from seeing him as a decent man? A seed of doubt had been sown. She needed to discover whether there was any valid reason for her feelings of unease.

Appearing to have regained her poise, Susana stalked out of the room. She had, however, already started planning how to exact her revenge. She didn't like being made a fool of, especially by a jumped-up Jew like Bernard Morris. And as for Max Freedland, she had every intention of exposing *him* as a fraud.

The solicitor thanked Bernard for his hospitality, then followed his wife out of the room.

'Well, it really has been a most entertaining dinner party,' the banker beamed, going up to Bernard. 'I'd better go and get hold of the old girl then we should be off. I must say, Lucinda would have loved your *pièce de résistance*.'

'Never a dull moment, eh, Rupert?' the host grinned, indicating that he had relished it himself.

'Next time, you must come down to Sussex - though I can't quite see you fitting in at a polo match,' the huge man smirked.

Bernard laughed, ignoring the joke at his expense. 'Don't forget we're meeting on Tuesday,' he reminded the banker.

'Looking forward to it already,' the other man replied smoothly, slapping his host on the back. With that, he strode out of the room to find his wife.

Fifteen minutes later, the Merediths had also departed.

Bernard returned to the drawing room, where he found Charlotte's attention fixed on the Renoir that she was holding away from her.

'Had them all fooled, didn't it?' he said, smiling contentedly.

Charlotte didn't reply. Despite the fact that he had exonerated himself, she was worried about working for a man who so obviously enjoyed courting controversy. Worse, he had allowed her to believe that the two paintings were originals.

'Listen, young lady,' he said from a few feet away, 'I know what's going through your pretty little mind, but business is business.'

'But I have no experience of that world,' Charlotte protested. Turning to face her employer, she felt close to tears.

'Then I'll teach you. Together, we can make a great team. Now come here,' Bernard said.

Charlotte put the painting down. Still in her stockinged feet, she moved closer until, feeling his warm breath on her, she willingly entered his open arms. Her doubts about him suddenly evaporated and she became calm. Bernard kissed the side of her head.

'You had those two blokes next to you eating out of your hand. I could see them thinking, *What's a classy bird like that doing with a common bloke like him*?'

He held her in a tight embrace, no words passing between them. She didn't want that moment to end. There was something about this man which evoked a strange mixture of emotions within her.

'It's getting late,' Bernard said after a while, separating himself from the young woman.

'I'm sorry. I must have had too much to drink,' Charlotte replied. 'Please could you find me a taxi?'

'I've given William the night off and you're not going

home on your own at this hour. There's a guest room already made up on the top floor. I'm sure you'll be comfortable, and there's a bathroom next door to it.'

'Well, only if you're sure that it won't be inconvenient,' Charlotte yawned, rubbing her eyes.

'It'll be a nice change having a guest for Sunday breakfast. It's the maid's day off, so I'm afraid you'll have to put up with my scrambled eggs,' Bernard said, grinning.

Taking Charlotte by the hand, he led her out into the hall, and together they proceeded up a winding staircase.

'Right then! So I'll see you in the morning,' Bernard told her as they approached the guest bedroom. 'Sleep well,' he whispered, letting go of her.

Looking back as the door closed gently behind her, Charlotte found that she was already missing Bernard's warmth against her. Alone in the large guest bed, her body weighed down with exhaustion, she felt herself falling into a deep sleep, disappointed that he had not asked her to spend the night with him.

Bernard stayed awake, sober and scheming how to get his hands on Bertie Chesterfield's Berkeley Square portfolio. He was already up to the limit of his overdraft and three months behind with his interest payments. What he really needed was a joint venture partner to share the risk. but he knew that would only be seen as a sign of weakness because he couldn't raise the three-and-a-half million for the purchase himself. Bernard sighed. He needed that deal badly and he would get it. Even if Tuesday's meeting with the bank meant re-mortgaging every single thing he had.

*

Just after 2 a.m. that same Saturday night, a young underage girl got out of a sports car parked on a derelict piece of land behind Kings Cross railway station. She tucked the seven one-pound notes down the front of her scruffy low-cut dress and walked briskly away, her long black hair blowing in the night breeze while the Jaguar sped off in the opposite direction.

Twenty minutes later, James Robson opened the front door of his house in South Kensington and crept up the stairs to the spare bedroom; why he bothered to be discreet, he really couldn't say. Susana turned a blind eye to his liking for young whores. Why wouldn't she? She was quite open about her own sexual exploits, having no compunction in allowing her predatory instincts to get the better of her in her private life. And she wasn't always perfect in public either, such as this evening when, having failed to discredit her host, hadn't she then focused her attentions on his female dinner companion?

His and Susana's relationship hadn't exactly started conventionally, so it was perhaps no surprise that their attitudes and boundaries were different to those of most other couples. After all, they were only together because of that business with her father and the priceless works of art that he had suddenly been in such a hurry to sell.

James knew all about men like Susana's father. He hadn't been in Military Intelligence for nothing. He had tracked all of the top Nazis who had sought refuge in South America at the end of the war. Most of them had obtained new identities by bribing the authorities, and so unless they were kidnapped, there was little chance that they would ever be brought to justice.

He and Susana had met at the 1949 Wimbledon Ladies

Lawn Tennis Finals when she was just nineteen. He was entertaining clients and Susana was sitting alone in the row in front. They soon got talking and James established that she was from a wealthy family in Buenos Aires. Susana explained that ideally, she was looking to move to London where she could put her expert knowledge of nineteenth-century art to good use. She had already started looking for a home and asked whether he might assist her with the name of a reputable bank since she wanted to make a sizeable deposit.

Three days later, a private car picked her up at the Savoy Hotel to take her to a meeting at Meredith's Bank in Lombard Street. James had known Rupert for ten years. He'd gone out with the banker's sister Elizabeth during the war but the relationship ended abruptly when she turned up one day unannounced at his flat in Notting Hill and caught him in a compromising position with his teenaged secretary. The men nevertheless had already established a professional relationship; even though it was no secret that they actively loathed each other.

Learning of the extent of her family's wealth, Meredith's were keen to take on Susana – or more accurately her father – as clients. There was a tacit understanding between the two of them that since James had effected the introduction, his firm would retain the client's legal work.

At first, James was no different from any of the others. Spellbound by Susana's extraordinary beauty and the raw passion that oozed effortlessly out of her, he had no compunction about starting an affair that, despite its physical intensity, was devoid of any real affection. The truth was, he was aware they both had agendas. He was her entrée into the London Establishment, and she would be instrumental in securing a great deal of money for him as his reward for facilitating a route out of South America for the plundered items of art that were in her family's possession. That was how he'd got her the position at Brockets. The latter weren't going to turn down the opportunity of a huge amount of commission.

It always amazed him that the people at Brockets never asked about the origins of the valuable pieces of art that found their way into the auction rooms. It was frankly incredible. However, James Robson had his own problems to worry about, such as how he was going to rid himself of his obsession with that dark-haired prostitute. His meetings with the young girl were becoming a bit too regular.

7

The newspaper editor, an overweight fellow with a pock-marked face and chronic bad breath, slammed down the phone.

''Ere, Francis!' he bellowed across the noisy Fleet Street office. 'I've got something you can get your teeth into, lad.'

The young, bright-eyed journalist in an ill-fitting suit which made him look like an overgrown schoolboy peered up from behind his typewriter.

'Be with you in two jiffs, sir,' he said. Retrieving his morning's work from his machine, he quickly scanned the content, got off his swivel chair and scurried over to the editor's desk.

'Got a tip there's some dodgy paintings doing the rounds by a bloke named Max Freedland,' the editor divulged.

'Why didn't you tell them to go to the police?' the young man asked naively.

'What, and ruin the chance of a good story?' the fat man berated him. 'Call yourself a newspaperman? Don't suppose you'd even recognise pussy if it was stuck in front of your nose.'

'No, sir,' Francis replied, standing with his hands in his pockets. He had learned from bitter experience that it was always safer to let the old man vent his bad temper.

'Talking of pussy, got any further news on that young prostitute?'

'I'm meeting her at the Angel this afternoon, sir,' the young reporter informed him, looking pleased with himself.

'If she's willing to spill the beans on certain members of the Establishment, I want the exclusive,' the editor warned him. 'Make sure you get the names of who she's been knobbing.' He took out his wallet and peeled off some five-pound notes, thinking that he would be most surprised if the young man did not help himself to what was on offer.

'Here, give her twenty-five quid and tell her there's more where that came from. Then bugger off down to those poncey Bond Street galleries and see what you can find out about our Max Freedland.'

In the weeks that followed the dinner party, Charlotte began to see more of Bernard. However, the experience with Susana had left her wondering whether there might have been an element of truth in the woman's aspersions against her employer. The unexpected visit by the fresh-faced reporter, asking probing questions about the artist Max Freedland whilst pretending to be interested in his paintings, only added to her unease. Nevertheless, she found herself growing increasingly fond of Bernard. She enjoyed his company and was now a regular visitor to the house in Mayfair. Bernard himself felt comfortable with Charlotte and always took her as his chosen companion whenever he dined out.

After the night spent in his home, Charlotte had expected that a romantic relationship would ensue, but Bernard never took advantage of the private moments between them to become more intimate with her. They were more like good friends. She just assumed that there were aspects of his private life that he didn't wish to share with her. Nor did he ever ask her about her own. It seemed enough for him to have her by his side. He often said that she had 'class'. It was as if, in some strange way, she provided him with the respectability that he felt he lacked. In Bernard, Charlotte found a warm-hearted father-like figure who gave her a feeling of security without demanding anything in return.

Over the course of the summer of 1956, feeling settled in her job, Charlotte's confidence grew, enabling her to identify several young artists whom she considered showed potential, and was given a free hand to promote their works. None, however, proved as popular as Max Freedland. She was relieved that Bernard had managed to persuade his friend to increase the output of his original paintings, and the artist, grateful for the extra income, had even agreed to come up with further posthumous works by the 'deceased' Daniel Petrovitch.

The only bone of contention was Bernard's refusal to allow her to visit the artist. When she tried to explain that his intransigence was hindering her ability to do her job, he just said that she should be patient. She again became suspicious, convinced that he was hiding something from her, but she didn't know what or why. She often wondered whether his reluctance to talk about himself or divulge any details of his family meant that, like her, he too was trying to escape from his past. Perhaps Max was part of that past?

Charlotte consoled herself with the thought that Bernard had agreed to her proposal for a spring exhibition the following year featuring Max Freedland's work. In less than six months, Bernard would have no choice but to acquaint her with their most popular artist.

As she got out of the tube at West Hampstead station, Charlotte buttoned her coat. The days were drawing in and there was a distinct hint of autumn in the air. She was feeling happy. Bernard had informed her that he had secured the Earl of Chesterfield's Berkeley Square portfolio and was now the owner of thirty-five properties in one of the most exclusive parts of London. In his own words, he had joined the 'big league'. He planned a celebration trip to the South of France for Christmas. The gallery would be closed over the holiday period and he had asked her to go with him. He knew the Cote d'Azur well, he said, and wanted to show her where the 'rich' lived it up.

She didn't know that he had already booked the car train to Avignon and that Joan, to her disgust, had been asked to make the hotel reservations in Nice.

Charlotte let herself into the flat in Gladys Road and went straight to the kitchen. She had been too busy for lunch and, once again, had got through the day on black coffee and a packet of ginger biscuits. From the kitchen cabinet, she took out a couple of eggs and a slice of cheese to make herself an omelette for her dinner. Before cooking, she put the geyser on to heat the water. She was looking forward to relaxing in a hot bath scented with a bath cube, and having an early night.

Taking her plate over to the kitchen table, Charlotte began sifting through the handful of letters she'd picked up from the front door mat. The tenants downstairs always put her post through her door. One letter in particular stood out from the others. It had a Swiss stamp and a Davos postmark. Her first thoughts were that it must be from Frau Goldstein, the woman who had befriended her at the sanatorium. Only she couldn't recall giving her the

London address.

Charlotte sliced open the thin blue envelope with her finger and started reading the two pages of German writing. It was from Johann. After examining it for a second time, she sat stunned, unable to move. Johann wrote that he was coming to London in a fortnight's time for a three-day medical conference and needed to see her urgently. He would be staying in a hotel nearby in Swiss Cottage.

Discarding her half-eaten dinner, Charlotte tried to come to terms with the contents of the letter. Johann mentioned that he was getting a divorce and wanted her to go back and live with him in Switzerland. He said that he loved her and that he had only let her leave because his father-in-law had threatened to remove him from his position as Director unless he terminated their relationship.

Charlotte got up from the table. A dull ache penetrated her insides. She moved into the lounge, lit a cigarette and slumped back into the worn-out sofa. 'Why now?' she asked herself. She took another drag, emitting a small stream of smoke upwards. She could refuse to meet him ... Yes, that was the answer. After all, she hadn't accepted his invitation when she was at the sanatorium, so it wouldn't exactly be unexpected. She would write back immediately, telling him that she was settled in a good job in London and would prefer them to just remain friends.

She felt better once she had made the right decision.

Charlotte then went into the bathroom and ran the hot tap. It had been a long day. She passed into the bedroom and began removing her clothes. Looking at herself in the full-length mirror, she placed her hands over her small breasts. Not for her the latest tight-fitting fashions to accentuate a voluptuous figure she was destined never to have. Johann was the one who had taught her to love her boyish shape. He had awakened her sexuality, shown her how to please him, and in turn had satisfied every single one of her desires.

Charlotte stepped into the soothingly hot bath and began to soap herself down. She leaned back and submerged her shoulders under the surface of the water. Against her will, Johann's image appeared so vividly that she was suddenly filled with an uncontrollable need. She knew then that she was powerless to stop herself from meeting him.

Over the next two weeks, Charlotte immersed herself in her work, happy to be distracted from thinking about her personal life. Her first priority was to arrange the dispatch of Max Freedland's paintings to their purchasers. A new batch of his works was again overdue, leaving the walls in serious danger of looking bare. The reliance on the enigmatic artist for such a major part of their business worried Charlotte, and she knew she would have to redouble her efforts to find other talented painters who would prove equally popular to their customers.

She felt aggrieved that Bernard was perfectly content for her to take responsibility for the enterprise without providing her with the means to make it a success. To him, it was just another one of his interests, whereas she was dependent on the gallery for her livelihood.

On the day that Johann was arriving, Charlotte awoke with a sense of great expectation. The morning was bright, and since it was still early, after breakfast she decided to walk the three miles to work. She would then leave promptly at five in the afternoon and be home in plenty of time to prepare herself to meet Johann at his hotel at seven.

'Morning, Charlotte,' a familiar voice called out from behind her desk, when she arrived at the gallery an hour later.

'Bernard!' Charlotte was startled and a little put out by her employer's unexpected appearance. Why did he have to show up today of all days? A feeling of unease gripped her.

'Just wanted to let you know that I've got a few things to sort out and so I won't be around for a while – maybe a good week or two,' he announced. 'I'm sure you won't mind looking after the shop until I get back?'

'No, of course not,' Charlotte answered hesitantly.

Bernard then got up and, without showing his usual warmth, walked straight past her towards the gallery door. She was baffled by his uncharacteristic aloofness. It was almost as if he knew about the rendezvous with Johann.

'Oh, and I've topped up the bank account with a couple of grand,' he said, turning around. 'Joan's a signatory so you won't run short. She knows where to find me if there's an emergency.' These were his parting words as he stepped out onto the pavement.

Charlotte was a bit shaken. She had no idea why Bernard had chosen to exclude her. Taking off her coat, she sat down at her desk, but before she could start work she heard the sound of heavy footsteps coming down the stairs. Looking up, she saw the secretary striding towards her. It was clear from her expression that Joan was in a confrontational mood.

'The guv'nor said you were to have this,' she stated curtly, holding out a buff-coloured envelope.

'Did Bernard say when he might be returning?' Charlotte enquired. She took the packet and without thinking put it in her desk drawer.

'All *you* need to know is that Mr Morris is going to be indisposed for several weeks. He has given strict instructions that he is *not* to be contacted. I've been left in charge, so you're just going to have to deal with me!' Joan was standing with her hands on her broad hips, doing her utmost to be unfriendly.

Charlotte was now convinced that something was seriously amiss.

'And you can take that stupid look off your face for a start,' the woman said nastily. 'If you hadn't had the guv'nor running after you like a bee around a honey pot, none of this would have happened.'

'Are you saying he's unwell?' Charlotte asked, beginning to get angry. How dare the woman speak to her like this.

'Didn't take *you* long to get your claws into him, did it?'

'I don't know what you mean,' Charlotte said, recoiling into her chair. 'Bernard asked me to come and work for him. *He's* the one who approached *me!*'

'You're lying, just like the rest of them. Because he's loaded you think he's a soft touch. Well, I'll tell you a thing or two, young lady,' Joan sneered, continuing with her diatribe. 'As soon as he's seen what you're really after, it'll be bye, bye and out the door for you!' She gestured with a wave of her flabby hand. 'Then you'll be on the first train back to Switzerland - or wherever else it is you really come from.'

The large woman then turned her back on Charlotte

and stomped off up to her office on the first floor.

The onslaught had left Charlotte badly shaken. It was clear from the first day she met her that the older woman had felt threatened by her presence. Charlotte now suspected that the antagonism towards her was because Joan had designs on Bernard herself and had now seen her chances disappear.

Calming herself, Charlotte took a deep breath. She had a job to do and had no intention of being distracted from it by something that she could do little about.

At the same time, Bernard's Rolls-Royce pulled up outside the private hospital in Central London. The results of the X-ray three weeks before had come as a shock. When he first received the news, Bernard went into denial. Despite the pain in his chest, he tried to carry on as normal. The specialist had confirmed that he had two badly blocked arteries that needed urgent attention.

The same afternoon, Bernard visited James Robson in his office at Pall Mall to grant him Power of Attorney over his business affairs. He also instructed his lawyer to draw up a will in the event of his sudden demise. There were many people who depended upon him and he wasn't going to leave them wanting.

William opened the rear passenger door for his employer. He then removed two smart leather suitcases from the boot of the car and carried them into the clinic. Bernard followed behind. For the first time, it truly sunk in that he was seriously ill and that he might not pull through.

Accompanied by his chauffeur, he joined a small queue of patients waiting to be admitted.

'William, look after Charlotte, will you?' Bernard said. 'I don't want her worrying. All she knows is that I won't be in for a while.'

'Don't worry, guv, I'll take care of everything,' the chauffeur replied, putting on a brave face. Hospitals made him squeamish however posh they were, and he just wanted to get the hell out of the place.

'You've got the cash and fags for my mother,' his boss reminded him. 'Give her a call, will you? Even better, drop in from time to time to see if she's all right, but remember to keep shtum. I've primed Max that we need more paintings, but he was probably pissed and has forgotten by now. Give him fifty quid. That should keep him sweet until I'm back on my feet.' Bernard took out a wad of new five-pound notes and handed it over. 'Tell him he can go and buy some new paintbrushes.'

And then suddenly it was his turn. 'Bernard Morris,' he announced to the admissions clerk.

'You are under Mr Peter Glazer, I believe,' the man behind the desk remarked, casting his eye down at the list of the day's admissions. 'You'll be in Room Eight on the first floor. Your procedure is scheduled for six o'clock. The porter will take your cases. I assume that you've been nil by mouth since last night?'

Bernard nodded.

'Splendid. Please fill in your details and sign the disclaimer at the back and we'll get started, shall we? How will you be settling your account, cash or by cheque?'

'That's a bit quick, isn't it? I haven't even had the bloody operation yet,' Bernard replied, nettled.

'Sir, this is a *private* hospital,' the administrator said condescendingly. 'It is quite normal practice, I can assure you.'

'You'd better get Joan to draw some more cash,' Bernard sighed, turning to his driver. 'Now go on – sod off.'

A porter appeared. He took hold of Bernard's cases and escorted the patient to the lift for the first floor.

William returned to his parked vehicle. He helped himself to ten pounds, which he stuffed in his back pocket, then put the rest into the glove compartment of the Rolls. Max would be none the wiser, he chuckled to himself. He then sped off for an early lunch.

8

Charlotte hurried out of the gallery and hailed a taxi. What with the strange encounter with Bernard and then being subjected to such unpleasantness from his secretary, she felt emotionally drained, hardly in the right frame of mind for a romantic reunion with Johann. Maybe she had been too hasty in dismissing the possibility of a life with him? London, it was true, had provided her with valuable experience, but she had forgone the chance of happiness to pursue a career. She now realised that she wanted something more. If Johann asked her, she would seriously consider moving back to Switzerland with him.

Charlotte glanced at her watch. It was nearly twenty past seven when she arrived at the quaint three-star hotel tucked away in a side street behind Swiss Cottage tube station. The rain that had persisted all day snarled up the traffic and had made her short cab journey seem endless. Not bothering to check her make-up, she hurried up the steps and went over to the front desk. She announced herself to a lethargic-looking receptionist and asked her to inform Dr Weber that she had arrived. The young woman pointed to a tanned man in a blue blazer sitting in an armchair next to an open fire in the small lounge area. He was casually flipping through an evening newspaper when he saw her familiar figure approaching.

'Charlotte!' he called out, getting up from his chair to

greet his former mistress. 'You look wonderful.' Placing his perfectly manicured hands on her shoulders, he kissed her on both cheeks.

'It's been a long time,' she replied, smiling, allowing herself a prolonged look at the man she had never been able to forget. Charlotte could feel her heart beating loudly. Johann always had that effect on her. He had been so handsome, with his Roman looks and strong dimpled chin, but she could see that over the years he had become greyer, more distinguished. Other than a doctor, he could easily have passed for a Hollywood actor. Someone like Cary Grant.

'Come! I have a table reserved in the restaurant. I hope that you don't mind eating here. I'm a little tired from the journey. Anyway, at least we can speak privately,' Johann said, taking her arm.

They passed through the hall into a cosy dining room, which was occupied at only one other table, and which looked out onto an illuminated garden.

'I regret that tonight, we only have the set menu,' the waiter said, placing two creased pieces of paper in front of them. 'May I recommend the consommé followed by the sole Meunière? You would care for an apéritif perhaps, while you are deciding?'

'We would like some white wine,' Johann said, busily studying the menu.

'Then you must try our vin de la maison. It is a Chassagne-Montrachet premier cru 1949,' the waiter announced proudly.

'That is most acceptable,' Johann decided. 'Please ensure that it is suitably chilled. And we will take your suggestion for the starter and the main course.' He glanced at Charlotte, who nodded her approval.

'Thank you! I will bring the wine immediately.' The waiter retrieved the menus and scurried away to the kitchen.

'I didn't expect to hear from you. It was a nice surprise,' Charlotte said, trying not to appear overly keen.

'Well, I could hardly come to London without looking you up,' Johann answered. 'Anyway, since you refused my invitation in Davos, you left me with little choice.' He smiled and reached out for her hand.

'You left it rather late. I was leaving the next morning,' Charlotte reminded him. 'I had expected to see you when I arrived.' She recalled how disappointed she had felt when he hadn't contacted her.

'Well, I'm here now, and over the next few days I'm sure that I can find a way of making it up to you,' he replied.

Charlotte looked into his eyes, and in that briefest of moments, it was as if they had never been apart. She remembered the first time. It was shortly after she arrived in Switzerland. They were in his top- floor apartment in the sanatorium surrounded by the snow-capped mountains. A fire was burning cosily in the huge living room. They spent the whole weekend in bed. To avoid suspicion from other members of the staff, Johann had arranged for their meals to be sent up to them from the dining room, on the pretext that he was entertaining an important foreign dignitary. What she remembered most was them waking up in each other's arms. Johann had made her feel complete.

'So, what brings you to London?' she asked. 'I thought you couldn't afford time away from the sanatorium? That is what you always told me when you made me travel to you from Basel.'

Just then, the waiter arrived with the wine. Seeing that his guests were engrossed in private conversation, he placed the bottle in an ice bucket by the side of the table and slid discreetly away.

'Margaretha and I are finally divorced. I thought I could do with some time off so I accepted the invitation to come to London,' Johann lied glibly. 'But the important thing is that we can now be together.'

Noticing that the other couple had left and that they were now alone in the restaurant, he moved his chair around and drawing Charlotte close to him, he kissed her passionately. Underneath the long white tablecloth, his hand slipped between her legs. Charlotte started to moan and then, remembering where she was, she opened her eyes and looked at him beseechingly.

'Johann, stop, please,' she begged half-heartedly, wanting him to continue but afraid of being seen by the waiter.

Satisfied that he still had that power over Charlotte, Johann gradually withdrew from their embrace. Perhaps the trip to London might be able to salvage his career, after all.

The investigation had taken its toll. The sanatorium was forced to close and he'd been severely censured. He had never expected that Trudi Weiss would testify against him. Naturally, she was upset when he finished with her. She'd been his mistress for three years. But that didn't mean she had any claim to him! However, the degree of vitriol that poured out of her mouth about the draconian practices that she was forced to carry out on the patients, left him stunned. In the circumstances, he thought he had got off lightly with a 25,000 franc fine.

Responding to Charlotte's gaze of arousal, he took out his wallet and withdrew two five-pound notes, which he left on the table. Not waiting for their meal to arrive, the couple got up together and left the restaurant, taking the bottle of wine and two glasses with them.

Ignoring the receptionist's knowing look, they proceeded up the main staircase to Johann's bedroom on the second floor. He unlocked the door and entered the darkened room, placing the bottle down on the dressing-table next to the two glasses.

Taking the initiative, which she knew excited him, Charlotte kicked the door closed with her high-heeled shoe and pushed him backwards towards the small double bed.

Afterwards, Charlotte lay on her back, panting for breath.

'Johann, please don't leave me again,' she implored, her arms stretching out to embrace him. 'You will take me back with you, won't you?'

'I think there's a reasonable possibility, assuming of course that there's more where that came from,' he said breathlessly. 'Now I don't know about you, but I'm ravenous.'

'Me too, but it's late and I don't suppose they offer room service,' Charlotte replied. She felt so exhilarated; it hadn't registered until now that she hadn't eaten all day, having been first upset and then letting her nerves get the better of her.

Johann switched on the bedside light, picked up the phone and ordered a selection of sandwiches and a pot of coffee. The same receptionist who had been on duty all evening, responding to her guest's charm, said that she would go into the kitchen and make them herself.

Johann went over and poured out two glasses of wine. He handed one to Charlotte, and when a few minutes later, there was a faint sound of knocking, Johann quickly put on his trousers and went to the door. The receptionist entered the dimly lit bedroom carrying a silver tray. Charlotte, hoping that she hadn't been spotted, pulled the blanket over her head.

'Breakfast is served between seven and nine-thirty,' the young woman informed him, placing the tray down on the dressing-table. 'I assume that you will want it brought to the room?'

'Yes, please,' Johann said.

'The kitchen is closed for our full English, so I'm afraid it'll just be our continental breakfast. Will you require orange juice and tea or coffee with your breadbasket?'

'Orange juice and coffee will be just fine,' Johann replied impatiently.

'Will there be anything else, sir?' the hotel employee then asked. Glancing at the sight of two feet sticking out from the bedcovers, a smirk appeared on her pasty face.

'No, that will be all. How much will that be?' Johann asked.

'It's already been paid for, sir.'

'Really? By whom?'

'The ten pounds you left in the dining room when madam was feeling unwell was more than sufficient. Please accept the sandwiches with the compliments of the hotel.'

'That's very kind of you,' Johann replied, looking surprised.

The receptionist then made to leave the room.

'Just one moment!' Johann called out. He went over to

the wardrobe and pulled out some loose change from his overcoat and gave it to her.

'Thank you, sir,' she said. Followed by a cheeky, 'I'm glad to see that madam is feeling better,' as she opened the door and sped away.

Charlotte bobbed up from beneath the covers and burst out laughing. 'I think we gave that poor girl quite a shock,' she said, allowing the covers to fall away.

'And probably an education,' Johann retorted. He helped himself to a sandwich and carried the tray to the bed.

'You are certainly qualified to give lessons,' Charlotte told him. Then, planting herself on his lap, she took a large bite out of his sandwich.

'I wonder what your father would say if he could see us now,' Johann mused.

'I used to dream that you would sweep me away,' Charlotte said, completely absorbed in her own thoughts. 'Anywhere to escape the misery of war!'

'You were so immersed in your painting I'm surprised that you noticed what was going on around you. Although I do remember you being quite upset when that Jewish boy you were friendly with upstairs got taken away. What was his name?'

Charlotte batted away the question. 'I just remember a fourteen-year-old girl being smitten with this older man,' she answered, placing her arms around her lover's neck. 'But you never gave me any encouragement,' she added. 'You seemed to be far more interested in my mother.'

'That's absolute rubbish!' Johann blustered.

'Well, it was a bit strange that you always came to the apartment when Father was away,' Charlotte teased.

'Being in the Medical Corps, I was frequently home on leave having to attend some course or other,' Johann replied, trying to justify himself. 'Gerhart was always flying missions and he asked me to make sure that you were both all right.'

Moving Charlotte off his lap, he reached over to the bedside table for his cigarettes. 'She was a beautiful woman, your mother,' he murmured.

'So everyone told me,' Charlotte remarked without any hint of affection.

'I felt quite sorry for her, all that time on her own, never knowing when or whether your father might return.' Johann inhaled deeply, blowing the smoke out through his nose. 'But we were just friends,' he stressed.

Charlotte took a gulp of the lukewarm coffee. She wondered what her lover had meant by the last few words.

Johann stretched out on the bed.

'Then when Hans was killed,' he continued, 'your mother had her breakdown.'

'Hans was her favourite,' Charlotte revealed. 'That's why I was so close to Papa. Mother never loved me.'

'Hans was a disappointment to your father,' Johann said harshly. 'Gerhart often told me that he was worried that Hans would never amount to anything. It wasn't until he joined the *Hitlerjugend* that he found his true vocation. It turned him into a fine young man.'

Charlotte recalled her own uniform of white shirt and coarse blue skirt of the *Hitler Mädchen* - the girls' unit. It wasn't so much the outdoor activities, which in truth she quite enjoyed, but their attempt to instil in her the range of domestic skills to prepare her to be a good German housewife that she found so absurd. She wondered why

Johann had suddenly started talking about the years in Berlin. He had never mentioned the relationship with her mother before. And the look of distaste on his face when he referred to her father, who was supposed to have been a close friend, shocked her. It almost sounded as if he had been jealous of him.

She quickly put these thoughts out of her mind. She wasn't going to let anything that happened so long ago come between them.

'It's time we got some sleep. Some of us have to work tomorrow.' Johann yawned and proceeded to remove his trousers once more and get into bed.

'I've got a better idea,' Charlotte whispered, and crawled over to him.

Later, exhausted, they pulled the sheets over themselves. Charlotte, who felt more than ever that their bodies fitted perfectly together and that such compatibility must surely mean they were destined to be together for ever, fell asleep immediately. Johann stayed awake, happy that he had achieved the first part of his plan. Charlotte was clearly obsessed with him. He'd go the next morning to the conference at the British Medical Association and not bother with the other two days. That would give Charlotte enough time to quit her job and give notice on her apartment. They would return to Switzerland, where he would open his own clinic in Zurich. She could arrange to have her things shipped over to her, after she moved in with him. He knew how rich the Schlessingers were and that Charlotte had inherited a fortune. Lying dormant in some bank account in Switzerland was a vast amount of money which he was determined to benefit from, even if it meant having to marry the girl.

Charlotte was still half-asleep when she felt Johann leave her side. 'What time is it?' she asked groggily.

Johann reached over for his watch. 'Ten to seven. I'm going to take a shower,' he replied. 'Go back to sleep, and we can see each other this afternoon.'

'You do still want me to come back to Switzerland?' Charlotte asked, needing further reassurance. She suddenly realised that she hadn't given any thought to the gallery and Bernard. How would she be able to tell him that she was leaving? She couldn't just walk away without a valid reason.

It was then she remembered the unpleasant exchange with his secretary. That was it! She would write Bernard a letter, explaining that her life had been made intolerable and that she couldn't carry on working where she was the cause of such great resentment. She put her head back on the pillow and drifted off to sleep for a short while. She was awoken by a kiss on her forehead and saw that Johann, fully dressed in a dark suit, was about to leave.

'Keep the bed warm and I'll see you here later,' he whispered in her ear.

'Wait!' Charlotte called out after him. 'I didn't bring a nightie and I can hardly open the door for breakfast like this.'

'I've got a spare shirt in the case,' Johann answered. And not bothering to turn around at the door, he left the room.

Charlotte stretched out in the bed. The apprehension that had filled her as she counted down the days for Johann to arrive had been replaced by a warm glow. Together again with the person she had been in love with for half her life, she was the happiest she could remember.

Suspecting that the breakfast would soon be arriving, Charlotte sprang out of bed and went to the leather suitcase that lay open on the floor by the window. Sitting cross-legged on the carpet, she carefully removed the meticulously folded clothes that had been separated by layers of tissue paper until she came to Johann's shirts. She took out the first one and held it against her shoulders. Letting it unfurl, she saw it covered the tops of her knees. Charlotte slipped the shirt over her head and had started putting back the clothes when she noticed something protruding out of the side pocket of the suitcase. It was a crumpled photograph of a voluptuous naked woman lying on a bed. She picked it up and looked at it more closely. The face seemed familiar but it took her a few seconds to recall where she had seen the woman before. Then it came to her. It was the attractive nurse who had admitted her at the sanatorium. On the reverse was written *Forever yours, all my love,* and was signed *Trudi.*

Charlotte looked at it again to make sure. But there was no mistake; it was the same person. Then she saw that it was dated 30 June 1953: six months before she left for England. Johann had obviously been having an affair with the nurse during the entire time they had been together.

Charlotte felt herself start to cry. Why had Johann done this? Was he deliberately trying to hurt her? She didn't understand what had happened, and realised that nor did she understand Johann in the way she thought she did. Perhaps she didn't understand him at all. Charlotte felt devastated.

It was light outside now and she just needed to get out of the hotel as quickly as possible. She threw off Johann's shirt, got dressed and, taking her handbag, let herself out of the room. Rushing down the main staircase, she nearly collided with a waiter carrying a breakfast tray. Fortunately, there were other guests at reception so she wasn't spotted as she dashed through the lobby to the open front door and away, out into the drizzle of the cold November morning. With tears running down her face, the young woman blindly made her way along unfamiliar streets, eventually finding herself in a park. She took a steep path that led to the top of a hill, from where the silhouettes of the buildings of Central London were partially visible through the early-morning mist.

Charlotte stood shivering. How could she have been so naïve, thinking that she was the only one? Had he told all his other women that he was getting divorced purely to mislead them into thinking that one day he would be free? Her whole world had fallen apart. She felt totally alone – the only link to her old life was now broken.

Lost in her misery, Charlotte carried on walking, out of the park now and along a busy main thoroughfare. In the distance, a clock struck nine. She looked up and saw that she was standing opposite the big church on the Marylebone Road. She had been walking for well over an hour and was drenched to the bone. A thought passed through her mind. Was she being punished?

For a moment, she was tempted to enter the old church. Her father was a staunch Catholic but her mother wouldn't have anything to do with religion. She consented, however, to having her children baptised. Charlotte went up to the entrance but it was closed. Feeling dizzy, she sat down on a bench in the gravelled courtyard and placed her head in her hands.

''Ere, that's my seat you've parked yourself on!' a disgruntled voice called out.

Charlotte opened her eyes. A tramp with an unkempt beard appeared from the side of the church. Incensed, he was striding towards her in a pair of worn-out boots and a torn Army greatcoat, clasping a half-bottle of whisky protectively to his chest.

'Got a few coppers for a cup of tea, miss?' the man then whined, putting out his grimy hand. When Charlotte remained silent, hoping that he would go away, he jeered, 'What's the matter, dearie? Your punter run off without paying you? Get a lot of you tarts around here. Gives the place a bad name,' he grumbled and took a drink from the bottle before belching.

Just then, a black police car pulled up outside the church and two Metropolitan Police officers marched across the courtyard.

'Still here, Jim?' the younger one said.

'Thought we warned you about making a nuisance of yourself. Go on, clear off before we charge you with harassment,' snapped his older colleague.

'All right! All right! Keep your hair on. I'm going.' The tramp took another swig from the bottle and staggered off in the direction of Baker Street station.

'Everything all right, miss?' the older officer asked Charlotte. 'Bit early for church. It doesn't open till ten on a weekday.'

'No, I'm fine, thank you,' she replied, her teeth chattering in the cold wind. 'I'd lost my way and just wanted to rest for a while before going home.'

'And where's home, love?' the other asked, not quite believing her.

'I live in West Hampstead.'

The two policemen stepped away to talk to each other in private.

'I don't suppose you have any identification on you?' the young one said, turning back to her.

'My papers are at home,' Charlotte replied innocently, wondering why they were continuing to question her.

'All right, love,' the same one said. 'We'll give you a lift back to West Hampstead, see you safely home and then we'll be on our way.'

'Thank you, that's really most kind of you, but I have money for a bus.' Charlotte began rummaging through her bag for her purse.

'Come on,' the older policeman said kindly. 'Looks like you could do with getting home sharpish for a hot cup of tea.'

Charlotte accompanied the two policemen to their car, which sped off, heading up towards the suburbs of north-west London.

9

Charlotte got out her keys and let herself into the house. The police car had already gone by the time she closed the front door. She was emotionally drained but worst of all, she felt unclean. All she wanted to do was roll up in a ball and erase the last twenty-four hours. But before she could go to bed, she had to wash away any traces of Johann. Trudging upstairs to her flat, she went in and put the water on to heat. While waiting, she had a hot cup of tea as the policeman had advised. After filling the bath, she stripped off her clothes and flung them in a heap, and then scrubbed herself all over.

It was dark when Charlotte stirred. Apart from making herself more tea and some toast, she didn't have the will to face reality. For the next two days, she stayed in bed. Then, having completely lost track of time, on the third day she finally emerged from the bedroom. Unsteady on her feet, she tottered into the kitchen and boiled the kettle. Feeling hungry, she opened the cupboard and with a teaspoon scooped out the remaining contents of a tub of cheese spread. She glanced up at the clock on the wall; it was ten past five in the morning. The sound of a milk cart on its rounds resonated from outside her window. Making herself a mug of black coffee, she sat down at the kitchen table. She felt unexpectedly calm. Johann had hurt her, but at least she had found out what he was like before it was too late. There was still her job, and in Bernard, someone who genuinely cared for her. She decided she needed to forget the past and get on with her life.

Charlotte got up and wandered into the tiny box room that served as her studio. Displayed on the easel in the middle of the room was the half-finished canvas of a young girl with her father; she had started it months ago. Picking up her palette, she slowly began to mix her oils, gaining in confidence as she worked. As she was reproducing the features of her beloved father, she suddenly paused. The awful thought entered her head that all the time Gerhart Schlessinger had been away from home, fighting in the war, Johann and her mother had been lovers. When he made that strange comment in the hotel room, the one about just being friends, Charlotte had dismissed it on the grounds that a man like Johann was incapable of betraying a friend, of doing something like that, not with her own mother. But she now knew Johann was not the man she thought he was.

A feeling of intense loathing came over her. The man for whom, only hours before, she had been prepared to turn her life upside down, was a monster.

She carried on furiously trying to obliterate his image from her mind, while recreating the image of her father.

Johann had returned to the hotel shortly after four the same afternoon. He noticed that the room had been made up and that Charlotte had gone. He felt a huge sense of relief. She had obviously grown tired of waiting for him and had returned to her flat.

In a stroke of good fortune, at the conference he had

been placed next to the wealthy widow of the esteemed philanthropist Sir Hugh Marchant. Her husband had bequeathed millions of pounds to charitable causes and a substantial sum had been earmarked for a new psychiatric clinic bearing his name in Guildford, just thirty miles outside of London. Johann had spent the whole day ingratiating himself with Sir Hugh's widow, who was middle-aged and attractive. She soon fell for his charm and asked whether he might consider heading up the new hospital. In his dire financial straits, it was an offer that he was in no position to turn down.

Charlotte could wait. He would write a letter telling her that he had been summoned back to Switzerland urgently and would have to put their plans on hold. London was a big place. She would never know that he too had decided to move there. He washed and changed for the dinner invitation that he had accepted at Lady Marchant's house in Knightsbridge. Twenty minutes later, Johann left his room. He hadn't noticed the crumpled blue shirt on the dressing table, nor the photograph of the nude woman that it was resting upon.

Charlotte put down her brushes and left the studio. She washed and got dressed for work, feeling ready to face the world as she left the house and got on the tube. Surfacing around forty minutes later at Green Park station, she bought a morning newspaper and then proceeded the short distance down Bond Street to her favourite Italian coffee bar. Entering the small establishment of no more than half a dozen Formica-topped tables, she ordered a hearty breakfast of sausage, eggs and bacon with lashings of toast and marmalade, and the first of her two double espressos. Putting the paper down, she wondered whether Joan would make a point of telling Bernard that she had missed two days' work. She then remembered how unwell he had seemed. He'd said he'd be away for a while. Charlotte desperately needed to see him. Only now did she acknowledge just how much she missed his warmth, and how alone she was in the world. When she'd finished her breakfast, she paid her bill, leaving a generous tip, and walked the few hundred yards to Cork Street.

She was surprised to find the door to the gallery unlocked. It was not yet nine o'clock and they never opened before nine thirty. She stepped inside and was immediately struck by the new Max Freedland paintings that had arrived during her absence. Charlotte went over to her desk. To her astonishment, her correspondence had been tidied up and her post left in a neat pile. She tried to apply herself to the tasks that she had left unfinished, but found it difficult to concentrate. However hard she tried to block it, Johann's image kept reappearing in her mind. Perhaps there was a perfectly plausible explanation for the photograph? She sat back in her chair and shut her eyes. The sound of high heels approaching thumping across the oak parquet floor aroused her.

'Charlotte! I'm so glad to see that you're all right.' It was Joan.

'I was feeling unwell,' Charlotte replied hesitantly. She now felt guilty that she hadn't at least telephoned to explain her absence.

'I was just worried,' the large woman said, wringing her hands nervously. There were small beads of perspiration on her forehead. 'I didn't know what to think. Up to our necks in paintings we were – William doing his best to put the ruddy things up with me holding the ladder, sure that you were going to turn up at any minute. It was quite a sight, I can tell you!'

'Joan, there was really no need to be concerned. It's entirely my fault. I should have—'

'No, please let me continue,' Joan pleaded. 'I owe you an apology, dear. I had no right to interfere in your private affairs. Mr Bernard has always been very good to me. Things haven't been easy since my Reg came back from the war.' Tears started to fill her eyes. 'It was bad enough that he has only got one good arm, but what he saw in action changed him.'

Charlotte sat back in her chair, wondering what had brought about the change in the secretary's attitude towards her.

'He was an engineer before he joined up,' Joan rambled on. 'Now he's only good for feeding offcuts through a bleeding hopper or getting pissed with his mates down the local. It's not much of a life.'

Charlotte unexpectedly found herself feeling sympathy for the woman leaning against her desk. She hadn't appreciated what a harsh life Joan had been subjected to.

'The guv'nor paid for our holiday last year,' the secretary continued. 'He knew we were a bit short. Ten days caravanning in Devon. Reg was his old self – we had a lovely time. But as soon as we got home, the nightmares started up again. Many a time I'm up half the night with his screaming. Poor sod! Coming to work is a welcome release, I can tell you.'

'It must be very hard,' Charlotte said quietly. 'I'm sorry.' She still failed to understand the reason why the secretary had decided to confide in her.

'I need this job, Charlotte. We couldn't survive on Reg's wage. God knows what we would do if there was a family to support.'

'Bernard – I mean Mr Morris – depends upon you. He always says that you run the place and that he couldn't do without you,' Charlotte said kindly.

'So you don't bear me a grudge?' The secretary moved her heavy frame over to Charlotte's side of the desk. 'And we can start off on a new footing?'

'Joan, we are colleagues. There are really no problems between us,' Charlotte smiled, holding out her hand to the secretary.

The large woman bent down and kissed Charlotte on the cheek. 'Thank you, dear. You don't know how happy that's made me feel. And what do you make of the new stuff, by the way? That Max Freedland is a strange fellow,' she commented, peering at the latest works by the artist. 'Took William all morning to get the bloke to agree to let him into that hovel he calls his home. Apparently, some young whipper-snapper of a reporter had been pestering him, asking questions about this and that. Put the wind up the poor beggar. William reckons he wouldn't be surprised if he was preparing to do a runner.'

Charlotte sat up, alarmed. It sounded as if the gallery was in imminent danger of losing its main source of revenue. She had to talk to Bernard urgently.

'Did Mr Morris mention when he will be returning?' she asked.

'I'm sorry, dear, he'll be laid up in hospital for a good while yet,' Joan replied self-importantly. No longer worried that her previous outburst had jeopardised the cushy job she had made for herself, she could continue fiddling the expenses, which she felt she was fully entitled to do.

'Would it be possible for me to see him?' Charlotte asked beseechingly, their roles suddenly reversed.

'The doctors have forbidden all visitors until next week,' Joan said, giving the impression that she knew more than she was divulging. She then returned to the first floor, confident that she had regained the upper hand over her younger colleague.

Once again feeling insecure about her job, Charlotte casually opened the drawer of her desk. Not immediately recognising the buff-coloured envelope that had been thrust on her by the secretary just a few days before, she looked inside it and found two train tickets to the South of France in late December, along with a hotel reservation. Two rooms had been booked in the names of Bernard Morris and Charlotte Brown at the five-star Hotel Negresco – his celebration for the property deal that he had been so desperate to complete. Bernard had chosen to share his good fortune with her. Now he had been taken ill and she had been ready to throw away everything and return to Switzerland because of a childhood infatuation. Charlotte shook her head at her folly.

She was glad to be back at the gallery. Despite the renewed doubt about Max Freedland, she could start preparing the catalogue of newly arrived artworks for their first exhibition.

All of a sudden, something made her stop what she was doing and look up. Peering down from above were the haunting faces in Daniel Petrovich's painting *Blight*. It was as if it had moved by itself from one end of the gallery to the other, simply so it could continue placing her under its spell.

*

Several weeks passed and still she hadn't seen or heard anything from Bernard. On the occasions when she had enquired after his health, Joan merely informed her that there had been complications after the operation and that their boss had been sent to a nursing home in the country to recuperate.

Then, just before Christmas, a Rolls-Royce pulled up outside the gallery. Charlotte was busy in negotiation with an elderly male client when a heavy-set man dressed in a camel-coloured cashmere overcoat discreetly entered the gallery. She concluded the transaction and, clasping the customer's cheque tightly in her hand, escorted the gentleman to the door.

Turning around, she saw Bernard Morris gazing at the travel documents that had been left open on her desk.

'Thinking of going somewhere?' he said, holding the two tickets up in front of him.

10

South of France, Christmas 1956

Charlotte looked out at the palm trees and the
Mediterranean Sea glistening brightly in the late-
December sun. She and Bernard had arrived at the Hotel
Negresco three days before. With its imposing pink dome,
white facade and elaborately decorated brickwork, the
famous hotel gave the impression of a nineteenth-century
French palace. She loved it. The weather was unseasonably
mild, and a festive atmosphere filled the streets crowded
with families on their short holiday break.

They ate their meals in pretty little restaurants along
the bustling Promenade des Anglais, the wide area that
ran between the coast road and the beach-front and which
was named after wealthy English holidaymakers from the
Victorian era. Then, when it got chilly, they'd take a ride in
one of the horse-drawn carriages to the busy port where
freshly caught fish were displayed on the quayside, and
where they would sit and look at the cruise ships that had
docked, allowing their passengers to disembark for a tour
along the Cote d'Azur. But what Charlotte liked most was
the gentle ascent through picturesque villages filled with
the fragrance from yellow mimosa trees that lined their

narrow streets; and of course, she loved to visit the studios of local artists.

Captivated by the scenery and the breath-taking views of the coastline below, Charlotte saw immediately why so many artists had chosen to settle here. The magical light that the Impressionists, in particular, had managed to capture in their paintings was unlike anything she had ever seen before.

The journey from London had taken its toll on Bernard. Ignoring his doctor's advice, he had insisted on making the trip. His only concession was to take the train the whole way instead of driving to Dover and then the 160 miles from Avignon to Nice.

Despite the extra comfort of travelling first class, Charlotte was seriously concerned that Bernard could suddenly be taken ill again. To reassure her, he had explained that the thought of this holiday was what had kept him going through the long haul of his recuperation.

Charlotte had tried to resist accompanying him. After all, they hadn't seen each other for weeks on end, and then there was the episode with Johann. She thought it would be deceitful. But as the gallery was about to close for the holiday period and the agreement was that they would just be close friends travelling together, she had consented to go. Also, she hoped to use their time together to resolve the question once and for all of their dependence on Max Freedland.

It didn't feel like Christmas. Charlotte thought back to when she was a young child in Berlin before the war; the tree that her father had spent hours decorating, the excruciating wait to open her presents. Then trying to hide her disappointment when her brother Hans had been bought more than her. Christmas was a time for families to be together. However, she had spent several Christmases all alone in West Hampstead; counting the days until she could go back to work, hoping that Johann might write. These were the loneliest periods that she could remember. She was glad to be away.

As she sat at her dressing table in the hotel room, thinking about the past, there was a knock at the door.

'Are you decent?' Bernard called from outside.

'Yes. Come in, the door's open,' Charlotte called back, trying to compose herself. She was dressed in a full-length black satin evening gown with gold high-heeled shoes. Her hair was held in place by a diamanté clip, and the gleaming pearl choker accentuated her slender neck.

Bernard appeared, his white dinner jacket and cummerbund tied tightly around his full girth. He stood at the entrance and let out a soft whistle. 'You look a million dollars!' he exclaimed, his round face beaming with pleasure.

'I am glad you approve,' she blushed, returning his smile. Charlotte had made a special effort for the Christmas gala dinner in the hotel that evening. Knowing how much Bernard wanted her to share his enthusiasm for the South of France, she had no wish to disappoint him.

'I hope you can dance in those things,' he joked, 'because I'm not going to take no for an answer with what they're charging for tonight's do! Ready?' He crooked his arm, gesturing for his escort to join him for dinner.

It was one in the morning when they took the lift back to their rooms on the fifth floor.

Charlotte mustered all her strength to get Bernard

back to his room. The festive meal had consisted of several rich courses and the champagne had been flowing all evening; the event had left him exhausted. It was clear that he'd pushed himself to the limit. Despite his protests, Charlotte helped him off with his clothes and into bed, where he immediately fell fast asleep. Then, unsteady on her feet from too much to drink, she staggered into the room opposite, kicked off her shoes with a sigh of relief, slipped out of her evening dress and got into bed without even turning on the light, only to wake in a panic a few hours later. She had dreamed that Bernard had suffered a heart attack and had died alone at his house in London. Suddenly she needed to check whether he was all right.

Charlotte jumped out of bed and, still in her underwear, she darted across to his room, relieved to find that his key was still in the lock. Quietly, she opened the door and let herself in. Through the un-drawn curtains, the full moon lit up the spacious room, and she could see that Bernard was safe, alive and lying on his side, snoring peacefully. But the dream had left her disturbed. She couldn't drag herself away. Nimbly, she got into his bed so that she could be next to him. A feeling of calm swept over her as she entered a deep slumber.

Bernard stirred. Sensing the warmth of a body next to him and knowing it must be Charlotte, he drew her closer and enveloped her in his powerful arms. The wind had come up and had blown the balcony doors open. The sound of rain splattered against the glass panes. Still half-asleep, Charlotte responded, instinctively pressing herself against him, and now their relationship changed for ever.

*

Afterwards, they dozed in each other's arms until they were awoken by a clattering noise and a movement of wheels outside their room. There followed a muffled sound of knocking.

Bernard leaped out of bed, put on his dressing gown that had been left folded on an armchair and opened the door while Charlotte continued drowsing.

'*Joyeux Noel, monsieur et madame!* Merry Christmas!' exclaimed the young uniformed waiter as he pushed the breakfast trolley into the centre of the chilly room and closed the balcony doors. He lifted the flaps at both ends of the table and arranged two place settings. The smell of strong black coffee and freshly baked croissants instantly filled the room.

'The champagne is with the compliments of the hotel,' he added, pointing to the chilled bottle of Dom Pérignon in the ice-bucket.

When the young fellow had left, Bernard walked over to the bureau and took out a small box that had been gift-wrapped in mauve paper. He returned to his bed and sat down next to Charlotte.

Charlotte opened her eyes. 'Bernard, about last night...' she began shamefacedly.

'Happy Christmas!' He kissed her affectionately on the forehead and placed the box on the bedcovers in front of her.

'But I haven't bought *you* anything,' she said, stricken.

Bernard smiled. 'Come on,' he said, 'open it before the breakfast gets cold.' He got up, grabbed a chair from the dressing table and another from the bureau, and dragged them over to the breakfast table.

Charlotte tore open the paper and took out a small

red leather box. She gasped at the pair of large emerald earrings staring up at her.

'Bernard, this is too much. I can't possibly accept.' With no warning, she burst out crying. She had never intended for it to go this far. She would have to explain to him that he had made a mistake. Tell him that there had been someone else in her life. She couldn't let him continue under the misapprehension that she was a virtuous woman. Bernard rushed over to her.

'Charlotte, it's all right. If you don't like them, they can be changed for something else. They're just a present. Please don't cry.' He took her in his arms to comfort her.

'No, they are beautiful. It's just that I didn't expect . . .' She stopped herself from continuing. She knew that she wasn't thinking clearly. Ashamed about her outpouring of emotion, she put on her slip and went over to the table.

'Here, take this,' Bernard called, handing her a blue cashmere V-neck sweater from the chest of drawers. 'It matches the colour of your eyes,' he said, trying to cheer her up.

The next few days flew by. Charlotte discovered that she felt a deep affection for Bernard and didn't want to be apart from him. In the beginning, she longed to tell him everything. That Charlotte Brown from Switzerland was really Eva Schlessinger from Berlin. That she had only moved to London after the end of a love affair, which had been rekindled while he lay ill in hospital. She wasn't prepared, however, to destroy what might be her last chance of happiness.

The hotel hadn't batted an eyelid when Bernard informed them that he and Charlotte would only be requiring one room for the remainder of their stay. Charlotte's things had already been moved by the time they returned from an early-morning boat trip to Monte Carlo. How different, she thought, from the disapproving looks she had received in that small hotel in north London.

For their last evening, Bernard had planned a surprise. He told her to dress up. After dining in a seafood restaurant behind the hotel, they made their way back to the Promenade des Anglais to the Casino Palais de la Méditerranée, a magnificent Belle Epoque building where handsome, tanned men with cigars and glamorous bejewelled women in evening dress were posing on a red carpet for photographers.

Bernard had told her that you couldn't experience the South of France without a visit to the casino. They ascended the steps of the many-arched building, entered a grand marble entrance hall, lit up by crystal chandeliers, then proceeded up the ornate staircase to the first floor. Bernard changed a large quantity of francs at the counter and gave Charlotte her own stack of multi-coloured chips. They followed a small stream of people into the first of three gaming rooms to the roulette wheel. For several minutes, they just stood watching the action of bets being placed on the green felt table while Bernard explained the intricacies of the game.

After a while, and a couple of vodkas to steady her nerves, Charlotte decided to play, and soon managed to double her stake. Bernard, who was playing with the confidence of one who feels completely at ease, had recovered after a slow start and was winning heavily.

An hour later, the pair decided to cash in their chips while they were still ahead and left the casino, which would remain in full swing until the early hours of the morning. It was just after midnight when in high spirits they arrived back at their hotel and went straight up to their room without noticing the letter that had been placed under the door.

They were preparing for bed when Bernard suddenly caught sight of the white envelope on the carpet.

'Can't say they're not on the ball here,' he grumbled. 'They've only given us the bloody bill, and we're not leaving till tomorrow evening.' He opened the envelope, read the telegram inside from his secretary, then, trying to come to terms with its contents, he read it again. He stood completely still, his expression displaying the fullness of his grief.

'Is it bad news?' Charlotte asked softly.

'My mother passed away last night,' he replied, tears forming in his eyes. 'The funeral's at midday tomorrow.'

'I'm so sorry.' Charlotte went over and put her arms out to comfort him. 'But surely it can be delayed until you get home?'

Without offering an explanation, Bernard quickly got dressed.

'Where are you going?' Charlotte asked.

'To see if we can get a flight to London,' he answered.

'But we already have our train tickets,' Charlotte protested.

It was too late. Bernard was already on his way down to the front desk to make the travel arrangements. He would pay whatever it cost to be back in East London by tomorrow morning.

11

The British European Airways Viscount touched down on time at London's Heathrow airport. Bernard looked at his watch; adjusting for the hour's time difference, it was two minutes before nine o'clock. He calculated that they would be through customs by ten, which would give them a couple of hours for the journey across London. The flight was nearly full and they had managed to pick up the last two seats. His brother Joe had telephoned Joan as soon as they found their mother's body. The old lady was in her fireside chair wrapped in her frayed woollen housecoat. The neighbours thought it was odd that no one had seen her for a while and had gone to check on her. When there was no answer at the door, they suspected the worst and called the family.

Annie Moscovitch had been dead for over a week and the gas meter had run out of money. The likelihood was that she had frozen to death. Knowing that Bernard was the closest to his mother and that he would blame himself for not being there, the family thought it best to withhold the full details and let him think that her passing was sudden.

He looked over at his companion. Charlotte had remained glued to him for the whole journey, terrified by the experience of her first flight.

'You do want me there?' she asked nervously.

Bernard squeezed her hand without replying. The truth was that he hadn't considered whether turning up at his mother's funeral with a woman friend who had never been introduced to the family was the right thing to do. So what that she wasn't Jewish? She would turn a few heads, that's for sure, but that was their problem. He had supported each and every one of his brothers or sisters at one time or other, and if they wanted to pass judgement on him, so be it.

William was waiting with a suitably lugubrious expression as his two passengers made their way through the arrivals gate.

'My condolences, guv'nor,' the chauffeur said, removing his cap. 'Your mum was a wonderful woman.' He chuckled wryly. 'Always gave me a right telling-off.'

Within minutes, the Rolls was speeding away down the A40 towards Central London. Bernard, stretching out on the back seat, had fallen asleep. The strain of the last twelve hours had caught up with him.

'Nice weather was it over there?' the chauffeur asked, trying to make conversation. 'Christmas Day here was a right wash-out. Couldn't even get down the pub, the rain was so bad. Still, we managed to listen to the Queen on the wireless, God bless her.'

'We were lucky. It was beautiful where we were,' Charlotte said.

'I wouldn't know. Never been overseas, miss. Did my service in Aldershot, preparing draft papers for those lucky blighters who got to fight. Me emphysema kept me out of the forces.' He overtook a lorry approaching the Hammersmith roundabout. 'Suppose you were too young to remember the war?'

'Well, I was still at school,' Charlotte replied hesitantly.

'I bet you could get all the tea, sugar and butter you wanted where you came from. And now they've started restricting petrol again,' William remarked resentfully.

'No, we did have rationing in Switzerland,' Charlotte replied, trying to sound sure of herself. She couldn't reveal that there weren't any noticeable shortages in Berlin until the latter stages of the war, by which time events had turned against Germany. Not having witnessed any deprivation before, she remembered feeling hard done by when she could no longer get her favourite chocolate biscuits.

When the car eventually turned down a narrow lane and came to a halt at the entrance to the East London Jewish Cemetery, Charlotte placed her hand on her companion's arm to wake him.

'We've arrived,' she said gently as he opened his eyes.

The car bounced along the uneven road surrounded on both sides by rows of headstones in various states of disrepair.

'Drop us off here, William,' Bernard instructed his driver. 'We'll walk the rest of the way.'

The sleet that had persisted throughout the whole journey from the airport resumed with even greater intensity as the two passengers got out of the car and proceeded along a gravel path. In the distance, a small gathering of people had congregated outside a simple hut-like structure, their coat collars pulled up high. It was sparse protection against the bitter morning.

Amongst the fifteen mourners that Charlotte counted, there were just two other women. Scarves covering their heads, they were standing together with arms interlocked, as one in their grief. She assumed that they were Millie and Rose, Bernard's two sisters.

The men were in two distinctly separate groups. The first, a kindly bunch of individuals who had rended their clothes, were busily chatting, attempting to keep up each other's spirits. A man of above average height and with particularly handsome features stood out from the rest. Charlotte caught him looking at her as she joined the gathering. Bernard had described Lenny perfectly – a ladies' man through and through, 'a real charmer' is what he called him. Next to him was the youngest, Joe, a stocky man with a round friendly face whose similarity to Bernard was unmistakable. It seemed odd that after all the months they had known each other, it was only in the past few days that she had learned the names of the members of the Morris family.

Several feet away stood three men with beards, dressed in long black coats and wide-brimmed hats. They were reading from small books held up close to their faces, mumbling the words. Charlotte couldn't keep her eyes off them. She had encountered similar groups in Berlin and had been instructed by her parents to give them a wide berth if they passed her in the street. These same people were jeered at and spat upon by children not much older than herself. She could still hear the abuse directed at them. They hadn't formed part of her world, so their plight had been of no concern to her. And then, little by little, they were nowhere to be seen. What were they doing here now?

Charlotte looked around her. Each of the headstones she had passed was inscribed with a familiar symbol: she recalled the yellow star worn by Jews on the outside of their clothes to distinguish them from the rest of the German population. How strange that she hadn't really thought of Bernard as being Jewish before.

'Berel!' Joe shouted out, coming to greet his older brother with outstretched arms. 'We never thought you were going to make it in time.'

The two men kissed, showing the deep affection they felt for each other.

'Only got the telegram last night. We were in France,' Bernard explained. 'Sorry, this is Charlotte,' he added, indicating his female companion.

'I'm Joe. We should meet on happier occasions,' the younger brother responded to the woman he was meeting for the first time.

'How are the girls taking it?' Bernard asked his brother.

'You know what Mum was like. As far as she was concerned, her daughters never existed. But they insisted on travelling in the car with her. They've always blamed themselves,' Joe replied sadly.

Just then the beadle, a stout man in a top hat armed with prayer books, opened the doors of the prayer hall and ushered in the mourners, men to the left and women to the right. In the middle of the hall sat the coffin on a trolley draped in a black cloth. A frail-looking old man with a long grey beard and piercing blue eyes stood leaning on a wooden lectern.

At the end of the short service, the coffin was slowly wheeled out of the cold hall through the grounds of the overgrown cemetery while the elderly rabbi recited from the book of Psalms. The old woman was laid to rest in a freshly dug grave filled in by her three sons and few surviving male relatives.

The small crowd returned to the hall where Bernard and his two brothers recited *Kaddish*, the prayer for the departed. The attendees then formed a line to pay their respects to the mourners before dispersing to resume their ordinary lives.

Charlotte returned alone to her flat in West Hampstead, while Bernard accompanied his family back to their mother's two rooms in the East End buildings for the commencement of the traditional seven-day mourning period.

Lenny was eager to get away. He hated the East End. He felt the same way about his brothers and sisters, especially Berel. Just because he'd changed his name and drove around in a flashy Rolls-Royce as if he owned the place, Berel seemed to think he was a *ganze macher,* a real big shot. He, Lenny, wasn't like the rest of them, dependent on their elder brother for handouts. The others had never forgiven Lenny for feigning madness to get out of being called up to do his military service. He'd wanted to be an actor and had gone to evening classes after he'd finished work at his father's tailor's shop, but when he saw that there was no way he was going to make a living on the stage, he decided to put his charm and good looks to a more productive use.

Refusing to be seen without a beautiful lady on his arm, he often fixed up his friends who were too timid or lacked his self-confidence to find their own women. The idea then occurred to him that he should charge a commission for his efforts. When the war came, there was no shortage of takers. Hanging around the seedy clubs of Soho, he regularly gave backhanders to the management to turn a blind eye as he plied his trade to American servicemen with seemingly unlimited amounts of money to spend on English girls. Then, after the end of hostilities, having managed to amass a substantial amount of capital, he used his connections with organised crime to begin mixing in higher levels of society. He was facilitated by certain senior members of the Metropolitan Police Force. They wanted their share of the action, which they were happy to take in cash or in kind. It wasn't long before his clients included politicians and wealthy members of the Establishment, none of whom had any qualms about using his services.

Everyone in Soho knew Lenny Moss; he was a somebody.

It was already getting dark when Lenny made his way down Greek Street to the Coach and Horses pub. The man he wanted to see was sitting at the bar.

'Hello, Lenny,' the man called out, swivelling his huge frame around on his stool. 'What will it be?'

'That's very nice of you, Mr Meredith. I'll have a double scotch, if you're paying,' Lenny replied, taking up the seat next to the banker.

'My brother's about to be married,' the banker announced, getting straight to the point. 'The thing is, he's rather landed me in it because he's asked me to arrange his stag do.'

'And you want me to help you out?' Lenny said.

'Yes. I'm going to want about twenty of your choicest stock.'

'That shouldn't be a problem. When do you need them for?'

'It's on Saturday, at my house in Sussex. Here's the address. It's going to be a masked ball, so your girls are going to need to be in full costume. Dressing up should be a bit of a change for them, I shouldn't wonder,' the banker smirked.

'Leave that to me, Mr Meredith. I know a place; we use them all the time. Martin's most reliable. He'll deck out the groom's party as well if you like.'

'Perfect. I'll give you a list of the guests, but better make sure you keep them well apart. Wouldn't want them bumping into each other before the big day. Here's a couple of hundred to keep you going. Let me know what I owe you for the rest. Right, I must be off.' The large man levered himself off his bar stool.

'One more thing,' he added, lowering his voice. 'There's one or two there who like them young.' He had James Robson specifically in mind. 'As they say in French, *chacun à son gout.*' With that, the banker put up the velvet collar of his coat and walked out of the pub.

The doorways of Soho were beginning to fill up with scantily dressed women waiting for their first customers of the evening. The banker crouched into the back of a black cab and instructed the driver to take him to the City. A late meeting had been arranged with a group of investors intent on purchasing as much prime Central London property as they could get their hands on.

Gaining James Robson's complete submission was crucial to making the plan a success, the scheming banker knew. He would pay one of Lenny's under-age prostitutes to proposition the solicitor. Then, after their relationship developed, she would threaten to expose him to the press. At that point, James Robson would come grovelling, ready to do anything to save himself. Rupert would help him, but would exact a heavy price in return.

Rupert Meredith stretched out his massive legs and smiled.

12

Two weeks after the funeral, Charlotte sub-let her flat and had the last of her belongings taken over to Bernard's house in Mayfair. She hadn't hesitated when he asked her to move in with him and it was convenient, living so close to work.

Activity in the gallery during the first few weeks of 1957 was sluggish. The cold spell at the start of the year had been replaced with an unseasonably warm spring. The first consignment of works by the contemporary artists that she and Bernard had identified during their visit to the South of France had just arrived. The lighter style and pastel colours of their landscapes gave the gallery a wider appeal. Charlotte procrastinated about including the painting by Daniel Petrovitch, one moment determined to rid herself of it, the next realising that she couldn't bear to be parted from it.

Everything was in place for the Private View today, but Charlotte was becoming increasingly apprehensive. She lit another cigarette. Surely Max would appear? Bernard had given his word. The enigmatic artist had already established a following and the clients who had bought his paintings were expecting to meet him in person.

The trouble was that although Bernard had left the running of the gallery to her, she suspected that he had lost interest. He explained this by saying he needed to make up for the time away from his businesses because of his illness. Even though he had taken on his brother Joe to do a lot of the running around, he had repeatedly ignored medical advice to slow down. Bernard carried on relentlessly adding to his portfolio of luxury Central London properties in pursuit of the one deal that would give him the status that, in his view, continued to elude him.

Although they were living together and he was unquestionably the warmest and most generous man that Charlotte had ever met, there was still so much of him that remained hidden from her. It was as if he had compartmentalised his life and she filled just a small part of it.

The day before, a police van had arrived outside a run-down building in Whitechapel High Street. Two burly officers armed with arrest warrants slammed on the broken front door, trying to attract the attention of its top-floor occupant. Receiving no response, they forced their way in and climbed the stone stairs to the fourth floor. Apart from several empty half-bottles of whisky and a lop-sided easel displaying a canvas of a nude woman that appeared to have been slashed with a sharp implement, the place was deserted.

Not getting any joy out of the press, Susana had contacted the authorities and informed them about the Max Freedland fakes that were circulating around London. The police raided a number of Sunday markets in the capital, knowing from previous experience that they were havens for illicit merchandise. They thought they'd struck lucky when they identified several paintings by the artist that were on sale in Petticoat Lane. However, they couldn't get the stallholders to reveal any information about the man's whereabouts. The police lacked sufficient nous to realise that what they had confiscated were merely copies of famous works. Max Freedland's name was duly erased by them from the reverse side of the specimens so that they could be used as evidence against him, although any art expert would point to the lack of the original artist's signature as proof that these were intended merely to be copies rather than fakes.

Early that morning, the partly decomposed body of a middle-aged man was retrieved from the Regent's Canal at Mile End. The only form of identification was a tin leg that was found upstream and on which a name had been illegibly scratched. A post-mortem was ordered to determine the cause of death. Despite the large quantity of alcohol detected in the victim's bloodstream, the Coroner's findings proved inconclusive. The verdict was death by misadventure.

It was after nine in the evening when the last customer left the gallery. Charlotte locked up behind her and walked the short distance home, paying for the final edition of the evening paper on the way. The first day had gone reasonably well. They had sold five of Max Freedland's paintings and two of Daniel Petrovitch's still lifes. However, she was disappointed by the cursory interest in the new works from the South of France. Even worse, Bernard hadn't kept his word. He'd been unable to persuade their most popular artist to attend the Private View of his own work.

Bernard was already at home when she arrived at the

house feeling disgruntled. Still in her coat, she found him dozing with his feet up on the drawing-room sofa.

'Good day?' he asked groggily.

Charlotte threw the evening paper at him and stormed out of the room.

Bernard sat up and rubbed his eyes. 'What's wrong?' he called out, startled by her angry demeanour. 'Charlotte! Would you mind telling me what's going on?' He followed her to the study, where she had already opened the drinks cabinet and poured herself a sherry.

'You gave me your word,' she hissed.

'I tried to be there, but something came up at the last minute. I swear it!'

'I've known for a long time that you only do what you say when it suits you.'

'And what's that supposed to mean?' Bernard demanded, his face flushed with anger.

'It was agreed that Max would be there,' Charlotte said heatedly, trying to hold back her tears. 'Well, he wasn't.'

'What do you mean not there?' Bernard shouted. 'It was all arranged. I spoke to him two days ago. I even made sure that he had money for a cab because he's always pissed!'

'It was so embarrassing. The clients who bought his paintings came especially to see him. And I thought . . .'

'I know what you thought,' Bernard said grimly. 'You thought I had let you down.' Suddenly his expression softened. He moved towards Charlotte and drew her to him. 'I don't suppose I can do anything about the fact that you always think the worst of me?'

'I'm sorry,' she wept. 'I didn't mean what I said. I'm trying my best to make the gallery a success for you.'

'For us,' Bernard corrected her, smiling.

'Yes, for us. But I don't know how much longer I can keep making excuses. Collectors can easily change their preferences and we're reliant on Max Freedland. None of the other artists sell as well.'

Bernard assumed that his friend had allowed drink to get the better of him and had slept through the day.

'If we could obtain more works by Daniel Petrovitch, it would help,' Charlotte commented dolefully, still unaware that the artist didn't exist.

'Please don't worry,' Bernard said gently. He kissed her forehead. 'Something will turn up. It always does. Annette left you out some supper. Come on, you've been on your feet all day. Go into the dining room and I'll wait on you.' Bernard made his way to the kitchen.

Charlotte slowly finished her sherry and proceeded along the hall to where her dinner was waiting for her. She devoured her meal in silence, overseen by the man in whose house she was living but once again unsure of her feelings towards him.

Bernard returned to the study while Charlotte went up to bed. She needed to sleep. Perhaps Bernard was right and things would work out for the best. All she knew as she entered the bedroom they shared was that he hadn't been able to allay her feelings of insecurity.

Downstairs, Bernard sat back in his favourite armchair and took a large gulp of brandy from the balloon glass. To hell with doctors telling him to give up drinking. They should have had the day he just had! It had gone from bad to worse. First, Rupert had informed him that he was up to his limit and the bank wasn't prepared to extend his line of credit. Then Lenny had got into debt with some lowlifes in East London and he had had to bail him out again. And now Charlotte had accused him of being a liar. It didn't matter, he had broad shoulders; he wouldn't let it get to him.

He picked up the evening paper she had brought home and starting browsing through the headlines. His attention was caught by the brief description of an unidentified man who had been found dead in the Regent's Canal. Bernard read it again to make sure - but there it was in black and white. The corpse had only one leg; the other, made of tin, had been recovered, washed up on the bank of the canal. He would have put money on the fact that it was Max. That explained why he never showed up at the gallery. Poor sod! Since the report stated that there were no witnesses, Bernard knew he would have to go down to Lime Street police station first thing in the morning to make a positive identification.

Sighing heavily, Bernard got up from his chair, turned off the downstairs lights and went slowly up to his bedroom. Once in bed, he lay awake wondering how he was going to break the news to the woman sleeping peacefully beside him.

14

Charlotte was pleased. The Bernard Morris Gallery was doing good business. Max Freedland's canvases had been snapped up and so had three of her own paintings. Also, to her amazement, the entire collection from the artists in the South of France had been sold to an anonymous group of investors. As soon as the Private View was over, Charlotte had travelled back to Nice to procure further paintings from her sources. At the same time, she entered into agreements with six of the artists for exclusive representation of their works.

Unbeknownst to Charlotte, Bernard had sanctioned the deal; it had bought him time. He had come to an agreement with a few trusted associates to buy the French landscapes, on the understanding that the gallery would buy them back in a year's time at a higher price. In the meantime, it would help keep the place afloat and detract Charlotte's attention away from Max Freedland. This was a dangerous ploy, but with far graver problems facing his property group, it was a chance he was prepared to take.

He sat back as his chauffeur drove around Hyde Park Corner. Things had gone from bad to worse after his mother's death. First, identifying his old friend Max's body had left him feeling uncharacteristically despondent. Then there was the pressure from Meredith's Bank to repay a huge loan that had fallen due. For the first time, Bernard had started to wonder whether, in his desire to prove himself, he had let his obsession overcome his judgement.

Reaching into the inside pocket of his sports jacket he withdrew a small square box. Opening it, his large fingers began carefully unfolding the smooth blue paper inside. Suddenly a three-carat emerald-shaped diamond appeared, radiating a brilliant beam of light. He had intended to propose to Charlotte when they returned from France but he could never find the right moment. Now, with everything he had built up crumbling around him, there was no way he could offer her the kind of life she deserved. Bernard quickly wrapped up the stone and replaced it in his pocket as the Rolls came to a halt at Victoria station. He could already make out Charlotte's slender figure waiting at the taxi rank.

James Robson proceeded briskly up St James's Street towards Piccadilly. A few minutes later, he stopped outside an undistinguished-looking building. From its exterior, one would never have guessed that it was the most exclusive gentleman's club in London. Watts' was generally closed to anyone other than members of the aristocracy. Joining was by invitation only, and applications had to be accompanied by two recommendations from existing members.

The solicitor checked his watch again. He was early for his midday meeting. Rupert had reluctantly agreed to see him, but the knot in his stomach told James it wouldn't prove fruitful. After all, it was his fault for getting involved with that new young prostitute in the first place – but how was he to know that she was under-age? If the girl pressed charges, not only would he be struck off by the Law

Society, he could also be facing a lengthy prison sentence. James Robson was here to ask Rupert if he would use his influence with the police at West End Central to get the brothel in Soho's St Anne's Court shut down and then the girl would as good as disappear. Anyway, it wasn't as if Rupert didn't owe him. Susana's introduction to the South American connection had made the fellow a fortune. It ensured that the proceeds of art and precious gems sold through Brockets remained in the UK with Meredith's Bank, where it had been miraculously transformed into a deposit of the highest repute.

It was too hot to wait outside. James Robson hurried up the steps and rang the bell on the front of the building. Almost immediately, he was let into the haughty establishment by an unsmiling man with an upright stance and regulation haircut who looked better suited to be a member of the Queen's Royal Horse Guards. After he had satisfied the fellow with his credentials and the reason for his visit, the solicitor was escorted into the members' study, where he found Rupert Meredith sat smoking a cigar and reading the *Financial Times*.

'James!' he called out, peering over his newspaper. 'It's always a pleasure.' Pointing to an empty chair, he summoned his guest to join him. 'How's Susana?' he asked, his expression failing to disguise his loathing for the man who had asked for the meeting.

'She's well, as far as I know,' replied the solicitor.

'I forgot – she did tell me the last time I bumped into her that you were living apart. Sorry to hear it,' the banker said in a completely false show of sympathy.

'Rupert, I'm in a wee spot of bother,' the solicitor began.

'Not got a young lady into trouble, have you?' the

banker tutted, shaking his huge head.

'Actually, there is a woman involved. I've tried to pay her off, but now she's threatening to take matters further,' James Robson whispered. 'God knows what will happen if the press gets hold of it.'

'Not really my problem, old boy,' the banker replied smugly. He then took a large gulp from the glass of champagne standing on the side table next to him, feeling pleased that the young whore had followed his instructions. He would pay the rest of her money to Lenny, the next time he was in the area.

'Rupert, I know that we haven't always seen eye to eye, but Meredith's have done very well over the years out of my firm. We go back a long way. I wouldn't demean myself if I weren't desperate.'

'Sounds as if you've got yourself in a bit of a fix, old chap,' the banker replied. 'However, there may be a way that you can extricate yourself.'

'What do I need to do?' the solicitor asked, feeling slightly more hopeful about his predicament.

'There are many I could name who have become disillusioned with your good friend Bernard Morris,' the banker began.

'What's that got to do with me?' James Robson asked, completely bemused.

'He owes a number of very influential people a great deal of money. They feel, and I have to say with some justification, that drastic action has to be taken; otherwise they could be facing huge write-offs on their loan book.'

'I still don't understand where I come in,' the solicitor repeated.

'You are going to see to it that his entire Mayfair

property portfolio gets delivered into a safer pair of hands.'

'And how am I supposed to ensure that happens?' the solicitor queried, worried about what was expected of him.

'He's lost the support of the banks, poor chap,' the banker continued. 'We've had a meeting, and I have to tell you that all parties concerned have decided that their best chance of recouping our debt is to break up his company.'

'You mean you're putting him into liquidation?' James asked.

'Indeed. And as you are a non-executive director, you will persuade Bernard that it is in his best interests to resign. You will be appointed as chairman in the interim and see to it that the first offer forthcoming for the company is accepted.'

'But Rupert, you know as well as I do that the Receiver is obliged to go to the open market to get the best price.'

'That's where you come in, my dear fellow. Because you're going to ensure that doesn't happen.'

The solicitor's mouth fell open. He could think of only one way to make it happen. 'You mean bribe the Receiver?' He was stunned at what was being suggested.

'Something you've been quite adept at over the years, by all accounts.'

'I don't know what you are referring to,' James Robson said angrily.

'Not raking off all that money for yourself from Susana's family when you were supposed to be representing their interests?' the banker said coolly.

'That was different. It was an introductory commission to help facilitate the transfer of their assets out of Argentina.'

'Ten years is a hell of a long introduction,' the other

man retorted.

The solicitor, his face flushed with embarrassment, was speechless. How on earth did Rupert find out about the secret deal he had made with Susana's father – a deal to which even his wife wasn't privy? They had obviously all been conspiring against him; he was being attacked from all sides. Perhaps it would be simpler if he ended it all. Jumping off Blackfriars Bridge was definitely an option. It wasn't as if he hadn't thought about it. At first, his obsession with money, seeing how those with privilege had it all so easy, had actually driven him on. But he could never get away from the fact that his father was only a docker and couldn't afford to send him to public school, which meant that no matter how much money he accumulated or how many connections he made, he would never really be one of them. Did that give Rupert and his ilk the right to look down upon him? He had worked bloody hard for what he had achieved and he would *never* let these bastards get the better of him. He took a deep breath. He needed to think clearly.

'Bernard's no fool, he's hardly going to relinquish his empire without putting up a fight,' was all he could come up with.

'Now he's breached his loan covenants, there's not a bank in London that will do business with him. He's also signed a number of personal guarantees, which if we decide to call them in would probably bankrupt him. Take it from me, the poor fellow is finished around here. I dare say, in time, he'll pick himself up. Those East End types are really quite resilient. Right, I have got a lunch meeting.' Rupert Meredith heaved himself to his feet.

'But we haven't finished!' James Robson protested.

'I'll be in touch. Things should start to move quite quickly.'

'And the girl?' the solicitor asked in a panic.

'Now we've reached agreement, it'll be taken care of. She's unlikely to cause you any more trouble. But a bit of advice - next time stick to the older ones, eh? That girl was only thirteen.'

The solicitor looked down sheepishly as Rupert turned to leave, calling out in a loud whisper: 'Sorry, old chap, better push off and collect your things. They're quite strict about the attendance of non-members.'

With that, the banker strode out of the room, feeling satisfied. The meeting had gone as expected. The man was completely beholden to him. In a few months, he would be of no further use. Robson Benson would be replaced by a much more prestigious firm and, like Bernard Morris, James Robson would be history.

As James retraced his steps out of Watts', he asked himself what exactly he had achieved this morning, other than merely substituting one crude form of blackmail with a more sophisticated version? However, he had got used to the fact that business was full of compromising situations. If he had to sacrifice Bernard Morris, even though Bernard was a decent individual, so be it. Rupert Meredith and his sort would always come out on top. That was the benefit of being part of the Establishment.

James Robson strolled back to his office feeling somewhat less fearful. It had been an expensive mistake on his part, he admitted, but now it looked as if Bernard Morris, not he, would be paying for it.

15

At first, Charlotte didn't notice the change in Bernard. She had grown accustomed to not seeing him during the day, but lately he was always at home before she arrived back from work. Worse, he had started drinking heavily. It was as if he'd adopted a death wish. Although he'd lost none of his warmth, he had become dispirited and withdrawn. The intimacy that they had enjoyed just a few months previously had evaporated, and despite living together, their relationship had reverted to its former platonic state. Whenever she asked what was wrong, Bernard just smiled, his eyes showing the deep affection that he still felt for her, but he said nothing. At those moments, Charlotte assumed that his mother's death was playing on his mind but that it would eventually pass and they would become close again. She could do nothing more.

One bright autumn morning, Bernard's secretary, Joan, was waiting for Charlotte when she arrived at work. The woman's cumbersome body was positioned awkwardly on her former desk and she wore a defiant look on her face. Charlotte sensed that, once again, she was going to bear the brunt of the woman's bad mood.

'Perhaps *she* can tell us what's going on,' Joan said accusingly, giving a sideways look at William who was loitering in the corner of the room.

'What's the matter?' Charlotte asked.

'Thought that you might be able to tell us that!' Joan snarled.

'I have no idea what you are talking about. Perhaps you want to explain?' Charlotte was curt. She had had more than enough of the woman's rudeness.

'It's obvious that something's going on. The guv'nor's got the worries of the world on his shoulders. He's not the same Bernard Morris that's employed me for the last fifteen years.'

William stood at a distance, nodding his agreement.

'And you think I'm to blame?' Charlotte said angrily.

'Well, I'm sure he tells you things. Like why for the last month he's been paying William and me out of his own pocket,' the woman persisted, unwilling to be deterred.

'Joan, I know nothing about this. You have my word.'

'Never been the same since that poor old sod was washed up in the Regent's Canal,' William interjected.

'Who do you mean?' Charlotte asked, wondering what he was talking about.

'Don't play the little innocent, it don't wash with me,' the fat woman said scornfully, making no attempt to get down from her perch. 'Max Freedland. He's dead, you idiot.'

Charlotte put her hand over her mouth, unable to absorb what she had just heard. 'He's dead?' she gasped.

William nodded. 'It made the morning paper.'

'Must have been while you were gallivanting abroad at the gaffer's expense,' Joan sneered.

There was a short pause. Charlotte was confused. She had believed Bernard when he denied any knowledge of the enigmatic artist's failure to appear at the Private View. Not for the first time, she suspected that Bernard had deceived her. Why hadn't he said anything? Then there was the sudden increase of interest in the other works on show. Maybe it wasn't just a coincidence. There was a strange feeling in her stomach. Bernard was keeping something from her and she had to find out what it was.

'If we're going to have to cut back on expenses, this place will have to go for a start,' Joan said sourly.

Charlotte stared at the other woman.

'Well, it's obvious that he's up to his neck in debt,' Joan told her.

'You mean he has financial problems?' Charlotte asked naively.

'That would be putting it mildly. I see the correspondence from the banks,' the large woman gloated. 'They're pressing him to repay them.'

Charlotte remained silent. How much more was there that she didn't know about the man with whom she had been living for the last eight months?

'I've never trusted that bloke Meredith,' the secretary ranted on. 'The guv'nor thought he was his friend, but what's a toff got in common with a real gent like Bernard?'

Charlotte thought back to the first time she'd met Rupert Meredith at the opening party of the gallery, and that curious comment of his warning her to be wary of her new employer. Perhaps she should have heeded his advice.

'The money probably doesn't mean much to you,' Joan continued spitefully, 'but for William and me, well, it's different. Now Reg has been sectioned, we're getting married when our divorces come through. We're going to need every penny for our new home. Isn't that right, love?' she said, looking over at her intended.

'Can't come quick enough as far as I'm concerned,' the

chauffeur confirmed, smiling mischievously.

'So you see, we need to know that we've still got jobs to come to tomorrow morning,' added Joan. Then, easing herself down from the desk, she gestured to William that they had accomplished their purpose. Without another word, both returned to their work.

Charlotte was stunned. Joan couldn't be telling the truth, could she? She knew that the other woman had always resented her relationship with Bernard. Yet too much of what she had said, especially about Max Freedland, rang true. Charlotte found it hard to concentrate on paperwork and spent the rest of the day going over in her mind what she would say to Bernard when she got home that evening. What did seem certain as she cleared her desk was that she would soon be looking for another job.

Bernard made his way up the stairs to the third-floor offices of Robson Benson, responding to the call he'd received an hour ago from James Robson, advising that they should meet as a matter of urgency. Bernard had been expecting the summons. He should have known that it would come via his non-executive director. Rupert Meredith always got someone else to do his dirty work for him. And he knew that James had the banker's ear, which was why he had appointed him in the first place.

Bernard was shown into a stuffy meeting room.

'Mr Robson is on an important call, but he knows you're here,' the secretary told him. She then turned around and left the room. Bernard sat down at the boardroom table and mulled over the various scenarios in his mind. He had worked into the night on a schedule of property disposals that would reduce the bank's exposure. Who could have foreseen that damned rise in interest rates? He just needed a few months, which he felt confident Rupert would grant him. After all, he had already lined up buyers willing to pay a fair price for several of his properties. It wasn't the first time that he'd encountered financial difficulties. He would get through it. Bernard Morris hadn't worked his way up from nothing to cave into pressure just because the going had got tough.

'Ah, Bernard,' said James Robson as he entered the room. He was perfectly groomed in a navy-blue suit and carried a yellow folder marked *Highly Confidential*. 'Sorry to keep you waiting. International call,' he explained.

Taking a seat at the head of the table, he placed the file in front of him. 'It's not terribly good news, I'm afraid,' he announced in his mild voice.

'I've been working on restructuring the company,' Bernard told him. 'I can get the gearing down to fifty per cent.'

The solicitor cleared his throat. 'I'm sorry, but it's a tad too late for that,' he said, trying his utmost to sound sympathetic.

'By the end of our financial year, the sales will be complete and we'll all be able to breathe more easily,' Bernard carried on, completely unaware of his dire predicament.

'Bernard, listen to me carefully. I was on the phone to Rupert. He called me from Buenos Aires. The banks have withdrawn their support.'

'What?' Bernard spluttered. 'But how? They can't do that without giving me notice.' He felt a tightening in his throat and began perspiring, his face turning pale under the sheen of sweat.

'Perhaps you should have something to drink,' the solicitor advised calmly.

'So, what exactly is my position?' Bernard asked shakily.

The solicitor opened his folder and removed a board Minute which he passed to Bernard, the Chairman of the company. He then picked up the phone from the sideboard behind him and instructed his secretary to bring in a glass of water.

Bernard looked up from the document that he had finished reading. 'And if I don't agree to resign?' he said.

There was a knock at the door and the secretary entered the room. Her expression indicated that she was in no doubt which one of the men was in need of the refreshment. She placed the tumbler of water in front of the visitor.

'Bernard, I am afraid that really isn't an option,' the solicitor responded, returning to his place. 'The bank is threatening to call in your personal guarantees, which means you'll lose the house and all of your other assets.'

'So you're saying I'll be left with nothing.'

'I've got Meredith's to agree to give you six months to sort out your affairs.'

'How very generous of them,' Bernard said sarcastically. 'Their best customer for fifteen years and you're telling me that in five minutes, I've lost the lot!'

'I wish there was some other way,' the solicitor murmured.

'And what is *your* position in all this?' Bernard asked, focusing his attention on the man he had entrusted with his affairs.

'Sorry, Bernard, I'm not with you.'

'I bet they paid you plenty so they could get their hands

on my company.'

'I don't know what you mean.' James sounded deeply offended.

'I know Rupert never felt comfortable doing business with a Jew, but I never thought that he was capable of such double-dealing.' Bernard took out his handkerchief and wiped the moisture from his face. 'My guess is that someone else put him up to it. Not that you would have the faintest idea who that might be,' he said accusingly.

The solicitor just stared back, his lips firmly sealed.

'Sorry, Bernard, but I've got another meeting at four,' James said after a short pause. 'So if you wouldn't mind?' He pointed to the unsigned board Minute. 'Here, take mine,' he said, offering his gold Parker pen.

'I've got my own,' Bernard replied disdainfully, reaching into his jacket. He then signed the document tendering his resignation and agreeing to appoint James Robson in his place. Angrily pushing the board Minute aside, he got up from his chair to leave.

'Rylands have been appointed as Receivers,' the solicitor informed him. 'They'll be at your office at nine a.m. tomorrow morning. Obviously, they'll need access to all the records so they can get moving on the Sales Memorandum. With any luck, they'll be out of the way in a couple of weeks.'

'And in the meantime, what am I supposed to tell my staff? William and Joan have been with me for fifteen years!' Bernard was only now becoming aware of the true extent of the calamity that he was facing.

'I can see that it's most unfortunate for all concerned,' the solicitor acknowledged, only interested in ending the meeting. 'Oh, and just so you know,' he added, 'the bank accounts have been frozen, so I'm afraid that to all intents and purposes, the business has ceased trading.'

Refusing to take the outstretched hand of the man whom he was convinced had been party to his demise, Bernard Morris shuffled dejectedly out of the boardroom. Before he had left the building, James Robson was already on the phone to Rupert Meredith.

Out in the bustle of the evening rush hour, Bernard began walking in the direction of his home in Mayfair. Suddenly, the tightness in his throat returned, followed by a shooting pain in his arm. The last thing he thought about before he fell to the ground unconscious was how he had failed Charlotte.

16

Charlotte stayed late at work, not that there was anything in particular to keep her there. Apart from two of her own paintings and the Daniel Petrovitch oil, the walls were completely bare. Now that there would be no further works by their most popular artist, she doubted whether the gallery would remain viable. She reached for her pack of cigarettes but saw it was empty. Glancing across her desk at the full ashtray, she couldn't believe how many she was getting through. The congestion in her chest had got worse. She breathed in deeply, trying to release the tension, but it was no use.

Charlotte was in no rush to go home. After the confrontation with Joan, old feelings of disenchantment with Bernard had resurfaced in her mind. Admittedly, she still felt a certain amount of affection towards him. But if she was honest, she couldn't envisage spending the rest of her life with someone who constantly challenged her trust. More importantly, if his financial affairs were as dire as had been indicated to her, the last thing he would be interested in would be the gallery.

It was past seven by the time Charlotte had locked up and left the premises. Walking briskly through Berkeley Square in the mild October evening, she made up her mind. She was going to leave Bernard. She would quit her job and apply for another position back at the National

Gallery.

Drumming up the courage to tell Bernard of her decision, she let herself into the house. It was a relief to find the place empty. She hurried upstairs and headed into the main bedroom. Taking her two suitcases from Bernard's dressing room, she frantically started packing. If she wrote him a note, with a bit of luck she could be gone by the time he returned. Fortunately, the tenants had moved out of her flat. It would only take a couple of journeys by taxi to move her things back to West Hampstead.

Twenty minutes later, Charlotte placed her suitcases down in the entrance hall. Then, passing along to the study, she sat down at the small French bureau by the window, took a pen and piece of headed notepaper from the leather writing folder and started to compose her letter.

When she was halfway through, there was the sound of knocking at the front door. She sat up abruptly. For a moment, she was tempted to ignore it but the caller was not to be deterred. This time, the knocking was louder, more urgent. Charlotte stopped what she was doing and went to see who was outside.

Opening the front door, she was confronted by the sight of a burly man in a zipped bomber jacket, his huge neck spilling over the collar of his woollen sports shirt. It was Joe, Bernard's brother. His round, friendly face looked worried.

'Bernard's not home yet, Joe,' Charlotte told him, not imagining there was anything untoward.

'I'm afraid I've got some bad news,' he said.

'You'd better come in.' Passing the two suitcases, she led the way through the hall to the drawing room, where she turned on the lights and beckoned the visitor to join her on the sofa nearest to them.

'Bernard has been taken seriously ill,' his younger brother revealed. Tears began to form in his deep-set eyes.

'Is it his heart again?' Charlotte enquired. As yet she was not worried. Bernard always bounced back. 'He will be all right, won't he?'

'The ambulance got to him just in time,' Joe said hoarsely.

Charlotte gasped.

'He told me that he was meeting his solicitor this afternoon,' Joe said. 'He did his best to put on a brave face, but I know Berel – sorry, I mean Bernard. I could tell there was something seriously troubling him.'

'I tried so many times to get him to confide in me,' Charlotte blurted out, feeling the need to justify herself.

'I knew where their offices were,' Joe continued, 'so I decided to hang around outside.'

Charlotte sat anxiously wringing her hands. 'What happened?' she asked.

'I waited for about an hour. Then Bernard came out of the building. It was as if he'd been drinking, the way he staggered unsteady on his feet, trying to find his bearings. Suddenly, I saw his legs give way and a bunch of people gathering around him shouting for help. Fortunately, there was a phone box a few feet away. I dialled 999 and said it was an emergency.'

'Bernard *is* going to be all right?' Charlotte asked again. 'I mean, he's not going to . . .?'

'If it hadn't been for that passing medical student, who knew what to do . . . He'd stopped breathing, you see. I travelled in the ambulance with him. The hospital said there wouldn't be any news until late this evening. But from what I could find out, it'll be a miracle if he makes it.'

Charlotte looked at the man next to her, overwhelmed in his distress for his beloved elder brother.

'I really had no idea,' she whispered.

'He didn't want to worry you.' Joe forced a smile. 'Bernard's very old-fashioned like that. He often told me that he couldn't believe his luck when he ran into you.'

There was a moment of silence as they both sat immersed in their own thoughts.

'Can I get you some tea or something else to drink?' Charlotte asked eventually.

'I wouldn't say no to a large scotch, if you're offering,' Joe replied, recovering some of his usual perkiness. 'But I can see I've stopped you from going somewhere.'

'I was only planning to stay with a friend for a few days,' Charlotte replied. She was fidgeting with the buttons on her coat. 'I'll phone her and tell her that there's been an emergency and I can't get away.'

'Look, love, if he pulls through, he's going to need a good woman to look after him.' By the expression on Joe's face, it was clear that he knew what she had really been planning to do.

Charlotte got up and went back to the study. The news about Bernard had left her stunned. She went over to the drinks cabinet, took out a bottle of Dimple whisky and poured out two generous measures. She then picked up the half-written letter and tore it into small pieces. Removing her coat and throwing it over a chair, she took the two tumblers and returned to the drawing room in a more settled frame of mind.

As Charlotte handed Joe his drink and sat down in an armchair facing him, she could see that he was making an extreme effort to compose himself for her benefit.

'To Bernard!' They both toasted him spontaneously.

'May he make a full recovery,' Joe added with intense feeling. He took a large gulp of his whisky.

'Joan is convinced that he has financial problems,' Charlotte stated.

'Nothing that he can't handle,' Joe replied, too quickly to sound convincing. 'Bernard's a fighter!' He punched the air with his huge fists to emphasise the point. 'That's what coming from the East End does for you.'

'He's never talked to me about his past. The first time I knew anything about his brothers or sisters was when your mother died,' Charlotte said.

'Must have been quite a shock to you,' Joe remarked. 'To be honest, I'm surprised he brought you along.'

'We'd just arrived back from the South of France. He wanted to get home as quickly as possible.'

'You don't know Bernard the way I do.' The visitor's round face broke into a warm grin. 'He wanted to show you off to the rest of the family.'

'But we had only just got to know each other,' Charlotte objected.

'Berel – sorry, Bernard – is very decisive. He makes up his mind quickly.'

Charlotte recalled the first time she had encountered him at the National Gallery and his persistence when he wanted her to come and work for him.

Joe reached into his jacket pocket and took out a small black leather box.

'He wanted you to have this,' he said, handing the item across.

'What is it?' Charlotte's face flushed with embarrassment. She opened the lid and inside some blue paper was a single diamond.

'Bernard was going to ask you to marry him. He told me so himself. But when all the problems in business flared up, he was convinced that you would turn him down. He made me promise that if anything happened to him, I would give this to you. After all, I was going to be his best man.'

'You mean he suspected that he was seriously ill?' Charlotte uttered softly.

'Bernard had been getting pains in his chest. He'd been in and out of specialists' clinics ever since Mum passed away.'

Charlotte felt a wave of sadness come over her. How could she not have noticed that his aloofness was merely a ruse so she shouldn't get too close to him?

She began to weep.

Joe sprang up out of his seat and went over to comfort her. Charlotte stood up and willingly entered into the embrace of Bernard's warm-hearted youngest brother.

They clung together, each one praying for the recovery of the man who meant so very much to them.

17

It was mid-morning when Charlotte eventually awoke, still disturbed by her dream. In it, Bernard was amongst the same group of religious Jews that she had encountered at the decrepit cemetery. They were being herded mercilessly onto open trucks by a strapping fair-haired guard whose face seemed familiar. Suddenly it came to her. It was the same young recruit who had helped with her luggage on the train from Zurich to Davos. Shuddering, she quickly put the image out of her mind as she went over the events of the previous evening.

Joe had stayed until one a.m. It was as if he had taken over responsibility for Charlotte. He had only agreed to leave when he was sure that she was all right to be left on her own. She had insisted that he telephone the hospital on the hour, every hour, to try and get an update on Bernard's condition. Each time, he was told the same story: there had been no change in the patient's condition. Bernard still hadn't regained consciousness. Then finally, just before one in the morning, the specialist informed them that Bernard had stirred. Although it was too soon for him to give an accurate prognosis, or for Bernard to receive visitors, the doctor did say that the patient was breathing on his own without assistance.

Charlotte remembered seeing Joe to the door and wondering why such a caring man had never settled down.

All he was prepared to tell her was that he had a long-term girlfriend who was married, and that they saw each other whenever they could at weekends in a cottage they shared in North Wales. She decided that since he wasn't too forthcoming, she wouldn't press him further. More problematic was Lenny, the handsome other brother. Joe had informed her that he'd just been arrested by the police, accused of living off the immoral earnings of women in his employ. With all his other troubles, Bernard didn't need to hear this. Joe had concealed the news from him and tried in vain to arrange bail for the normally phlegmatic Lenny. The magistrate wouldn't budge, however. Unbeknownst to Joe, it was Lenny's third offence and the police were determined to hand him a custodial sentence to teach him a lesson.

Charlotte bathed and dressed quickly. When she went downstairs, Annette the maid was busy on her hands and knees scrubbing the kitchen floor. Not wanting to raise the woman's concerns about her employer's sudden absence, Charlotte moved stealthily towards the front door and quietly let herself out of the house.

The temperature had dropped overnight. Braving a sudden rush of cold air against her face, Charlotte put up her coat collar and started on the short journey to work. Albeit feeling more optimistic about Bernard's recovery, she still felt remorseful that in a moment of pique, she had been prepared to walk away. Was she really so easily influenced that she would side with that devious woman in the office, who was clearly solely focused on her own interests? If only she had realised how deeply Bernard had cared for her. She would try never to think badly of him again. Perhaps she would agree to marry him. After all, being in her thirties, what other man would want her?

Feeling hungry, Charlotte stopped briefly at the coffee bar down the street from the gallery and ordered a custard doughnut and a double espresso. When she arrived at the gallery, to her surprise she found it in darkness. She didn't understand – Joan always opened up in the mornings. Maybe she was ill? Charlotte let herself in and switched on the lights. At that moment, she heard footsteps coming down the stairs from the first floor. A very tall man with slicked-back hair and a smarmy expression appeared carrying a pile of papers.

'You are Miss Brown, I assume,' he said, peering at his documents.

'Yes, I am Charlotte Brown,' she answered, confused by the sight of this stranger.

'George Harris is the name,' the man introduced himself, striding towards her. 'I gather that you weren't expecting me. Think I've already caused a bit of a stir,' he smirked. 'Anyway, can't be helped. I've got a job to do, so it's probably best if we get on with it.'

'And what exactly is the reason you are here?' Charlotte wanted to know.

'Well, it's not to purchase a painting. Although I must say that the one of a father and child on his knee did rather catch my eye,' the man said, gesturing at one of Charlotte's most recent works. 'No, I've been appointed by your bankers to wind up the company.'

'I'm sorry, I don't understand.' Charlotte was becoming alarmed. 'Bernard Morris owns the gallery. He didn't give any instruction about handing it over to anyone else.'

'As of this morning, Bernard Morris has no further involvement with the company. You need to understand that the group has been put into liquidation. It's my job to sell off all the assets at the best price so that the creditors get paid.'

Charlotte was in a renewed state of shock. Joe certainly hadn't given her the impression that things were this serious. The only plausible explanation was that Bernard had kept his dire financial situation to himself.

What on earth was she going to do? For the second time in less than twenty-four hours she began to reassess her future. She got up from behind her desk and headed towards the stairs. She needed to talk to Joan. Even though she had good reason not to trust the woman, Joan was the only one around who could confirm what the man had just told her.

'I assume that you want to share some thoughts with your colleagues,' the tall man commented perceptively. 'I'm afraid you'll find no one upstairs. It appears that the other employees knew more than you did about the state of play.'

Charlotte stopped and turned around, looking bemused.

'Did a runner, I think the expression is. Appears they tried helping themselves to the company chequebook before they left. They didn't realise, of course, that the account was frozen. Probably had to make do with what was left in the petty cash box.'

Charlotte was speechless. Once again, she appeared to be the last person to know what was going on. She had been left completely out in the cold, all on her own.

'So you see, you're the only one left, Miss Brown. Obviously, I shall need you to carry on here until all the stock is sold. Then the building can be marketed with vacant possession. Anyway, consider it a chance for us to become better acquainted.'

He looked her up and down in a suggestive way, making her feel uncomfortable.

'Apparently, I can be quite charming when you get to know me better,' he beamed. Patting her arm, he left her in no doubt about his intentions.

'Feel free to call me George,' he added. Then he turned around and walked back upstairs. 'Oh – and I do hope that Bernard Morris gets better soon,' he called down before disappearing into his office on the floor above.

Charlotte returned to her desk feeling unsettled. How could things have changed so radically and so quickly? She found it odd that Mr Harris had made no reference to Joe, who was also working for Bernard. She needed to speak to him. There were too many unanswered questions. Maybe Joe could provide her with some assurance about her future.

Charlotte didn't have to wait long. After she finished work, she found Joe outside, sitting behind the wheel of his car. Seeing Charlotte approaching in his rear-view mirror, he reached over and opened the passenger door.

Charlotte noticed as she got into the seat next to him that his eyes were bloodshot and that he'd been crying.

'Bernard died at three o'clock this afternoon,' he said.

18

Bernard Morris was buried early the next morning in the same Jewish cemetery where his mother had been laid to rest only ten months earlier. Charlotte, emulating a few of the other mourners, took a handful of pebbles, in accordance with Jewish tradition, and placed them on the freshly dug grave. She felt drained of any emotion. The last forty-eight hours had been a complete haze, and by the time of the burial Charlotte was numb. A huge crowd had turned up to pay their respects to a good man. Men and women whom Charlotte didn't recognise came up to her offering words of comfort, but they left no impression on her. Joe was completely distraught and had to be supported by his two sisters. No mention was made of Lenny, who had brought disgrace upon the family.

Charlotte had already spent her last night at the house in Mayfair and left it in the capable hands of Annette the maid. The same evening, her two cases still packed, she went back to her flat in West Hampstead.

For the next three weeks, Charlotte turned up for work as if nothing had changed. At first she found it hard, seeing Bernard's name on the gallery. But gradually, he no longer formed part of her thoughts. She resorted to what she had always done when confronted with a painful experience: she denied its existence. She found it strange that she was still being paid and the man in the upstairs office appeared in no hurry to dispense with her services. She was also relieved that he had apparently decided to keep his distance. Theirs was, in the circumstances, a normal working relationship. However, whenever she brought up the question of her position and whether the gallery would remain open, he became evasive, and she was sure that he was keeping something from her.

Then one afternoon, and without any prior notice, she was summoned into his office and informed that he had completed his assignment. Her position, he told her, would be clarified the next day with the new owners.

The same evening, three smartly dressed men and a stunningly beautiful woman sat back in comfortable armchairs, sipping champagne in Rupert Meredith's private suite on the seventh floor of the Ritz Hotel. The atmosphere, however, was tense.

'Robson made the final payment a few hours ago,' the ruddy-faced banker proclaimed. 'He's fulfilled his function. Now your offer should go through without any hitches.'

'Have to say that chap Harris is a cool character,' young Bertie Chesterfield remarked.

'Been lining his pockets for years at shareholders' expense, I expect,' the banker surmised.

'Gentlemen, if you don't mind, can we get down to details? I've a plane leaving for Buenos Aires in a few hours,' the craggy-faced elderly man declared in a thick German accent.

'Papa, it's all been decided,' said the woman sitting next to him. She placed her hand on his frail arm. 'Together with the Chesterfield Estate, we will each own fifty per cent of the company.'

'And what happens if you cannot agree?' the elderly man demanded. It was clear from his expression that he was deeply suspicious of the arrangement.

'Mere formality, old chap. As Chairman, I will hold the casting vote,' the banker said smoothly. Rupert Meredith wanted to avoid any further delay in signing the agreement, lest it jeopardise his £500,000 arrangement fee.

'And if I'm correct, Rupert, each side does have pre-emption rights?' Bertie Chesterfield checked.

'Absolutely. So there's no need for concern, Herr Muller,' the banker confirmed, attempting to placate the man who was now openly scowling at him.

'Susana, it's your decision,' said the German. 'But I would never enter into an agreement where I didn't have complete control.'

'Sounds familiar,' Bertie Chesterfield muttered under his breath.

'You wanted to say something?' Herr Muller snapped at the youngest person in the room.

'Only that the agreement works both ways,' Bertie snapped back. He got up from his chair and went over to where Susana's father was sitting. 'We have to trust each other. I'm willing to take that chance if you are.'

Bertie then extended his hand to the man who was threatening to scupper the deal. He didn't disclose that even with Meredith's extortionate fee, he was buying back part of the family heritage at a fraction of the price at which it had been sold to Bernard Morris. The deal with the German was only an expedient until Bertie got back the other half of his Mayfair portfolio. He had learned his lesson: that when it came to property, it paid to be patient.

The banker picked up his briefcase from down the side of his chair and produced the agreement, which he strategically handed first to Bertie Chesterfield. The young aristocrat gave the document a cursory examination before taking out his fountain pen and signing his name. He then passed the pen and agreement to Susana, who added her signature without looking at it.

The meeting broke up amidst the shaking of hands and fake camaraderie. Bertie Chesterfield, realising that Susana's father still wielded the main influence over his family affairs, accompanied the old man as they left the private suite, each one attempting to hide their mutual distrust.

Susana walked seductively up to the banker and pressed her voluptuous body against his.

'Rupert, darling, you're a genius,' she breathed, looking up at him. She then reached for his hand and cupped it around her full breast.

'I thought you'd be pleased that you finally helped bury Bernard Morris,' the banker smirked.

'And I get my own gallery with someone already there to run it for me.'

'Assuming, of course, she's prepared to stay. I must say, I expected her to put up more of a fight handing Park Street to us,' Rupert shrugged, referring to Charlotte, who unwittingly had signed over the half share in Bernard Morris's house that had been put in her name.

Susana began undoing the buttons on the banker's shirt. A determined expression appeared on her exquisite face.

'I can be *most* persuasive, if I want to be,' she murmured.

Rupert Meredith needed no further encouragement.

He lifted her up in his huge arms and walked slowly to the bedroom.

The day had turned out rather well, he thought. He'd finally managed to get rid of all the Muller family money from the bank and got paid a decent amount in the process. That old Nazi was shrewder than he gave him credit for. There would, of course, be dissension between the two parties, which he would engineer. Then, as Chairman, he would cast his vote with the Chesterfields. The old man would find himself in a position of weakness with a minority stake in the company, which would only prove saleable to the major shareholder.

Placing his mistress on the large double bed, he smiled to himself at the cleverness of his deception.

19

One day in December, Charlotte got to work, shivering in the cold spell that continued to grip the capital. It was nearly noon, and she had come from a medical appointment. This morning's X-ray had shown that her lungs were badly congested; also, she was suffering from high blood pressure. She had been told in no uncertain terms by the consultant that unless she gave up smoking, the probability was that she wouldn't live past forty. Unfortunately, over and over again, she had proved to herself that she couldn't do without cigarettes.

On arriving at the gallery, Charlotte looked up at the new sign above the awning. She was stunned. Bernard Morris's name had disappeared! It had become the Muller Gallery.

How, she asked herself, could a business that was thriving one moment have gone wrong, so quickly? It was all a mystery.

As she rummaged around in her bag for her key, a chill went through her at the thought that the locks might have been changed.

'I can see that I have managed to surprise you,' a woman's voice whispered.

As the fragrance of expensive perfume wafted over her shoulder, Charlotte turned around. The solicitor's wife was standing behind her. Despite the sub-zero temperature,

Susana was dressed in a revealing silk blouse and a tight-fitting black suit that showed off her curvaceous figure.

'I d-didn't expect . . .' Charlotte stammered, trying to find the words to convey her astonishment.

'That you would be working for me? I do hope that you're not *too* disappointed,' Susana replied, pouting.

'You mean that you want me to stay!' Charlotte exclaimed.

'But of course. Now why don't we go and have some lunch? It will give us a chance to get to know each other a little better.'

'Yes, I would like that very much,' Charlotte said, suddenly feeling much more optimistic.

The two women started walking briskly towards Piccadilly.

'There's a quiet hotel just around the corner from here. Brockets use it all the time for entertaining. It's really quite conducive for intimate conversations,' Susana remarked. She was paying more attention to the stares of admiration from passers-by than to the woman accompanying her. Charlotte wondered how she could have gained such confidence, to relish the looks she was receiving. Walking next to her was a little intoxicating.

After they had entered through the revolving doors of the exclusive fifty-room hotel, Susana led Charlotte through a hallway lined with cabinets displaying fashion accessories and costly items of jewellery. At the end was the bar, a cosy wood-panelled room that gave off the aroma of beeswax polish. They sat down at a small table by the window.

'I think champagne would be appropriate, don't you?' The new gallery-owner clicked her fingers to attract the attention of the lounging barman. 'A bottle of 1955 Cristal and some olives - and make sure the champagne is suitably chilled,' she instructed the flushed-faced bartender, who had scurried over to take their order.

'Of course, right away, madam. Will you be requiring your usual table in the dining room?' the man asked.

Susanna nodded.

'I'll bring the menus,' he said, before slinking off.

'I've been so looking forward to this moment,' Susana said then, reaching across the table for her companion's hand. 'I knew when we first met that we had so much in common. Now I've got you all to myself.'

Charlotte blushed at the unexpected attention being directed towards her.

'Naturally, Brockets know nothing about my new venture,' the woman went on. 'They would be most displeased if they thought I wasn't giving full attention to my job. So you see, it's worked out well that you will be running the gallery for me.'

Susana couldn't reveal the real reason why she needed the gallery. Her family in South America was making so much money from their art sold through Brockets that they didn't know what to do with it. She had therefore come up with the idea of creating a legitimate front for their unsavoury activities.

'And what direction will you want the gallery to take?' Charlotte was eager to know, already adapting to the new situation.

'I was thinking that we shouldn't ignore the Pre-Raphaelite period.'

Charlotte's face lit up at the mention of her main area of expertise.

'That is your speciality, if I remember correctly?'

Charlotte recalled the first time the two of them had met – at the dinner party at Bernard's house, just over a year ago. The unpleasant scene that had marred the evening, and which had stayed with her for weeks afterwards, now seemed a distant memory. Strangely, she found herself looking forward to working for this woman.

'In fact,' Susana confided, 'I've a Millais and two Rossettis arriving in London approximately ten days from now.'

Charlotte's eyes widened in astonishment. She knew the woman was enterprising, but how she had managed to procure paintings by such famous artists was beyond her.

'Most of the major works are still held in private collections, but as I'm sure you are aware, that movement is not currently in vogue. We have been most successful in persuading the owners to part with the paintings at extremely reasonable prices.' Susana was clearly proud of her achievement. 'In a few months, the walls of the Muller Gallery will be full of exquisite pieces of art.'

The barman appeared, carrying a tray with two fluted glasses and a bowl of large green olives, which he placed on the table in front of the two women. He then rushed back to fetch the champagne, which was already embedded in the ice-bucket, and presented it to his customer. Relieved when Susana nodded her approval, he opened the bottle and began carefully filling the glasses before returning the champagne to its cooler.

'I should like to drink to a close relationship,' Susana announced, looking intensely at her companion.

Charlotte followed by raising her glass. 'I'm grateful of course that you should want me to continue,' she said, sipping her champagne, 'but what exactly will be my function? Bernard allowed me to run the gallery and . . .'

'Please, Charlotte, let's not talk about the past,' Susana interrupted. 'I realise the two of you were close, but to be completely honest, he was not the right man for you.'

Charlotte was taken back by the other woman's frankness. But maybe she was right. Hadn't she often doubted Bernard herself?

'I mean, anyone could tell by his garish home that the man had absolutely no taste.' Susana gestured to the barman to pour more champagne.

'We did very well with one particular artist,' Charlotte replied. She felt that she needed to defend Bernard's memory.

'Surely you can't be referring to that Max Freedland?' Susana scoffed.

'His paintings were beginning to achieve quite respectable prices, but then he seemed to just disappear,' Charlotte responded.

'Darling, didn't you know? The police were after him. Anyway, it's best that you're no longer involved with those types of people. Now, I don't know about you, but I'm starving!' Susana exclaimed.

Charlotte had no interest in hearing anything more about Max Freedland. As far as she was concerned, he was part of an unhappy episode that thankfully was now over. Two menus were put in front of the women and the barman began refilling their glasses. Their order was taken.

Lunch was a two-hour affair. By the time Susana had called for the bill, it was three in the afternoon.

'It's most remiss of me, but we haven't settled on your

salary,' she said to Charlotte. 'What do you think you're worth?'

'I'm sorry, I don't know what you expect me to say,' Charlotte replied, feeling embarrassed.

The other woman threw back her mane of magnificent dark hair and laughed. 'I'm only teasing, I'm sure we can come to a mutually satisfactory arrangement,' she said, and got up from the table. Taking Charlotte by the arm, she walked with her back to the gallery.

'You know, I think we could become more than just work colleagues,' Susana murmured, looking at Charlotte.

'I would like that,' Charlotte said shyly.

'Forgive me for mentioning it, but you really don't make the best of yourself.'

Charlotte, her senses numbed from too much champagne, looked down at the grey pleated dress that covered her knees.

'I should like to take you shopping. We could have lunch in Knightsbridge and then I'll take you to my hairdresser. I think you would look quite magnificent with it cut short.'

Charlotte's heart was pounding. The attention from this woman, who seemed so far away from her socially, had blended with their lunchtime alcohol to form a potent cocktail.

'Charlotte, darling, I have some errands to run,' Susana said. 'Why don't you come up with some suggestions of how to fill the rest of the walls and we can discuss it tomorrow?'

Charlotte stood motionless, unable to react.

'Don't look so sad. We've only just got reacquainted,' the other woman said sweetly, noting with satisfaction the clear disappointment on Charlotte's face.

'Oh, and you'll need new keys,' she announced, and tossed her own set over to her employee. 'And darling, you simply must get rid of that *dreadful* painting,' she ended, starting to walk away.

It took Charlotte a moment to grasp that Susana was referring to *Blight*, Daniel Petrovitch's disturbing scene above her desk.

For the rest of the day, she was unable to get the charismatic woman out of her mind.

That evening, Charlotte inspected herself in the mirror and was pleased with the results of her labour. Straight after work, she had gone to a Mayfair salon and had her hair skilfully cut to show off her high cheekbones. The new style gave her a striking appearance. She pictured herself in one of the films portraying Berlin's decadent reputation of the 1920s.

She went into the bedroom, opened the wardrobe and flipped through the half-dozen dresses that she possessed. She told herself she really should, as Susana had pointed out, make more of an effort. There were still some savings left; Bernard had always been more than generous with her. She would treat herself to two new outfits.

The latest transformation of Eva Schlessinger had begun.

James Robson carried the last of the cardboard packing boxes up the three flights of stairs into the dingy one-bedroom flat he was now renting at the rear of Euston station. He shut the front door, went into the sparsely decorated living room and slumped back into the solitary armchair. The divorce from Susana had cost him dearly.

Not only had he lost the house in Kensington, but also most of his capital. More seriously, he had taken the blame for his firm losing Meredith's Bank as clients. It was a miracle that the other partners had taken pity on him and given him the opportunity to rebuild his reputation.

James knew, however, that he was far more resilient than people imagined. He also held a personal grudge against his wife and the man whose mistress she had become, Rupert Meredith. Together, those two had tried to destroy him. The day would come, he vowed, when he would exact his revenge.

20

For the next few days, Charlotte attempted to occupy herself at work while she waited expectantly for Susana to appear. However, it was as if their intimate conversation had never happened. More curious was her employer's sudden loss of interest in the gallery. Perhaps she had been unable to get away from Brockets, Charlotte tried convincing herself. But whatever the reason, she was desperate to see her again. Although she wouldn't admit it, she had become infatuated with the exotic-looking woman.

Early one morning at the beginning of her second week, a van drew up outside the gallery. Two men in smart uniforms appeared at the front door with a wooden crate marked *Fragile*. It took Charlotte a moment to ascertain that it must be the delivery of the Pre-Raphaelite paintings that Susana had mentioned over lunch. The men helped her unpack the works of art and then left. The last remaining items had been sold, their hooks still inserted in the empty walls. Charlotte decided that she would hang the paintings herself.

Later that afternoon, while she was admiring the new pieces, Susana breezed in unexpectedly.

'Absolutely perfect!' she exclaimed, looking at the works on display.

'I'm pleased that you approve,' Charlotte replied,

anxious for Susana to notice her new appearance.

'So, these are the selling prices of similar pieces that have just been sold at auction,' Susana said, producing a card from her handbag, which she passed to her employee. 'Put them up straight away. With luck, you may achieve your first sale for me,' she added condescendingly.

Unbeknownst to Charlotte, the Millais and the two Rossettis had been purchased by the Muller family at Brockets auction so as to establish their credibility as authentic collectors. Susana was now intending to sell the paintings on in her own gallery so they could recoup their investment.

'I'll catalogue them immediately. They've already attracted some interest,' Charlotte proffered, still trying to make a good impression.

Ignoring her assistant, the chic woman glided past her to the rear of the gallery. She picked up a handful of letters addressed to the previous owner, Bernard Morris, and perched on the edge of Charlotte's desk.

'More wretched demands for payment,' she scowled. 'Charlotte, you need to move your things. I shall be sitting here in future. You'll be far more use to me upstairs running the office.'

'But Susana, we can't leave the gallery unattended,' Charlotte protested.

'Our clientele will expect the owner to serve them personally,' her new boss said curtly. 'It was a different matter when they were spending a few hundred pounds. We're now in a much higher league. Some of the works on display are going to be in the hundreds of thousands.'

Charlotte couldn't believe that the woman in front of her was the same one who had fawned over her just days before. In a matter of minutes, she had been demoted to the upstairs office and told in no uncertain terms that she would have no say whatsoever in the running of the gallery. It was humiliating. Running her hands through her cropped hair, she turned away.

'Oh Charlotte!' Susana called after her. 'I do hope that I can rely on you.'

Charlotte stopped and looked back, using all her resolve to keep calm.

'I'm sorry that I gave you any reason to doubt me,' she replied with a quiet dignity.

'I've been notified that a large shipment of twenty paintings I was expecting has just docked at Southampton,' Susana informed her. 'Once they've cleared customs, they should be here well in time for our New Year opening.'

Charlotte again was taken by surprise.

'Oh, didn't I mention it to you?' Susana said carelessly, knowing full well that she hadn't. 'I've arranged delivery for next Thursday, so you'll need to cancel whatever else you might be doing and be prepared to stay late.'

'I'm quite used to working long hours,' Charlotte responded, keeping her distance. 'When I was at the National Gallery, we often—'

'There's really no need to keep justifying yourself,' Susana interrupted.

'And who are the artists whose works will be arriving?' Charlotte enquired, not showing much enthusiasm.

'You'll just have to wait and see,' the owner replied with a mischievous smile that recaptured some of her previous charm. 'But I can tell you that you won't have to put them up yourself. I've got the people that Brockets use to do that. Obviously, you'll need to arrange to have the gallery alarmed. The insurance company has insisted.'

'I will deal with it immediately,' Charlotte said.

'Now I have to run,' Susana said airily. 'Problems with the builders again. It's always the same in this country. Can't interfere with their precious tea breaks. They don't know what hard work is.'

The moment Susana had marched out of the gallery, Charlotte sat down at the desk that had just been taken away from her and started to weep bitterly. At that moment, she couldn't remember ever having felt more alone. She looked back on her life. On the few occasions that she thought she'd found happiness, something always happened that dragged her back to reality. Not for the first time, she felt as though she was being punished.

Gathering up her things from her desk, she placed them in one of the packing boxes that had been left by the deliverymen, went up to the first floor and entered the small office that had previously been occupied by Bernard's secretary, Joan. She dropped the box on the floor. It could wait till the next day to sort everything out.

The weather after Christmas had turned milder and so Charlotte decided to walk back to her flat. She needed to clear her head, and the stroll through Regent's Park always managed to lift her spirits. She arrived home just before seven and noticed a woman in a drab brown coat sitting on the step outside the house in Gladys Road, an old leather suitcase beside her.

It took a moment for Charlotte to recognise Annette, Bernard's maid-housekeeper.

'Hello, madam,' the woman called out, trying her best to appear cheerful.

'Annette, hello. What are you doing here?' Charlotte asked. She was surprised that the woman knew where she lived.

'Nowhere else to go, madam,' the maid shrugged, looking exhausted.

'You'd better come in,' Charlotte said kindly.

'That's very nice of you, so long as I won't be any trouble,' the woman answered. She got up and followed Charlotte into the house and up the stairs.

'The living room is just through there,' Charlotte said, unlocking the door. 'Make yourself comfortable. I'll go and put the kettle on.'

The woman dumped her coat on top of her suitcase and, still in her apron, accompanied Charlotte into the compact kitchen at the end of the hallway.

'I assumed you had just got another job,' Charlotte said as she lit the stove, made a pot of tea and set two places at the table. She then brought over a fresh loaf, butter, a piece of Cheddar cheese, some slices of corned beef on a plate and a tin of biscuits, and sat down opposite her visitor. As she poured out a cup of tea for them both, Annette began to speak.

'Been with Mr Bernard for fifteen years, I had, God rest his soul. Me and my brother William, we was brought up as kids in a Dr Barnardo's home. Mr Morris gave us both a job and put a roof over our heads.'

'You mean that Bernard's chauffeur is your brother?' Charlotte asked, her face showing genuine surprise. She had often thought about the chatty little man and Joan the secretary running off together.

'We left school at thirteen,' the scrawny woman continued. 'Neither of us had any qualifications so I went into service. William wanted to join up but he had a weak chest, see. Spent the war as a clerk in an office, driving Civil Servants around.'

'So how did you meet Bernard?' Charlotte asked.

'We was living in the East End around the corner from his old mum. Everyone knew Annie Moss. You would have liked her, madam. No airs and graces with her.' The woman laughed, slurping some tea and beginning to make herself a corned-beef sandwich.

'I'm afraid I never did meet her,' Charlotte said, passing her guest the pickle.

'Only at her funeral,' the other woman quickly corrected her, then carried on eating.

Charlotte could see that there was little that Annette didn't know about Bernard's family.

'Even when he made all his money, Mr Bernard always came back. The East End was in his blood, see. So one day he saw our William hanging around the Lane with time on his hands. He asked him if he wanted a job as his driver. Naturally, William jumped at the chance. Before you know it, he's only got hissself dressed up in a smart cap and grey chauffeur's uniform. A nice cuppa this is,' she said approvingly, finishing her sandwich and taking a couple of ginger biscuits to dunk in her tea.

'And how did you come to work for him?' Charlotte asked, buttering a slice of bread and cutting a chunk of cheese to go with it.

'The first thing he does, my brother, is to ask the gaffer whether he needs any help around the house. He had this smashing place in Bloomsbury. Lovely it was.'

'When was that?' Charlotte enquired, wondering why Bernard had never mentioned it.

'Must be a couple of years after the war ended,' answered the housekeeper. 'We weren't there long. The guv'nor always had big eyes, see. He moves to Mayfair and starts mixing with all them lah-di-dah types. You know, the country-house and champagne brigade.'

A piece of biscuit went down the wrong way and she suddenly started coughing so violently that her sparrow-like frame shook with the force.

'But they could see right through him,' she gasped, taking a gulp of tea and trying to catch her breath. 'It suited them while he was in the money, but when he hit hard times, none of them wanted to know. Cruel they was.' She scowled. 'That Meredith bloke was the worst. Wouldn't trust him if you paid me. Couldn't wait to get his greedy hands on that lovely house of the guvnor's – *you* know how clean I kept it. And when he moved in his fancy woman, that foreign tart, the cheeky mare only told me to pack me bags.'

'Which woman do you mean?' Charlotte asked, unsure whether she had heard correctly.

'You know her, the solicitor's wife. They'd been carrying on behind her husband's back. Disgusting, that's what it is.' Annette snorted. Then, 'Haven't got a fag by any chance, have you, love? Sorry, I mean a cigarette,' she corrected herself.

'Yes, of course.' Charlotte got up and went to fetch her handbag from the coat-stand in the hall. She still couldn't absorb the housekeeper's words. It was one thing about Bernard's business – she had come to terms with the fact that the gallery had been taken over by new owners. But to have lost his house to the person now living in it was too much. She shivered at Susana's callous nature.

Charlotte returned to the kitchen with the packet of cigarettes, fetched the box of matches from the cooker and handed both of them to her visitor.

'Not going to have one yourself?' Annette asked.

'I've been told to stop,' Charlotte replied.

'Have to say that your new hairstyle suits you,' the woman commented. She blew a stream of smoke across the table.

'When did Mrs Robson move in?' Charlotte asked, still in a state of shock.

'Two weeks after Bernard died,' Annette replied, looking downcast. 'I've been at the Salvation Army ever since. But I can't stay there for ever.' She bristled. 'I've still got some pride left.'

'And how about Joe and his sisters? Weren't they able to offer you something?' Charlotte asked, feeling sympathy for the other woman.

'Joe fell to pieces after his brother passed away. He couldn't even bring himself to come to the house and help clear out the guv'nor's clothes. Last I heard of him, he was trying to become a cabbie.'

Charlotte had expected that Joe would have remained in contact. It was only now she began to comprehend the extent of his loss.

'Mr Bernard had some smashing suits and dozens of pairs of shoes,' Annette said wistfully 'Anybody would have been glad of them. Shame our William wasn't the right size.'

Charlotte couldn't help smiling at the vision of the diminutive chauffeur in Bernard's clothes that were several sizes too big for him.

'Oh, well, we got a few bob for them down the Lane.

Never had much to do with Rose and Millie though,' the housekeeper commented. 'They have their own lives. And as for Lenny, well! Always getting himself into trouble, he is. A right spiv. And now he's doing time, courtesy of Her Majesty.'

Charlotte was only half-listening to the woman's rambling. How was she ever going to face Susana? At that moment, it seemed inconceivable that she could continue working at the gallery.

'Well, this is a very nice place you have,' Annette said approvingly, looking around the room. 'Of course, nothing like the house in Park Street but it's cosy, that's what I'd call it.' She finished her second cup of tea, then added slyly, adopting a knowing look, 'So what I was thinking was that Mr Bernard must have seen you all right.'

'Sorry, Annette, what exactly do you mean?' Charlotte asked, puzzled.

'Money!' the other woman hissed, rubbing her thumb and forefinger together.

'And that's the reason why you were waiting outside my house?' Charlotte asked.

'Mr Bernard, may he rest in peace, never left me short. So since you and him were close, like,' the maid said, leaning her bony frame forward in her chair, 'I was thinking that I might call on your generosity.'

'Yes, of course, I'll give you what I can.' Charlotte reached into her handbag beside her on the kitchen floor. 'But I'm afraid you'd be mistaken if you think that there is anything more substantial.'

The visitor's expression became pinched. 'In that case, I'll take what you have and be on my way,' she said tightly.

Charlotte opened her purse and withdrew twenty-five

pounds in five-pound notes, which she handed over to the disgruntled maid.

'Would you like some more tea before you leave?'

'I've had quite enough, thank you,' the woman replied sourly. She got up from the table. 'I can see that I have already outstayed my welcome.' She looked down again at the paltry sum of money she had been palmed off with.

'But where will you go?' Charlotte asked, following the bony little woman out of the kitchen.

'There's always a bed at William's place now he's moved out. Janice will probably be pleased of the company,' Annette said peevishly, fabricating a recently abandoned sister-in-law. She then put on her coat and picked up her suitcase.

'I can see meself out,' she announced. And without looking back, she marched out of the small flat and thumped down the stairs. A few seconds later, there was the sound of the front door being slammed.

Out of Charlotte's sight, Annette scuttled up the road, dragging her empty suitcase to where an old green Ford Anglia was waiting for her. She put the bag in the boot, moved around to the front and got into the passenger side.

'How did you get on, love?' William asked.

'Got twenty-five quid out of her,' the maid replied. 'Said Bernard never left her nothing.'

'The tight sod was too smart for that. Wouldn't surprise me if he knew she was only after his money,' the chauffeur sneered. He then turned the car around and sped off in the other direction. 'Still, don't forget them emerald earrings you nicked, girl. They must be worth a few hundred quid.'

'Yeah. Flashy, ain't they? Woolworth's probably do a

pair just like them. Anyway, she fell for the story that you were my brother.' Annette ran her fingers through her hair and applied a coat of lipstick.

'She never? You should be on the stage, you should,' William chuckled.

'I suppose you're going straight back to your fancy woman now,' Annette remarked.

'Nah! Joan's old man is out of hospital and he has no intention of giving her a divorce, so it's over,' William said indifferently.

'I suppose that means you're stuck with me,' his wife said, gazing through the window, a resigned expression on her face.

Charlotte stood motionless in the small hallway. Feeling particularly unsettled, she retreated into the small box room and went over to her easel and the unfinished painting of the kind-faced man. She stared at the image of Bernard Morris and thought, not for the first time, that she hadn't been worthy of him.

21

Charlotte stood staring at the vast oil painting of three nude women by Rubens. In a period of a few weeks the gallery had been completely transformed. Works by Lautrec, Cezanne and Van Gogh, as well as Matisse and Picasso, now adorned its walls. All but a few had red 'Sold' stickers by their side.

The February opening had been a huge success. For these few hours, Susana had reverted to her more amiable self. She'd introduced Charlotte to her most important clients as her 'indispensable assistant', apportioning most of the credit to her for the displays, and as a result Charlotte had had second thoughts about confronting her. The visit from Annette had left a bad taste, but the maid, however badly she may have been treated, was clearly unreliable. Perhaps there was a perfectly logical reason why Susana had moved into the house in Mayfair. Yes, Charlotte had been happy living there with Bernard, but she certainly had no claim to it.

During the months that followed, the relationship with Susana became of a friendlier nature. Contrary to what Charlotte had anticipated, her employer's absences became more frequent, and she delegated more of the running of the gallery to her. Charlotte even resumed her old position at the desk on the ground floor. There was something else. Susana had changed, become more subdued. She had lost the intensity that had made her such a formidable adversary and so charismatic a woman. Perhaps she was experiencing turmoil in her personal life? When things were going well, she'd often share with Charlotte the most intimate details of her relationship with Rupert Meredith.

The dry spring of 1958 was followed by a cold, wet summer. One day, the heating in the Muller Gallery had broken down again and Charlotte sat in her lightweight coat and scarf, trying to put the finishing touches to their catalogue for the June exhibition.

Susana had been summoned home to Buenos Aires. Her father had suffered a stroke and wasn't expected to survive. She had asked Charlotte to attend an auction of French nineteenth-century artists at Brockets on her behalf later that week, and send the results of the prices achieved via Telex to South America.

By the time Charlotte arrived at the auction house, the atmosphere in the packed room was tense. She had highlighted the lots of special interest and sat back to await the commencement of proceedings.

Several minutes into the auction, a dark-haired young man in a short blue raincoat, carrying a tattered leather briefcase, negotiated his way through Charlotte's row to the empty seat next to her. He immediately began studying the catalogue with great concentration. Then, from the inside pocket of his jacket, he removed a large white envelope and took out what appeared to be several photographs of paintings.

Doing her best to pay attention to the sale-price of the particular lots she'd been asked to observe, Charlotte couldn't help glancing over her shoulder at the young man.

Something about his mop of black hair and his delicate features seemed familiar. As the auction proceeded, the young man became visibly agitated. Each time a painting was brought onto the podium, he held up a photograph that, to judge from his expression, he clearly believed corresponded to the item. By the end of the sale, his face had become deathly pale. He remained impassive in his seat while the chattering crowd gradually vacated the stuffy room.

Curious to find out the cause of the young man's anguish, Charlotte said gently to him, 'Excuse me, but I couldn't help noticing that you seem in some distress. Can I help in some way?'

The young dark-haired man didn't reply. He sat motionless, grasping hold of the stack of black and white photographs. It was as if he had suffered a major shock.

'Do you perhaps have some connection with the items in the auction?' Charlotte tried again.

'Why do you want to know?' he asked in return, wary of this woman standing over him.

'You seem to have shown an unusual interest in some of our most sought-after items,' Charlotte explained, thinking that she recognised his distinctive accent.

'You mean that you work here?'

'No, but I do have contacts at Brockets.' Charlotte was careful not to disclose anything about her relationship with Susana.

'Then you can help me get back the paintings that belong to my family!' the young man exclaimed, suddenly coming to life.

'I'm sorry, but you're obviously mistaken. All the items in the auction are strictly documented. I'm afraid that you've wasted your journey.' Convinced that this individual was deluded, Charlotte got up and started to walk away.

'Wait, please! I have proof,' the fellow called out, getting to his feet.

Charlotte turned around. 'I really don't think I can help you. And now I must get back to work.'

'Let me come with you,' the young man pleaded. Holding his photographs close to his chest, he followed her to the exit. 'Excuse me for not introducing myself,' he added, remembering his manners. 'My name is David Goldstein.'

At first, she couldn't place where she had heard the name before. A few seconds later, it came to her: the image of the sad woman at the Blauerberg sanatorium in Davos flashed through her mind. Her name was also Goldstein – Margot Goldstein. Charlotte stopped and gazed at the slight young man next to her. The similarity was unmistakable. How could it be? She recalled the woman telling her that she had had a child who had died. Could David be this son? But how? Charlotte frowned, trying to understand. The war had created many chaotic situations; it wasn't unfeasible that this David Goldstein could be Margot's son. If this really was the child from whom Margot was so tragically separated, she had to find out more about him.

As they approached a coffee bar around the corner from the Muller Gallery, she invited David in for a drink.

'I thought that you needed to return to work?' he said.

'I don't know about you, but I could certainly do with some refreshment,' Charlotte answered, thinking that the gallery wouldn't be a suitable place to talk.

They ordered tea and toast as the last customers were

leaving. It was still light outside, but the place was ready to close. Charlotte, remembering Frau Goldstein's heart-breaking tale, waited patiently for David to talk.

'I have to find out the truth,' the young man stressed. He took a bite of his toast. 'You see, I'm the only one of my family to survive. My father was killed in the war and I was brought up by a woman whom I called Mother. It was only when she was dying that I discovered that she wasn't my real mother. She said that she needed to confess. You see, she was very religious, a good Catholic. I was even brought up a Catholic. It was only when I was told that my name was not Axel Schmidt but David Goldstein - and that I was a Jew - that I learned who I really was.'

'And what happened to your real mother?' Charlotte asked, convinced now that the young man was Frau Goldstein's lost son.

'Apparently, she'd been a cabaret artiste, living in Zurich.'

Charlotte had visions of the strange woman by the lake showing off her dancer's shapely legs.

'I searched all the clubs in the city trying to find her,' David went on doggedly. 'I was about to give up when one day, I was having lunch in a restaurant on the lake when I saw pictures of dancers and film stars all around the walls. I asked the manager if he knew the names of any of the artistes, hoping that one of them might have been my mother.'

Seeing the desperation on the young face opposite her, Charlotte had a sudden desire to cradle him in her arms.

'You see, I had no photograph of her,' David continued. 'The proprietor informed me that the club, which apparently used to be called Emile's, had been sold but he gave me the address of the former owner, saying he might be able to help me.'

'And what happened?' Charlotte asked, so absorbed in the young man's tale that she had forgotten it was the very same place where Margot said she had worked.

'He allowed me to take the picture. I found out where the man lived. He was very old and couldn't identify my mother from the photograph, but he said he remembered agreeing to help a Jewish dancer to escape from Germany. He also recalled that there had been a child involved and how distressed the mother had become when the father, who was the manager, took him away.'

'And you were that child?' Charlotte said, biting her lip to hold back the tears that were swelling up inside.

'I'd reached a dead end,' the young man said. 'I was about to leave Zurich and return to my studies in Germany, when for some reason I decided to visit the library in the town. I began casually sifting through old editions of Swiss newspapers when a headline caught my eye.' David drank down more of his tea that had now become tepid.

'It concerned your real mother?' Charlotte asked, fearful that she was about to learn the fate of the woman who had befriended her.

'There was a scandal concerning the Blauerberg sanatorium in Davos. It made front-page news,' the young man disclosed.

'What was it? When did it happen?' Charlotte's mind turned to Johann. Part of her had always suspected that there was another reason why he had been so keen to see her again. But as always, she had suppressed any thoughts that might cause her discomfort.

'Around two years ago. An action was brought against the Director of the sanatorium for gross negligence.'

'And your mother?' Charlotte asked.

David Goldstein swallowed, then managed: 'Only a reference to a patient named Margot Goldstein, who had committed suicide.'

Charlotte gasped. 'I'm so sorry!' she blurted out. 'Look, David, there's something I have to tell you.' She reached over and took hold of his hand.

'What is it?' the young man asked innocently.

'I knew your mother – well, we met briefly. I was suffering from bronchitis and went to the same sanatorium in Davos for a short respite.'

David Goldstein looked at her intently.

'One day, she stopped me in the grounds while I was on the way back from a walk. We talked until it got dark. She told me about her life, about her past as a top cabaret dancer when she'd been known as "the white Josephine Baker".'

The young man's jaw dropped. He was unable to speak. Eventually, he managed, with a whimper, 'Did she mention me?' His large brown eyes were full of emotion.

'Yes. She told me how much she had loved you and how deeply it had affected her, to have you adopted.' Charlotte couldn't bring herself to reveal the lie that had been told to his mother when Margot had come, full of hope, to reclaim her son. What was there to be gained by telling the young man the truth? Frau Schmidt saw herself rightly as the boy's mother. So if Margot Goldstein were to turn up unexpectedly, the woman had obviously had a story ready in order to keep the child she adored and whom she'd brought up single-handedly.

David Goldstein fell silent, a forlorn expression on his face.

Charlotte allowed him some moments of reflection before saying gently, 'We have to go, it's getting late.' She took some money out of her purse to pay the bill.

'But I haven't finished! What about our paintings?' the young man protested. He handed her the envelope containing the photographs that hadn't left his side. Charlotte herself had been so preoccupied with the tragic story of his mother that she hadn't considered his claim about his family's art collection.

'My train leaves for Germany at midnight,' he went on, 'and I still haven't achieved the purpose of my journey.'

'I don't live too far away,' Charlotte told him. 'It's only half past six. If we take the Underground, we can be back at my flat by seven. If you like, we can carry on talking over supper. Then I'll find you a taxi to take you to the station.'

The young man just nodded. He got up from his bench seat and followed Charlotte out of the empty coffee bar into the muggy evening.

In no time, they were sitting around the kitchen table in Charlotte's small flat, sipping more tea while a pot of home-made vegetable soup simmered on the stove.

'You still haven't told me how you were able to trace the paintings to London,' Charlotte said.

'After I arrived back from Switzerland, I contacted a Jewish organisation in Frankfurt which holds records of all businesses that existed before the war. It wasn't difficult to find the Goldstein Bank. Everybody had heard of it. In fact, there were even a few people in the office who had known my grandfather. His name was Walther.'

'But how did you prove who you were? I mean, the name on your birth certificate?'

'I already thought of that. You remember the old man

that I visited in Zurich? He eventually saw my resemblance to one of the dancers in the picture and kindly agreed to confirm in writing that she must have been my mother. Remember, he knew that she had borne a child.'

'But surely that couldn't have been sufficient evidence?' Charlotte queried.

'I offered to pay a few Swiss francs for the photograph, and the restaurant allowed me to keep it,' the young man divulged. 'Fortunately, the Jewish organisation had managed to piece together photographs of whole families that had lived in the city before the war. One of my family, the Goldsteins, showed a young woman who was almost identical to the dancer in my picture.'

'That was most inventive of you.' Charlotte began ladling the piping hot soup into two large bowls and passed him the basket of bread.

'Training as a forensic accountant does have its uses,' the young man sighed, picking up his spoon, eager to devour his first proper meal that day.

'But even if they believed that you were who you said you were, surely there must still have been a problem with your birth certificate?' Charlotte said.

'Another piece of good fortune.' Reaching down into his briefcase, David produced a paper folder containing a document which he handed across to Charlotte. 'You can see that the mother's name is stated as Margot Goldstein.'

'How is that possible?' Charlotte asked. 'The woman you believed was your mother . . .'

'Probably refused to have her name on the certificate,' the young man interjected, shrugging his shoulders. 'Look, she knew I was a Jew but she was still willing to take me in, at great risk to herself.'

'But you too could have been in mortal danger, if anyone had seen your birth certificate.'

'Thankfully it was an oversight by the authorities. But it didn't stop the Nazis from helping themselves to the considerable wealth that my family had accumulated over the last hundred years. There was nothing left, or so I believed.'

'When Frau Schmidt died, how did you live? I mean, who looked after you?' Charlotte felt overcome with emotion.

'I was nearly eighteen; I was about to start university. The house was granted to me in my adoptive parents' will. It was too big for one person, so I took in a couple of lodgers, which provided me with a small income. I was hardly destitute,' the young man reassured her.

'I'm sorry. I didn't mean to offend you,' Charlotte responded, touching David's arm. She thought about the woman who had raised the child, and wondered whether her final gesture of benevolence had helped clear her conscience.

'So how did you establish the existence of the photographs?' she asked.

'It only occurred to me recently that my mother must have had money from somewhere. Otherwise, how could she have supported herself for fifteen years?'

'Wait!' Charlotte said urgently. 'If I remember correctly, your mother told me that the sanatorium in Davos used to belong to your family. She told me that she moved there after the war, but that she couldn't afford its upkeep. It even had a Goldstein crest on the outside.'

'I didn't know that.' The young man tried to absorb this latest revelation. After a few moments, he continued with his tale. 'However, I did find a vault with the Goldstein name in a bank in Zurich. It took me two days to convince the manager that I was the sole surviving member of the family before he agreed to hand over the keys.'

'What did you find?'

'Only photographs of the paintings and their certificates of authenticity.'

Charlotte's first reaction was to assume that there must have been some mistake. She automatically rejected the possibility of any wrongdoing by Brockets.

'You can see them if you like,' David said, perking up. This time he removed a cluster of certificates and passed them across the table. 'Don't worry, they're only photographed copies,' he said, noting Charlotte's hesitancy. 'The originals are kept at my bank in Frankfurt.'

'How did you know that they were going to turn up at auction in London?' Charlotte was unable to dispel the thought that she had unwittingly been caught up in some sort of conspiracy. But she had witnessed the young man's tenacity and sensed that he wouldn't cease his efforts until he received the justice denied to his family.

'When I returned to Germany, I went on the mailing list of all the leading auction houses in Europe and the United States.' David looked at Charlotte. 'To tell you the truth, I never expected it would reap any dividends. The paintings could easily have been sold to a number of different galleries. It would have been a lifetime's work trying to track them down. I just took a chance.'

He broke off some bread and dipped it in his soup.

'One thing I'm still curious about is the people who claim to be the owners,' he told Charlotte. He was attempting to glean any information he could get that would substantiate his claim.

'We receive works on consignment from all over the world: Europe, the United States, South America.' Charlotte's attention was focused on the photographs on the table. If the paintings *did* belong to the Goldsteins, maybe there were collections belonging to other families that had also disappeared. She shuddered at the thought.

'How do you think I can help you?' she asked.

David smiled politely. There was no doubt that the woman who had known his mother meant well. But whether he could rely on her support was another matter. Frankly, he was sceptical. Picking up the certificates, he put them back in the folder and then packed them away in his briefcase.

It was time to leave, to catch the midnight train home.

22

After her visitor had left, Charlotte went to bed and lay awake, unable to get to sleep. The guilt that she felt for not doing enough to intercede on Margot Goldstein's behalf was now eclipsed by concern for Margot's son.

Before David departed, she had given him her home address and telephone number so they could continue to communicate privately. He had left his firm's business card on the kitchen table. Standing on the kerb as he climbed into the taxi, she could see a lost look in his eyes that reminded her of his mother.

Charlotte was impatient for the night to pass so she could get to work. Susana would be wondering why she hadn't received her Telex. Her mind turned to the auction. How enthralled she had been by Monet's flower garden, the Cezanne landscapes, the Degas ballerinas. The collection of twenty paintings had fetched record prices. She had difficulty reminding herself that these works might have been stolen from their original owners.

When Susana returned, Charlotte would inform her of what she had discovered, hoping for a plausible explanation. She wanted to be able to telephone David and tell him that his family's art collection were not the same paintings that had been sold by Brockets. After all, didn't some artists, especially the Impressionists, paint many versions of the same subject?

Back in Frankfurt, the young trainee accountant had no intention of leaving it to someone else to pursue his cause. Thanks to his visit to London, he had already built up enough evidence to commence his own recovery proceedings. Excited by his discovery, David Goldstein went straight to work. The grey, three-storey building in the city's central business district housed Weil Richter, a highly respected firm of forensic accountants. They also had a less publicised arm that concentrated exclusively on recovering property stolen from European Jews, working from an extensive database of those Nazis who had escaped to South America with their booty. The Muller clan was top of their list of suspects.

David handed in to his superior the report he had worked on during the night. Attached was Charlotte's business card from the Muller Gallery, which confirmed conclusively that the family's activities had infiltrated the most exclusive parts of London. Interpol was alerted and the department which dealt with such matters started an immediate investigation. However, David's superior knew from experience that when it came to the illicit movement of stolen artworks from South America, it could take years to retrieve the items. He chose not to share his doubts with his protégé.

Over the next few days, Charlotte spent her time catching up on paperwork and organising the guest list for the Muller Gallery's next big exhibition. A telegram from Susana had crossed with her own, demanding to know why Charlotte had not followed her instructions and sent the results of the auction.

On the morning that she was expecting her employer to return, Charlotte decided to take advantage of the break in the wet weather by walking to work. She needed to be fully alert for the confrontation that awaited her. As she passed Bond Street station, she noticed a crowd gathering at a news kiosk. The headline on the newspaper-stand read: *Plane Crashes Over Amazon, 200 Feared Dead*

Without taking much notice, Charlotte carried on with her journey, rehearsing her speech for when Susana strutted into the gallery. When her employer failed to appear, Charlotte merely thought she had been delayed.

On her way home that night, she purchased a copy of the *Evening News*, which contained the first photographs of carnage from the aeroplane crash. Still she failed to connect her employer's absence with the accident. She had, in addition, failed to notice the name of Susana Muller in the long list of missing persons.

A week later, when there was still no sign of her employer, Charlotte began to worry that something was seriously wrong. She decided to send another Telex to Buenos Aires on her way to work. When she reached the gallery, however, she found a small group of reporters gathered together on the pavement outside.

'Miss Brown!' the shortest of them called out as he saw Charlotte approaching. 'How well did you know Susana Muller?'

'Are you also originally from Germany?' another speculated.

Caught unaware, Charlotte froze. 'There must be some mistake,' she gulped, doing her utmost to hide her fear.

'I'm sure it's come as a shock, Miss Brown,' remarked

a well-spoken reporter in a long brown raincoat, who stepped out towards her. 'If you would be good enough to spare me a few minutes, just so that I can get your side of the story? I promise to keep it brief.'

Wishing only to be allowed into her place of work, Charlotte nodded her consent.

'OK, lads, let the lady through!' the same fellow shouted, clearing a path for her to enter the building. He then followed Charlotte into the gallery, leaving his disgruntled colleagues beginning to disperse, cheated of a story.

Charlotte switched on the lights that brought the displays magically to life. The reporter stood admiring the Rubens painting of the three voluptuous nudes.

'Absolutely magnificent,' he said. 'I was here a while back but the stuff you had then was nothing compared to this.'

'I'm sorry, I don't remember meeting you before,' Charlotte replied from behind her desk. Then suddenly, the stories of the air crash in South America began to make sense. That explained the presence of the reporters outside. Instinctively, she knew that something terrible must have happened to Susana. Dreadful images of charred bodies from the plane wreckage flashed through her mind.

'It was about that chappie, what was his name?' the reporter said, scratching his head of thinning hair. 'You know, the one who was found washed up in the East End – Max Something or other. Death by misadventure, the coroner called it. Covers a multitude of sins,' he said knowingly.

'Please tell me why you're here,' Charlotte asked shakily.

'I take it that you haven't read the morning news,' the man said, not unkindly. Pulling out the newspaper that was protruding from his coat pocket, he handed it to her. 'It appears that the owners of this place have been up to no good.'

'What do you mean?' Charlotte whispered, bewildered by the man's comment.

'Susana Muller, or so it's alleged—' he began.

'Is she still alive?' Charlotte interrupted. She prayed that she had been wrong to assume the worst.

'Still missing, by all accounts,' the reporter replied.

Charlotte breathed a sigh of relief.

'It seems her family have been implicated in handling works of art, plundered from victims of the Holocaust,' the man disclosed, his expression grim.

Charlotte gasped. So that was why the men outside had wanted to interview her. It had nothing to do with the air crash.

'Brockets, the auction house, are also mentioned. Apparently, they've not been too particular in vetting their clients.'

Charlotte felt a chill run down her spine. 'You have my word I don't know anything about this,' she told him.

'So you can't throw any light on why the woman you work for left the country nearly three weeks ago?'

'She told me that her father was seriously ill and that she had to return home. We've an exhibition opening next week. I had expected her back by now,' Charlotte said, trying to remain calm.

The reporter stood looking pensive. Then he said, 'Our sources say that Franz Muller died eight months ago.'

Charlotte was completely thrown. Susana had lied.

'His daughter had taken over the running of the family business,' the journalist went on.

'I know they were involved in the production of soya beans,' Charlotte proffered, recalling what had been mentioned at the dinner party, when she met Susana for the first time.

'No doubt just a front for the huge amounts of money they've been generating from their range of illicit activities,' the reporter said cynically.

'I'm only employed to run the gallery. You must believe me!' Charlotte blurted out. She was beginning to feel that she was already a suspect.

'The authorities have been after them for years. I wouldn't be surprised if they've got fortunes sitting in bank accounts all over South America, probably in the names of trustee companies that can't be traced.'

'So what am I supposed to do?' Charlotte asked.

'Well, since it appears that you didn't know what was going on, I shouldn't think anyone will bring charges against you,' the journalist remarked, closing his notebook. He turned to leave, stopping to look at the Rubens for a last time, and telling her, 'Just to be sure, I wouldn't be in a hurry to sell any more paintings. Now the police are involved, the gallery is likely to be closed at any time.'

The man then walked out of the gallery, whistling, and disappeared into the midday sun.

Charlotte slumped down on her chair. What had she become involved with? She suddenly wished Bernard were there to protect her. He would know what to do. She sat with her head in her hands, trying to bring her thoughts into some semblance of order. Maybe David Goldstein's claim was true, after all.

After a while, Charlotte came to a decision. She opened her address book, picked up the telephone and dialled the number of the only person she could turn to.

'Good morning, my name is Charlotte Brown. I wish to make an appointment to see Mr James Robson, please,' she said to the person at the other end of the line.

23

As Charlotte walked the short distance to the lawyer's offices in Piccadilly, she recalled that Bernard had made the same journey in not dissimilar circumstances just before he died. Robson Benson had remained her solicitors after Bernard's demise, for despite her initial reservations she had found James Robson to be a person she felt she could trust. He had arranged for her to gain access to the bank account that Bernard had opened for her, and the seven thousand pounds in it had kept her going, since Susana had only paid her wages sporadically.

The solicitor was standing at the window when Charlotte was shown into the meeting room on the third floor.

'My dear, how good to see you,' he greeted her, extending his hand.

Charlotte thought it strange that nothing had changed about the thin man with the officious demeanour. She had expected that, even though Susana and he were divorced, in the tragic circumstances he would at least be displaying some outward signs of grief.

'It's been a long time. But I must say, you're looking well. Come and sit down.' He drew out a chair.

'Thank you for seeing me at such short notice,' Charlotte said.

'I assume you wish to talk to me about all that stuff in

the newspapers,' he replied.

'Several reporters were waiting for me outside the gallery when I arrived for work today,' Charlotte told him, her shock still evident.

'How awful for you. I know what those people are like. Once they've got a sniff of a story, there's no letting go,' the lawyer sympathised.

'But I'm just running a gallery. I don't know anything about the rest of the Mullers' affairs!' Charlotte protested.

'I understand that this is a most upsetting time for you, but I'm not sure how I can help,' James Robson said in his mild Scottish accent. Then, seeing that his client was in distress, he reached over and took hold of her hand to try and comfort her.

'Susana was supposed to have returned two weeks ago. We've an exhibition starting in a few days. The invitations have already gone out,' Charlotte said. 'And now I've just been informed that I'm being investigated by the police. I don't know what to do.'

There was an awkward silence. The atmosphere in the room had become tense, each party waiting for the other to speak.

'My dear,' the lawyer said carefully, 'you seem to think, mistakenly, that I had some kind of influence over my ex-wife. I am afraid to tell you that that hasn't been the case for many years.'

James Robson failed to mention that he'd been assisting Interpol for the last three months with information about Nazi activities in South America. When, thanks to him, it became too precarious for Susana to remain in London, he had arranged - at a price - for her to disappear. With a new set of papers supplied by one of his contacts in the

Intelligence Service she had fled back to her family ranch outside of Buenos Aires, where she was told to lie low.

The plane crash provided a perfect opportunity to disappear. In exchange for a hefty bribe, the Argentinian authorities added the name of Susana Muller to the list of missing passengers, presumed dead. She was in the clear. In return, James Robson obtained possession of the house in Mayfair, along with half a million pounds for his trouble, now sitting in his offshore bank account in the Bahamas.

Revenge and a great deal of satisfaction had been gained in one master-stroke.

'But she owns the gallery!' Charlotte cried.

'That's not strictly correct,' James informed her.

'I'm sorry, I don't understand.'

'I'll try and explain as simply as I can,' he said, lowering his voice. 'The gallery, together with a substantial amount of property, is held in a company. The Muller family and the Chesterfield Estate each own fifty per cent.'

Charlotte was finding it hard to concentrate.

'But it belonged to Bernard,' she protested weakly. She was beginning to feel there was more to Bernard's demise than she had been led to believe.

'Quite so. But I'm afraid, my dear, the world of business can be a rather unkind place. In my experience, whenever there are large amounts of money at stake, people will resort to any methods to get what they want.'

'Are you saying that they took Bernard's company?' Charlotte asked.

'What I'm alluding to, and it pains me to say this, is that Bernard was becoming too successful for his own good. And when you are as reliant as he was on the goodwill of the banks . . . '

'You mean Rupert Meredith? But I thought he was Bernard's friend!'

'Charlotte, with the greatest respect, you are a wee touch naïve. Banks are, if you will excuse the expression, like a bunch of whores.'

Charlotte frowned at the sudden uncharacteristic crudeness of her legal adviser.

'So long as they think you're good for the money,' he went on, 'they'll bend over backwards for you, promise you the earth.'

'And when Bernard got into financial difficulty?'

'They dropped him as if he had never existed. They wanted their money back and so they forced Bernard to sell his business at a knock-down price. They'd already lined up a buyer behind his back.'

'That's unbelievable!' Charlotte exclaimed, horrified. 'And you couldn't find any way to help him?'

'I did everything I could,' the solicitor stated, lying about his role in the conspiracy. 'So you see, my dear young lady, Meredith's have a better idea than I do about what's going on.'

'But surely, when you were married, you must have known about Susana's family?'

'You certainly would have thought so,' James Robson nodded, hiding the fact that he was the one who had originally facilitated the movement of the stolen works of art from South America. 'I just did what I could to find Susana a position at Brockets so she could further her career. Believe me, what's in the news has come as much of a shock to me as it has to you.'

The lawyer moved towards his client and, putting his

arm around her shoulder, he drew her closer to him.

'I know you were fond of Susana but it's quite clear that there were no survivors. I think you should prepare yourself for the worst.' He helped Charlotte to her feet. 'My advice, for what it's worth, is to co-operate with the police and then go off and start afresh. You're still young, you'll soon put this unfortunate episode behind you.'

'But the gallery – it's my life,' she lamented.

'Naturally I'll do everything I can to help you,' James Robson said. 'My guess is that with all the adverse publicity, the owners will want to get shot as soon as possible.'

He accompanied his client out of the boardroom and waited at the top of the stairs until she had left the building. It couldn't be helped, he thought to himself. The weak got shat upon. That was all there was to it.

Charlotte walked slowly away. She was in a daze. Her whole world had fallen apart. She began to shake uncontrollably as she crossed Piccadilly. Was she going to suffer the same fate as Bernard? She felt a tightening in her chest.

The open horse-drawn carriage lurched forward and then came to a halt outside the quaint south-west London church. Men in grey morning dress and women in a range of colourful silk taffeta outfits stood milling around on the pavement in the late-August sun, waiting expectantly for the arrival of the wedding party.

And then the nervous-looking young groom, supported by the huge figure of his best man, appeared to the cheers of the crowd.

'I still don't know how you managed to pull it off, Rupert,' Bertie Chesterfield said. Both men began posing for the society photographers who had congregated on the steps of the church.

'All worked out rather well, I would say,' the banker replied smugly. 'But who could have foreseen the old German just dropping dead like that? And then the investigation into his Nazi past.' He smiled for the camera. 'Susana couldn't sign those share transfer forms over to you quickly enough.'

The groom glanced anxiously at his watch. 'What do you think will happen to her?' he remarked, distracted by the late arrival of his bride.

'Knowing Susana, she's probably already got some rich South American in tow,' the best man replied. 'Shouldn't think he's going to be too bothered what her family was up to. Anyway, I'm glad we're rid of her. Lucinda was beginning to think it was getting serious,' he said, roaring with laughter.

'Shame about that Charlotte Brown woman,' the groom commented.

'Who?' the banker asked.

'You know, the woman at the gallery.'

'Yes, I suppose so,' the banker replied carelessly.

'I'm thinking of turning the place into a studio for Davina. She's always been interested in photography,' Bertie said.

A huge cheer went up then as the bride's carriage pulled up outside the church. Lady Davina, looking radiant in a flowing wedding gown of white lace, with a crescent diamond tiara, appeared with her parents Lord and Lady Ambleforth. Photographers' flashing light bulbs accompanied the wedding party into the church, to the resounding chords of the Wedding March.

24

That evening, Charlotte was very relieved to reach the sanctuary of her flat on Gladys Road. Thoughts were racing around in her brain after the meeting with James Robson and she found it hard to sleep. Then, early the next morning, her life was turned upside down when the police knocked on the main front door, disturbing her neighbours and causing several curtains to twitch nearby. In a very shaken state, she was taken to the local station and questioned. To her horror, she was under suspicion. Her passport was confiscated and she was forbidden to leave the country. Then she was sent home, this time on a bus rather than in a police car.

Convinced that she was going to prison, the young woman sank into a deep depression. She shut herself away from the outside world, barely eating and drinking. Nightmares haunted her, leaving her exhausted and unable to get out of bed. Once again, the characters in the Daniel Petrovich painting came to life. Families with emaciated faces surrounded her, begging for food. But this time, amongst them stood the familiar figure of a dark-haired young man with his back to her. She called out to him, 'David! David!' but he didn't answer. She implored him to turn around so that she could see his face. Instead, he walked away as the throng of starving people began attacking her.

When, after several more days, she still hadn't emerged from her first-floor abode, the alarm was raised by Aileen Brookes, an elderly woman who lived on the floor above. Charlotte regularly helped her with the shopping, and the neighbour could tell that something was badly wrong when the young woman failed to appear and wasn't answering the door. With the spare key she apprehensively unlocked the flat door and found Charlotte in a semi-delirious state in bed. Aileen phoned for an ambulance and Charlotte was taken to the Whittington Hospital and immediately put on a drip to rehydrate her, and to replace the nourishment that she was lacking. She had lost a dramatic amount of weight. Unconsciously, she had become one of the characters in the painting on the wall above her bed.

Confined to the ward that she shared with several others, Charlotte gradually put back the weight she had lost and was then transferred to the Priory in Roehampton, a private institution specialising in a wide range of mental disorders. At first in denial, she finally reconciled herself to the fact that she had been affected by the same illness that had consumed her mother. But for Charlotte, there was hope. After an extended period of therapy, her consultant psychiatrist was sufficiently happy with her progress to allow her home at the start of the New Year 1959.

It was raining heavily when Charlotte let herself into her home. Putting down her suitcase, she passed through the flat, opening windows to bring in much-needed ventilation along with the distinctive scent of falling rain. She then picked up the post that had accumulated on the carpet and went to make some black coffee. Her head felt heavy, the result of the strong medication that she had been prescribed.

Filling the kettle, she sat down at the kitchen table and sorted through the pile of unpaid bills. There were two communications from Switzerland. The first was a condolence letter from Herr Grossman, informing her that her mother had passed away. The second stated that since there had been no response to their earlier communication, and in the absence of a next-of-kin to give specific instructions, the funeral arrangements had been made by the bank. Charlotte knew that she should feel some grief and remorse, but she was unable to react.

Putting the letters aside, she opened the heavy buff envelope that she had left till last. There, fastened by a rubber band, was her passport. She looked inside again for any letter of acknowledgement, but there was none. No recognition of, nor apology for, the turmoil to which she had been unjustly subjected and which had contributed to her breakdown.

During Charlotte's illness, the police had come no closer to being able to bring charges. The Muller Gallery remained impounded. Paintings, collectively worth vast sums, remained displayed with no one to claim them.

The case implicating Brockets was withdrawn after a few weeks. The auction house claimed that they had taken the works in good faith and denied any knowledge of the true owners of the paintings. Nor did they believe that it was their responsibility to carry out detailed checks.

Shortly afterwards, the Muller Gallery closed. Abandoned by its owners, the establishment, together with its stock of paintings, reverted to the company that had leased it to the Muller family. Thus, the Chesterfield Estate became the beneficiaries of immensely valuable works of art. Bertie Chesterfield, intent on distancing himself from anything that might tarnish his family's impeccable reputation, donated the entire collection to the person who had been instrumental in restoring his property empire. Rupert Meredith had no qualms about accepting the twenty paintings that had been the subject of so much controversy. He merely regarded them as satisfactory payment for his services.

It was good to be back home. Charlotte looked around her kitchen. The place felt better for the fresh air, but all the cupboards were bare. It was time to get her life back in order. Taking a small note pad from the shelf, she made a list of the things she needed. In her purse were three five-pound notes and some loose change, more than enough for her requirements. On the way out, she went upstairs to visit Mrs Brookes on the next floor. Charlotte hadn't had the opportunity to thank her. She knocked on the door but there was no answer.

Assuming that the woman must be taking her afternoon nap, Charlotte left and went to do her shopping. Reaching the main road, she saw two gleaming new supermarkets stacked with brightly packed goods at substantially lower prices than the corner shop. There were a couple of new establishments serving French and Italian food. Posters advertising live music events in West Hampstead and the adjoining Kilburn brought a vibrant atmosphere to a previously rather staid corner of north-west London.

The primary school across the road had finished for the day, and mothers waiting to collect their children had congregated outside the school gates. Charlotte thought about her maternal instinct, or lack of it. Perhaps if things had been different, she would have liked to have a family of her own. But the only two men in her life had never offered that opportunity. Johann, whom she once would have followed to the ends of the earth, had proved his unsuitability for a monogamous relationship, and Bernard hadn't lived long enough to become a father.

Turning back into her street, her string bag full of fruit and vegetables and her basket laden with a fresh loaf and other shopping, Charlotte noticed an unfamiliar young couple letting themselves in at the front door of the house. Entering the tiny front garden, she assumed they had taken the vacant ground-floor flat.

'Hello!' the bespectacled long-haired young man called out. 'We've just moved in. I'm Mike Crosby and this is my wife Dee.'

'I'm Charlotte Brown – first floor,' she replied, struggling to find her keys.

'Here, let me help you with those,' offered the friendly young man, who wore a black leather jacket.

'Have you lived here long?' his wife enquired.

'Locally, about five years,' Charlotte replied. She could see that beneath the mass of curly blonde hair, the young woman wearing striped cotton trousers had a pretty face. She imagined that the couple were in their early twenties.

'My aunt left us her flat in her will,' the young man announced, helping their new neighbour through the door with her shopping. 'It's on the second floor.'

'You mean poor Aileen has died?' A feeling of sorrow came over Charlotte.

'Four weeks ago.' From Mike's sad expression, it was clear that he had felt a great deal of affection for his elderly relation.

'I didn't know. I've been in hospital – I only came home today.'

'Well, if you need anything, don't hesitate to let us know,' Dee said sweetly. Then they bounded upstairs, leaving Charlotte alone to contemplate this new loss, of the woman who had no doubt saved her life.

Charlotte slept well. No longer confined to a hard hospital bed, she had the luxury of spreading herself out over her soft double divan. She woke feeling more optimistic. The fact that she didn't know what she was going to do that day – nor indeed how she was going to spend the rest of her life – didn't concern her unduly. After all, she was still convalescing. She reached for her medication and took a sip of water from the glass on the bedside table.

Several days of rain followed, before a period of dry weather. One day after breakfast, Charlotte decided to go for a long walk on Hampstead Heath. Crossing muddy paths, the sight of majestic trees and the distinctive smell of dew on the long grass filled her senses. She stopped and took a deep breath, exhilarated as a rush of cold air entered her lungs. Continuing her trek, Charlotte passed several families with small children calling for their dogs that had been let off their leashes. She thought back to the spacious apartment in Berlin and the Schlessinger family's German Shepherd, Goethe. He was her brother's dog but when Hans joined the forces, the animal had become hers. She was the one who had looked after Goethe when he became unwell. She still remembered crying the day he had to be put down. Charlotte sighed, feeling sad. It seemed such a long time ago.

In this reflective mood, she walked up the steep bank

to the main road and followed the signpost back to West Hampstead. In her flat, the stack of final gas and electric demands still cluttered the kitchen table. She hadn't worked in almost six months and her savings had dwindled. Charlotte shuddered at the thought that unless she found some money quickly, she would end up in the magistrate's court and possibly become homeless.

That evening, she began wording a telegram to Herr Grossman in Zurich. Perhaps she could draw on the money that had been left to her? Suddenly, she thought of her mother and stopped what she was doing. A delayed reaction of deep guilt prevented her from continuing and convinced her that she had forfeited any right to her inheritance.

Charlotte spent the rest of the evening on her living-room sofa, mulling over and then discarding ideas of how she could start to earn a living. Art was all she knew, and yet the prospect of finding another job in a gallery filled her with trepidation. Her mind turned to Bernard. She could still hear his voice in her head: hadn't he always advised her never to leave herself short of money? If only she hadn't left the emerald earrings behind at the house in Park Street, the beautiful ones Bernard had given her for Christmas in Nice, just before his mother died . . . Then in a flash it came to her. The diamond that Joe had brought round for her!

Getting up, she darted into the bedroom, took her jewellery box from the middle drawer of the dressing table and removed the gem that was still in its original blue paper in a small black box. She tried to feel some attachment to the gleaming stone, and wondered briefly what Bernard would say if he was still alive. Quickly blotting out any further memories of the past, she made her decision: the diamond had to be sold. There was a place near the gallery where she had once taken her watch to be repaired; Charlotte rummaged around until she located the jeweller's business card. First thing in the morning, she would ring for an appointment to show him the stone. If she was in luck, he'd buy it and the proceeds would cover her debts. She could then think more clearly about her future.

The elderly jeweller was stooped over his work-bench in the cluttered area at the back of the shop as Charlotte entered.

'I'll be with you in a minute,' he said, finishing the job he was working on. Then: 'Right, miss, how can I help you?' he asked, finally putting down his implement and coming over to the counter.

'Mr Price, we spoke on the telephone earlier about a diamond. My name is Charlotte Brown.'

'Yes, yes. I assume you have it with you?'

She opened her handbag, took out the small black box and passed it across to him.

'Good, good. Well, let's see what all the fuss is about,' he muttered and began examining the precious stone with his eyeglass.

'Does it have any value?' Charlotte asked anxiously.

The old man remained expressionless. He said, 'Miss, I should like to ask the opinion of a colleague before committing myself. If you don't mind leaving it with me, you can telephone me tomorrow.'

Charlotte nodded her agreement and left the old man with the precious stone still in his wrinkled hand.

The next day, when Charlotte replaced the receiver, she was stunned. Ten thousand pounds! 'A flawless blue-white diamond.' She could still hear the jeweller's words. That's how much I meant to Bernard, she thought emotionally.

Charlotte spent the rest of the evening wrestling with her conscience. What was she to do? She was desperate for the money, but on the other hand, she somehow felt she was letting Bernard down and just couldn't bring herself to part with it.

The next morning, she rang Mr Price and declined his offer. Unperturbed, the old man suggested that if she wasn't prepared to sell the diamond, she might like to consider pawning it instead. That would enable her to raise the money she needed, and when she had the funds, she could redeem the item, less what she owed.

Charlotte immediately agreed to the proposal.

The next day, she went to the address Mr Price had given her, in the City of London. She signed the pawnbroker's agreement and handed over the diamond. In return, she received a cheque for two thousand pounds, which she immediately deposited into her bank account. Over the next week, she paid off all her bills and still had a substantial sum left over, enough to live on until she found a job.

But there was a void in her life. She was lonely. Her figure was still slim and shapely, her face still free of lines and she only had a few grey strands of hair. Charlotte considered that she didn't look too bad for a woman of her age, yet she didn't have any romance in her life. That didn't bother her, however. She just needed companionship. Then the idea came to her.

The following morning, Charlotte ventured out to a

local pet shop, where she was shown half a dozen different puppies, finally settling on a brown male Boxer with a squashed nose. She picked out a wicker basket, a smart blue leather lead, a soft cushion for his bed and some Bonio dog biscuits; a chatty young assistant helped her carry the items home.

Charlotte named her puppy 'Hunter'.

Her new best friend.

25

As the winter of 1960 passed, Charlotte managed to regain most of her strength. She was, however, scrupulously careful not to miss her regular medical check-ups. The depressive illness had shaken her and she was determined never again to allow herself to sink to the same levels of despair. At long last, she was ready to work again. The problem was, what was she going to do with Hunter? She couldn't bear the thought of leaving him alone all day in the flat. On the rare occasions when it was too cold to take him with her to the shops, he created such a scene that she relented and carried him under her coat.

One evening, Charlotte was relaxing on the sofa with the dog fast asleep on her lap, listening to classical music on the BBC Third Programme, when there was a knock on the door. Hunter immediately leaped up and began barking. Shushing him, she got up to see who it was.

'Sorry to disturb you like this, but I don't suppose you've got a spare pint of milk, by any chance?' It was Mike Crosby from the flat upstairs.

'Yes, of course, I've got plenty. Come in. I'll just go and get it.' Hunter was still barking at the stranger who had entered his domain.

'Makes quite a racket for a little feller,' Mike grinned, stroking him. 'Your flat seems bigger than our place,' he remarked, unconcerned about the animal now sniffing his shoes.

'I thought all three flats were the same,' Charlotte called out from the other end of the hall.

'Yes, but your living room is definitely larger.'

'Well, I've only got the one bedroom.' Returning with the milk, Charlotte took him on an impromptu tour of her home.

'And what's in here?' the neighbour asked, peering through the open door of the tiny box room.

'I use it as my studio,' Charlotte said. She switched on the light.

'And did you do this?' Mike was looking at the unfinished portrait of a man, propped on the easel.

'Yes, but I haven't painted for a while,' Charlotte sighed.

'I'm no expert, statistics is my subject, but these are really good,' the young man said in admiration, examining some of the other works that were stacked up against the wall.

'So, you are a teacher?' Charlotte asked.

'Yes. I lecture at the Regent Street Polytechnic. That's where Dee and I met. She teaches German.'

'How interesting,' Charlotte replied hesitantly. It was strange that she still felt self-conscious about her original nationality. She had never been able to rid herself of the uneasy feeling of guilt, of being judged.

'I should be getting back,' Mike said then. 'Thanks for showing me around. I'll bring you down a bottle of milk tomorrow.'

'There's really no hurry,' Charlotte told him.

Picking up the milk from the hall table, the young man opened the door to let himself out, saying, 'You really should think about taking up your painting again. It's obvious that you are very talented.'

When Charlotte went to bed that night, she wondered whether there was any merit in the neighbour's suggestion. With the puppy resting peacefully at her feet, she fell into a deep slumber, and for the first time in many years, found herself back in Berlin . . .

It was summer. The sky was a deep blue and the sun was dazzling. She was sitting on a bench at the zoo with her father. She had taken her sketchbook and, peering at the pages from under the brim of her straw hat, was trying to draw from memory some of the animals they had visited that morning.

'Eva, my child, these are very good,' Gerhart Schlessinger said, peering down at her work. 'With the right tuition, I am sure that one day you will become an accomplished artist.'

'Thank you, Papa.' She threw her spindly arms around his neck. 'I love you more than anyone else in the whole world.'

The dream ended and Charlotte awoke early, knowing now what she was going to do. That morning, she wrote an advert for the local paper and also put a postcard in the newsagent's window in the High Street. She was going to start giving art lessons from her small studio in West Hampstead.

At first, the response was slow and she had to get by with just a trickle of pupils. She began to be plagued by self-doubt. Had she once again been too hasty and taken yet another wrong direction? However, this time, there was a difference. In the presence of young children, she found a certain tranquillity that had been absent in so much of her life. Charlotte knew that she had to persevere.

Gradually, word got around and she was contacted by more mothers in the area, keen to find interesting hobbies for their children. When she felt more secure about her number of pupils, Charlotte was able to put her fee up to five shillings per session per child. Two years of hard struggle followed, after which she was earning on average around fifteen pounds a week. Even though she had to pay for materials, she was bringing in enough to get by. More importantly, sharing some of her knowledge with the boys and girls in her care gave her a profound sense of fulfilment. Charlotte felt that she had finally found her true vocation.

Her one regret was that she had been unable to redeem the blue-white diamond from the pawnbroker on the due date. They had sold it on her behalf, less the original loan. The addition of several thousand pounds into her bank account, however, had given her a welcome feeling of financial security. She had Bernard to thank for this, Charlotte thought, as for so many things.

26

Just before the start of the new school year in September 1965, Charlotte was contacted by the headmistress of St Augustine's secondary school at the end of her road. Their art teacher had left to have a baby and Miss Hart was looking to fill the position for four mornings a week.

Even though she was flattered to be asked, Charlotte's first instinct was to decline the offer. She was already working every weekday afternoon and some weekends. The other problem was what to do about Hunter. The Boxer had long since grown to his full size and needed to be exercised. It was bad enough that she neglected him in the afternoons. She couldn't just leave him cooped up all day in the small flat on his own.

However, Miss Hart persisted. Several of the parents had enthused about Charlotte and the wily spinster wanted the chance to assess her abilities herself. Securing help from Dee who, with a young child of her own was at home and willing to look after Hunter, Charlotte finally relented. She threw herself headlong into her new job and after a short trial period, the position became hers.

Working full-time and often sitting up long into the night planning her class lessons, Charlotte neglected herself, and her health inevitably began to suffer. Against doctor's orders, she started smoking heavily again to cope with the stress. Her asthma got worse and there were days when it was hard to breathe. One morning, when she just couldn't muster sufficient strength to go to work, she acknowledged that something had to change before it was too late. Fortunately, the long summer school holidays came around again and provided the respite she so desperately needed.

Shortly after term ended, Charlotte was relaxing at home reading the Sunday papers when her attention was drawn to an advertisement for a cruise around the Western Mediterranean. Apart from the trip to the Cote d'Azur with Bernard, she had not been to Italy or Spain. The prospect of seeing Florence and Venice excited her. Unlike her father, Charlotte had never been an accomplished photographer but she still had his camera, and this would be the ideal opportunity to brush up on her skills.

The next morning, she rang the tour operator and secured a place on the fifteen-day cruise. She had one week to organise herself before departure. Mike and Dee Crosby had agreed to take care of Hunter during her absence, and to keep an eye on her flat.

Charlotte reached Southampton in the late afternoon. Passengers had already begun embarking on the pristine 500-foot ocean liner. Scores of middle-aged men dressed in white slacks, their blue blazers flapping in the gentle breeze, accompanied their wives who wore colourful summer frocks and open sandals, scurrying excitedly up the three roped gangways.

Carrying her own suitcase, Charlotte handed the details of her booking to a member of the blue-uniformed cruise staff. She was directed to the lower deck. Making her way slightly uneasily down a narrow corridor, she was accompanied by the sound of humming from the engine room below. Eventually, she located her cabin. Letting herself into the air-conditioned room, she was struck by its spacious size. There were two good-sized beds, separated by bedside tables on which stood a pair of brass reading lamps. Opposite was a large fitted wardrobe, together with a mirrored dressing-table and stool.

Placing her case on the luggage rack, she moved around to the folding door that opened into a compact shower room, containing a small sink and toilet. Sensing only a slight movement from the huge vessel, several blasts on the ship's horn were the only real indication that they had up anchored and were slowly being escorted out of port. Instinctively, Charlotte hurried over to the other side of the cabin, hoping to catch a glimpse of the view. Pulling aside the half-length curtain, she found herself staring at a blank wall. A feeling of disappointment came over her, then she remembered that she had only been allocated an internal cabin. Now she understood why the price, which included all her meals, had seemed so reasonable.

She unpacked her suitcase, showered and changed into a simple cotton dress for dinner. Walking up the stairs, she joined the long queue of passengers outside the main dining room. They were waiting to be allocated their table, which in most instances would remain theirs for the entire journey. The first-class travellers in luxury suites had their own separate dining facilities and a private chef for their exclusive use.

Charlotte gave her name, which was checked against a long list by a member of the restaurant staff perched on a high chair. The young man appeared overwhelmed by the onslaught of hungry passengers.

Charlotte was confronted by a sea of white linen

covering elaborately set tables for eight and ten as she entered the eating area. Huge buffet tables piled high with food were set out along three sides of the rectangular-shaped room. Behind them, French doors were opened to their full extent to allow air to circulate through the overcrowded area and supplement the ineffectual ceiling fans.

Charlotte passed through the room where, scattered haphazardly amongst the rest were a number of small square card-tables for passengers travelling on their own who might be on the look-out for some extra company.

Putting her handbag down on a chair, she went to the buffet, which already looked seriously depleted. Then, as if on cue, the swing doors at the far end of the room opened and a steady stream of kitchen staff appeared carrying full containers of food, ready to replenish the evening meal.

The fact that no one deigned to join her at her table didn't bother Charlotte one bit. Nor did she take advantage of the full programme of entertainment that took place every evening after dinner in the 350-seat auditorium. She preferred to go to bed early and sleep late.

Often missing breakfast, Charlotte spent her time in between the day excursions first to Gibraltar and then to the Spanish coastal town of Alicante, lazing on the sundeck. Self-conscious about exposing her pale body, she wrapped herself up in a beach robe and spread out on a shaded sun-lounger. Breathing in the warm sea air, she began to relax. The thoughts that worried her in London just seemed to evaporate, and the vivid dreams that would plague her without warning no longer came. She started to read again. Her two favourite writers, Schiller and Kleist, whose works she had mastered in German as a teenager, she now read in English, eager to rediscover her previous enjoyment.

On the day they were due to visit Nice, a violent thunderstorm came up, preventing the ship from being able to dock. Feeling queasy, Charlotte took to her cabin, waiting for the rough seas to subside. She was nevertheless relieved that the change in the ship's course had prevented her from being reminded of that Christmas she had spent in Nice with Bernard, when they had first become lovers.

The fine weather soon returned and with it, Charlotte's high spirits. Two days later, they docked at the coastal port of Livorno. On hand were six coaches to take passengers on the 90-minute journey to Florence.

Strolling in the Piazza della Signoria in one of Italy's most historic cities, the midday sun beating down on her uncovered shoulders, Charlotte was completely mesmerised. The sight of the Palazzo Vecchio, of Michelangelo's statue of *David* and the Duomo Cathedral simply took her breath away. But it was the visit to the Renaissance art collection at the Uffizi Gallery that really stirred her senses. She was overwhelmed by the desire to start painting again, to work seriously once more.

Before getting back on the coach, she went into the tourist shop next to the gallery and purchased some postcards, a large drawing pad and some fine-nib pens. She wouldn't be able to have the film in her camera developed until she got home. Instead, she would rely on the images while they were still fresh in her mind, and put them down on paper.

Venice had a similar effect upon her; this was where she used up her remaining film. Particularly memorable was the bustle of St Mark's Square and the view of the city from an open motorboat tour around the islands.

The last evening on board, Charlotte entered the packed dining room feeling particularly revitalised from a late-afternoon swim. From just a short distance away, she was surprised to see a petite woman with auburn hair, sitting at 'her' table. She was dressed in an immaculate navy linen dress. Around her neck was a double strand of white pearls, fastened with a diamond clasp.

'Good evening,' the woman said, a touch startled by the appearance of Charlotte's tall figure looming over her. 'I do hope that you don't mind me sitting here?'

'No, of course not. Please continue with your dinner,' Charlotte smiled. She took a seat at the other end of the table. 'I normally dine alone so it will be a pleasure to have some company.'

Because of her youthful complexion, it was difficult to tell the newcomer's age. The absence of any grey in the perfectly styled hair that fell to just above her shoulders led Charlotte to believe, however, that she must be a good deal younger than her own forty-one years.

'I felt I needed a change,' the woman confided, 'and there seems to be a much wider choice of dishes in the main dining room.' She glanced at the overflowing buffet tables.

Charlotte assumed that her new neighbour was travelling first class and the reason she hadn't noticed her before was because the other woman would have been keeping to the more exclusive area of the boat.

'I'm Charlotte Brown,' she said, introducing herself.

'And I'm Lillian Saunders,' the woman replied, taking Charlotte's hand. 'Please, don't let me stop you from getting your meal. I can recommend the prawn cocktail - and the coronet chicken was really quite excellent.'

Now she could see that the queue at the buffet had dwindled to just a few people, Charlotte got up from the table and went to choose her dinner. She tried to recall where she had eaten coronet chicken before: it suddenly came to her that it was when Bernard had first taken her to lunch at the restaurant in Mayfair. Walking carefully back to her table with her plate of food, she sighed. It seemed such a long time ago.

She sat down and placing the linen napkin on her lap, started enthusiastically on her meal. The exercise before dinner had given her a healthy appetite.

'Would you care for some white wine?' the woman asked.

'That would be lovely, thank you,' Charlotte replied.

'I didn't consider that there might be other people travelling on their own,' Lillian Saunders said, filling Charlotte's glass from the bottle in the ice-bucket beside her. 'It's very nice to make your acquaintance. I do hope the wine is to your taste?'

'Oh yes, thank you.' Charlotte touched her glass lightly against Lillian's. 'I don't particularly like travelling alone,' she admitted. 'I must confess to being a little apprehensive.'

'I know exactly what you mean,' remarked the other woman. 'You see, I'm recently widowed.'

'I'm so sorry.' Charlotte noticed that the woman was still wearing her wedding ring.

'It's only been three months. Even though my husband had been ill for a year, when he died it came as a great shock.'

'Do you have children?' Charlotte asked.

'Just one, a daughter of twelve, Elizabeth. She was very close to her father and she has taken his death very badly. Fortunately, I have a nanny at home who has been a great help.'

'Forgive me. I really didn't mean to pry.' Charlotte could see that her companion was trying her hardest to control her emotions.

'Well, I don't know about you but I'm going to treat myself to one of those meringues with whipped cream,' Lillian announced shakily.

Charlotte beamed. 'Why not? Since it is our last night.' Having finished her chicken, she got up from the table and went with Lillian to inspect the huge display of desserts. The pair made their selection and returned to their seats.

'And how about you?' Lillian asked, tucking into her meringue.

'I teach at a school,' Charlotte explained, scooping a small portion of ice cream onto her spoon. 'It was the end of term and I needed a break.'

'And what's your subject, may I ask?'

'Art,' Charlotte replied.

Lillian remembered how, as a child, she had wanted to be an artist. It was one of her biggest regrets that she had been deprived of that ambition.

'And do you paint yourself?' she asked Charlotte.

'Occasionally,' Charlotte responded. 'I have a small room in my flat that serves as my studio. In fact, the visit to Italy has given me the impetus to take it up again.'

The two women carried on chatting for a further hour while they finished their desserts and then said good night.

*

Charlotte slept fitfully. Whether it was the return to work in a few days that was making her anxious or just the return to face reality, she couldn't quite fathom. She suddenly realised that she hadn't sent postcards to Mike and Dee. Now it would have to wait until she got to England. However, she had found a Venetian glass vase for them, and a beautiful Florentine leather collar for Hunter.

After a light breakfast, she paid the ship's purser for the modest extras bill that she had incurred during the cruise and returned to her cabin to collect her suitcase.

The liner docked and the first passengers disembarked into the grey August morning. As Charlotte stood waiting for the bus to take her to the railway station, she heard her name being called. The woman with whom she had dined the previous night was waving frantically out of the rear window of a black limousine.

'Charlotte, my dear!' she called out. 'Do you need a lift?'

Lugging her case, Charlotte proceeded to where the car was parked.

'I'm going to London,' she shouted back, trying to make herself heard above the din of the lively quayside.

'That's all right – jump in! There's plenty of room.' Before she had a chance to object, a large man in a grey suit had sprung out from behind his wheel, grabbed hold of her suitcase and put it in the boot of the car.

'This is really very kind of you,' Charlotte said, getting into the back seat, 'but you will allow me to contribute to the petrol?'

'You don't have to worry, the business deals with that,' Lillian replied dismissively.

Charlotte thought better of querying it any further and sat back as the limousine sped away northwards towards

London.

'When Donald died, I decided to join the board of our publishing company,' Lillian said.

'So you do work?' Charlotte was surprised. 'What exactly do you do? I'd love to know.'

Lillian laughed. 'The world of business really isn't as glamorous as it appears,' she revealed. 'Mostly it's just attending meetings once a month in order to keep an eye on the figures. Things were so much simpler when it was a family concern but then we got taken over by one of the main publishers, who implemented much stricter financial reporting controls.'

'And who looks after your daughter?'

'I drop her off at school in the mornings and Nanny picks her up. It works reasonably well,' Lillian explained, without much conviction.

When the big car eventually approached the Chiswick roundabout in west London, Lillian said, 'Charlotte, my dear, it's most remiss of me but I have no idea where you live.'

'I have a flat in West Hampstead,' Charlotte replied. 'But you can drop me anywhere near a tube. I don't want to put you out of your way.'

'That is a coincidence. I'm in Maida Vale; we'll take you to the door.'

When the limousine turned into the quiet residential street, Lillian said sincerely, 'It's been wonderful having you to talk to. These long car journeys can be so tedious. Anyway, let me give you my card.' She opened her Chanel handbag and took out a small leather card-holder.

'I'm afraid I don't have one,' Charlotte said, blushing. 'I've never got around to having any printed, even though

I know I should.'

'You can write down your contact details on one of mine.' Lillian handed across two of her visiting cards.

Charlotte jotted down her address and then gave the other woman back her pen.

'Thank you again for taking me home,' she said, getting out of the car.

'I do hope that we shall see each other again!' Lillian called after her.

By the time Charlotte reached the front door, her suitcase was already on the doorstep. She looked around to thank the driver but he was moving smoothly away from the kerb, heading for Maida Vale.

27

As the summer of 1968 ushered in a mild autumn, Charlotte became close friends with Lillian. Despite leading such different lives, the two women soon realised how much they had in common. They'd accompany each other to art galleries, where Lillian was keen to learn from her friend's wide depth of knowledge, and in return, Charlotte was happy to share Lillian's enthusiasm for classical music and theatre. Other times, they would meet for dinner at a restaurant in town after Lillian finished work, or Charlotte would cycle round to the imposing house by the waterfront in Maida Vale and spend a cosy evening with Lillian and Elizabeth, the latter's twelve-year-old daughter, who fell in love with Hunter the first time she saw his squashed-up face.

Although it was clear to Charlotte from the beginning that mother and daughter often had a tense relationship, she adored the girl and would do anything for her. And she loved their house, which was situated in a place of exceptional beauty. Their avenue looked more like a street in Amsterdam than a suburb of west London.

Charlotte found it reassuring that Lillian felt sufficiently at ease to talk about the most intimate aspects of her own life without any inhibition. She, in turn, single for many years, told of the couple of occasions since Bernard had died when she thought there might have been a chance of happiness, but things hadn't worked out. The first time was with a widower, whose child she taught privately, and a few years afterwards a male teacher at the school where she worked. Neither relationship lasted more than a few weeks. She said that she was always making comparisons with the two older men in her life whom she had held most dear: Bernard Morris and her beloved father.

Just as Charlotte was preparing for bed after a particularly gruelling day at school, there was a ring on her bell. Charlotte ran down, the dog at her heels, and opened the front door. Standing there, with a suitcase and a defiant expression, was Elizabeth. The girl had put her coat on top of her pyjamas, and inside her shoes, her feet were bare.

Without any explanation, she marched straight up the stairs and into the small flat.

'My dear, what on earth are you doing here at this hour?' Charlotte asked, shocked by the impromptu visit of her friend's daughter. 'Is there some kind of emergency?'

'I want to stay here,' the girl replied, kneeling and putting her arms around Hunter.

'Does your mother know where you are?'

'I'm not going back there!' Elizabeth said fiercely, burying her face in the dog's comforting fur.

'I have to let her know you're all right. She'll be so worried about you. Go and take your coat off and get warm,' Charlotte said, and went straight over to the phone in the hall.

Charlotte had quickly formed a bond with Elizabeth. Despite not having a child of her own, it became clear that she could relate to the girl in a way that her mother was unable to. Soon, Elizabeth was allowed to stay over at the flat in West Hampstead on the odd occasion. During that precious time together, the ginger-haired girl became the daughter that Charlotte knew she would never have – but she was careful never to take advantage. Elizabeth was always delivered home at the time her mother had requested.

Charlotte dialled the number.

'Lillian, dear, it's Charlotte. Please don't worry, Elizabeth is safely here with me. She just turned up on the doorstep but thank goodness, she's fine.' She spoke softly to prevent the girl from overhearing her conversation.

'I hoped it was you,' replied the concerned voice at the other end of the line. 'Elizabeth had a tantrum and stormed out of the house. I was just about to call the police.' Lillian burst into tears.

'I'll bring her home in a taxi,' Charlotte promised gently. As she spoke, she looked up the number of a minicab.

'It's late, I don't want to put you out,' Lillian said tearfully. 'Look, I know it's a lot to ask, but perhaps if she can stay the night, you might be able to get through to her. She always seems to listen to you.'

'If you're sure, since it is the weekend,' Charlotte replied, secretly delighted. 'I'll bring her back after breakfast. And of course, I will try talking to her.'

'Thank you, Charlotte. Thank you so very much. I really don't know what I'd do without you.'

'Good night, Lillian.' Charlotte replaced the receiver and went off to tell Elizabeth the good news. When she got to the bedroom, however, she found Elizabeth with Hunter both fast asleep under the covers. Charlotte locked up, took a pillow and blanket from her laundry cupboard and made up the sofa for herself in the living room. Tomorrow, she decided, she would give her young uninvited guest a firm talking-to.

The next morning, Charlotte was in her dressing gown preparing breakfast when Elizabeth walked meekly into the kitchen.

'I trust you slept well?' Charlotte enquired coolly, devoid of her normal friendliness.

'Please don't be angry with me!' the child blurted out, sobbing. 'You don't understand how awful my life is.'

For one brief moment, all Charlotte could see was a spoiled child standing in front of her. How many other children enjoyed such a privileged upbringing? she wondered. Certainly none of the ones at the school where she taught. She then realised that she was doing the girl a grave disservice. Elizabeth had lost the one person in her life that she adored. Hadn't Charlotte herself felt equally devastated when her beloved father had finally succumbed to his injuries? And she had been twenty-one then, not twelve years old like Elizabeth. She felt ashamed of her unkind thoughts.

Holding back her own tears, she held out her arms to the weeping child.

'Come and have your boiled eggs and soldiers before they get cold. Then you can tell me what can possibly be so awful.' She took a lace handkerchief from her robe pocket and passed it to the distressed girl. They moved across to the table and sat down next to each other.

'Mother wants to sell the house,' Elizabeth revealed, dipping a finger of buttered toast into her egg yolk. 'Please, Charlotte, don't let her.'

'Elizabeth, dear, surely your mother knows best. It

wouldn't be right for me to interfere.'

'But you don't understand. It was my daddy's house. If we move somewhere else, I'll forget him. I know I will!' She began crying again.

Charlotte drew the child to her bosom, trying to comfort her. 'Sweetheart, I know it's been very hard for you. But believe me, you'll never forget your daddy. He will remain in your heart for ever.'

'Didn't your father die when you were my age?' Elizabeth asked chokily.

'I was considerably older than you, but I remember it was still very hard.'

'Did it happen when you were living in Switzerland?'

'It was few years before I came to England,' Charlotte replied obliquely. She had lived in England for so many years that she often had difficulty in remembering that she had once been Eva Schlessinger from Berlin.

'It's only because Mother is so unhappy that she blames me. It's just not fair!' Elizabeth complained.

'What do you mean?' Charlotte had always found Lillian to be so warm and generous.

'Daddy always said that I had to be more understanding. That she had gone through a very difficult period when she was a child.' Elizabeth looked sulky, then began to eat again. 'The only time she's nice is when I play the piano. That's what I keep telling that silly doctor she makes me go to.'

'Unfortunately, some people are faced with difficulties at an early age,' Charlotte replied, as she drank her coffee. 'The war did terrible things to many of us.'

'I've got proof,' the ginger-haired girl whispered excitedly. 'And I'll tell you if you promise not to say anything to her.'

Charlotte felt a sense of foreboding. She knew it would be totally inappropriate to let the girl continue. If there were things about Lillian's past that she was prepared to share, then Lillian herself should be the one to tell her.

'I found this old brown leather suitcase . . .' Elizabeth began.

'Stop, please, dear. You shouldn't be telling me these things.'

'It was in the attic, all covered in dust,' the girl went on regardless. 'Inside were loads of drawings of a man and a woman. They were standing outside a big house. A child was playing on a swing in the garden. There were also letters to my mother at an address in High Wycombe, which is just outside London. They had Austrian stamps – I think from Vienna. The dates on them said 1939 and 1940. I couldn't understand what they said because I think they were in German. But it was obvious that Mummy had been sent away. She must have been very naughty, but she spends all her time telling *me* off!'

Charlotte went to put the kettle on, thinking about the daughter's discovery.

'Finish your toast,' she said to the girl. 'I promised your mother you'd be home by ten o'clock.'

'Oh, please can't I stay a bit longer? We could take Hunter on the Heath.'

'I have pupils coming later.'

'Mother never works at weekends.'

'Your mother is a successful businesswoman. I'm just a simple teacher.'

'You mean that you need the money?' Elizabeth asked perceptively.

'Well, yes. Schools don't pay that well. I depend upon my private pupils.'

The young girl fell silent. A look of disappointment crossed her freckled face.

'I'll tell you what,' Charlotte said. 'The week after next is half-term, so why don't I ask Mummy if you can come and stay for a few days?'

'She won't let me,' the girl sighed dejectedly.

'I'm sure that if you promise to do all your homework, she'll agree.'

'I hate that school. I'm only interested in music,' Elizabeth said rebelliously.

Charlotte had witnessed the child's quite extraordinary talent on several occasions. It was clear that if she persevered, she was capable of gaining a scholarship to a musical academy.

'I know, but you also need to work hard in your other subjects. Now go and get dressed. I'll find you some socks and a cardigan to put on over your pyjamas. It's a lovely bright morning; we'll go for a walk now and take Hunter with us. How about that?' If they left soon, Charlotte anticipated she would still be back in time to prepare for her first pupil at midday.

When they arrived back in Maida Vale after their walk, Charlotte saw a large *For Sale* sign at the front of the house. As they closed the front gate behind them, Charlotte spotted Lillian peering through her bedroom curtains. The expression on her face was far from conciliatory, so Charlotte was rather relieved that it was the nanny who opened the door. She was in no doubt that Elizabeth was in for a severe dressing-down, which would place an even greater strain on the relationship with her mother.

On the way back to West Hampstead, Charlotte couldn't help wondering whether she had been too hasty in dismissing the girl's findings in the attic. Lillian was a very complex person, and maybe she, like Charlotte herself, had a past she would rather keep to herself.

Several weeks went by without any contact from Lillian. Charlotte assumed that the episode with Elizabeth had soured their relationship. Then, when she least expected it, Lillian telephoned and said that she wanted her advice on a certain matter. They agreed to meet the following afternoon at a little teashop overlooking the canal in the area that was known appropriately as Little Venice.

When Charlotte arrived, Lillian was already sat at a table by the window. She was occupied making notes on a small leather memo pad.

Flustered at being late, Charlotte said, 'Good afternoon, Lillian. I'm sorry, I couldn't get out of school any earlier.'

Lillian put down her pen and looked up. 'Please don't worry. I assumed that was the reason.'

Charlotte unbuttoned her coat and sat down.

'Shall we have tea and scones?' Lillian suggested.

'That would be very nice,' Charlotte said. She was tired, and both thirsty and hungry.

Lillian summoned a waitress and gave her their order. Then: 'How have you been? I've missed you.' Reaching across the table, she took hold of her friend's hands.

'I thought that I had offended you,' Charlotte said, feeling more at ease.

'You mean because of Elizabeth?'

'I only wanted to help, not to try and take your place.'

'You don't need to explain. I'm very grateful for everything you've done for her. No one could have been a better friend.'

'How is she?' All of a sudden, Charlotte had a premonition that something was amiss.

'My daughter has gone away to school,' Lillian divulged, pouring out the tea and offering Charlotte a scone.

'You mean to boarding school?' Charlotte asked, unable to disguise her shock. 'But I thought her work was improving. And her music, it was so important to her!'

'Her headmistress informed me just before half-term that Elizabeth was a disruptive influence on the other pupils. Apparently, the woman had received complaints from several of the other mothers, reporting that their daughters were being bullied.'

'I can't believe that she would do anything like that.'

'There was really no alternative,' Lillian continued. 'Even Dr Weber, her psychiatrist, said that constantly being surrounded by adults was unhealthy.'

Charlotte added jam and cream to her scone and took a bite. She knew that she had heard that name before, but at that moment she couldn't recall where.

'So you're saying that Elizabeth was asked to leave?'

But Lillian was unable to look her friend in the face. She just sipped her tea in silence, her expression sad. Was it perhaps an acknowledgement that she had failed her own child?

'She'll be coming home during the school holidays,' she said finally, sounding more sanguine.

'But surely you'll be able to visit her before that – at weekends?'

'The school discourage it when a child first joins. They

say it takes time for them to get bedded in to their new environment. But there's nothing stopping you from writing to her,' Lillian said. 'Before we leave, I'll give you the address.'

Charlotte wanted to respond but couldn't find the right words. She was convinced that the girl had been treated unfairly but the truth was that Elizabeth was not her child and she had no right to feel the way she did.

'You don't think very highly of me, do you?' the mother said.

'Lillian, forgive me. Who am I to query your judgement? It's just that I had grown attached to Elizabeth.'

'Charlotte, dear, as her psychiatrist said, it was for the best. Anyway, I have something else to tell you,' Lillian said, brushing crumbs from her mouth. 'I shall be moving in three weeks' time.'

'You've sold the house!' Charlotte exclaimed.

'I was very lucky. A banker and his wife fell in love with it. They offered the full asking price and said that they'd like to move in by the end of the month.'

'Where will you go?'

'I've found a very nice three-bedroom flat overlooking Regent's Park. I can't wait to show it to you.'

Charlotte thought better of mentioning her last conversation with Elizabeth, when the girl had confided that she couldn't bear the prospect of leaving the home where all the memories of her father were stored.

'Which is actually what I wanted to talk to you about,' Lillian went on. 'I'm afraid that I may have acted a little too hastily.'

'You mean in selling the house?' Charlotte asked hopefully.

'No, there's something else.'

Charlotte waited, curious to see what was coming next.

'I need to dispose of many of my paintings; there's simply not enough space in the new flat. I've placed most of them in an auction. They telephoned me yesterday with the reserve prices and I was just totting them up when you arrived.' Lillian pointed to the memo pad with her calculations. 'The thing is, I'm having second thoughts.'

'Have you signed their agreement?' Charlotte asked.

Lillian nodded sheepishly.

'When is the auction?'

'It's at Brockets next Wednesday at three. Look, I know it's a big favour to ask, but do you think you could get time off school? I've never been to one of those places before and I'd be really grateful if you could come with me.'

'Brockets?' Charlotte heard herself say faintly.

'Yes, why?'

Charlotte felt the blood drain from her face. The mention of the auction house had brought back bitter memories of the gallery in Cork Street and the interrogation that led to her illness.

'Are you feeling unwell?' Lillian asked, concerned at the sudden change in her friend.

'No, I'm fine.' Charlotte busied herself with her second scone, glad that Lillian knew very little of her past. She had been careful only to tell her about working at the National Gallery when she first came to London and then afterwards, managing a private art concern in Mayfair.

'You will come with me, won't you?' Lillian pleaded.

'Yes, of course,' came the muted response from across the table.

'That's a great relief, thank you. I'll get the bill.' Lillian raised her hand to attract the waitress's attention again. 'Sorry to rush you, but I've got a meeting at five o'clock at the flat with the architect.'

When she had paid, the two women got up from the table and made their way to the entrance.

'Are you certain you'll be all right?' Lillian said, grasping her friend's arm. 'You still look very pale. The car is outside and I can easily give you a lift home.'

'No, really, I'd prefer to walk. It's hot in here and the fresh air will do me good.' Charlotte forced a weak smile.

'I am really pleased that we'll be seeing more of each other from now on,' Lillian said. Reaching up, she kissed Charlotte on both cheeks and hurried out of the restaurant.

Charlotte walked slowly back to West Hampstead. She was ashamed of her reaction. After all, it had been many years since her illness and she had done her best to make a new life for herself.

She let herself into the flat and was just about to run a hot bath when she remembered that she had to collect Hunter from the downstairs flat. It had been rented by a musician, who spent most of the day asleep or watching television and was grateful to have the dog as company. She had housework to catch up on, and two pupils from six until eight o'clock. She needed to pull herself together. The trouble was, the rendezvous with Lillian had left her feeling completely unsettled.

That night, Charlotte went to bed early and immediately fell into a deep sleep. Johann appeared to her in a dream. He was in bed with the blonde nurse; they were making love. She was standing outside the open door in a corridor, watching them. Tears were pouring down her face and they just ignored her as if she wasn't there. Then, when they had finished, the big-busted woman got out of the bed, put on her white nurse's uniform and walked straight past her as if she didn't exist. The wind blew the door closed with such force behind Trudi Weiss that Charlotte physically jerked awake. The last thing she saw before becoming fully conscious was Johann Weber's nameplate on the door.

The dream left her feeling disturbed all of the next day. During the morning break, she asked to borrow a phone directory from the school office, frantic to check whether Johann's name was there. Running her eye down the list of doctors in Central London, sure enough, she found him listed under the Weber Group Psychiatric Practice. Charlotte made a note of the number and immediately went out into the school grounds and across the road to a phone box. She put a coin in the slot and dialled the Harley Street telephone number. She *had* to know whether it was really him. But what was she going to say? Suddenly, inspiration came to her. She knew that it was unethical, but her obsession drove her on.

'Hello, this is Elizabeth Saunders's mother. I would like to speak to Dr Weber.'

Charlotte held her breath as she waited to be connected.

Just then, a man's voice answered. 'Mrs Saunders, Dr Weber here. I believe you wanted to talk to me about Elizabeth. What seems to be the trouble?'

She immediately recognised her ex-lover's distinctive intonation. There was no doubt: it was the same person.

As Charlotte replaced the receiver, for some unknown reason she found that she felt better for knowing the truth. The fact that Johann had settled in London didn't even surprise her. Her assessment of him all those years ago, even though it had caused her a great deal of pain, had proven accurate.

28

Charlotte gazed around the stuffy auction room. The last time she had been here was more than ten years ago. Thankfully, the painful memories she had dreaded failed to materialise. She thought again of David Goldstein, the intense dark-haired young man with his postcards and photographs, and recalled his expression when he saw that they matched with the paintings on the podium. Then later, when she had taken him back to Gladys Road for a meal, his complete astonishment when Charlotte related how she had encountered his mother at the clinic in Davos, years before.

She wondered what had happened to David Goldstein and whether he had continued his relentless pursuit of the justice that had so far been denied to his family.

Apart from just three paintings that were sold, Lillian managed to take back the remainder of her collection that luckily hadn't reached their reserve price. They were delivered to the newly decorated third-floor flat in St John's Wood and hung in their pre-determined places.

Another Christmas approached. Once more, Charlotte resigned herself to being on her own. She had written to Elizabeth and, at first, the young girl wrote back, describing how miserable she was and saying she would never forgive her mother for sending her away. Charlotte did her best to offer encouragement and make her see that she should take advantage of the broad range of facilities offered by the school. She didn't give any hint of the wrench that she felt by her absence. When, gradually, Elizabeth's letters stopped, Charlotte assumed that she had got used to her surroundings.

Lillian had suggested that Charlotte should accompany them to a hotel on the South Coast for a week of Christmas festivities. Although she was tempted, Charlotte declined the invitation. Elizabeth hadn't been home in nearly three months; it would be an opportunity for mother and daughter to bond. She consoled herself with the thought that there would still be a few days before the child went back to school, in which they could see each other. They could go to Madame Tussauds, and if there was still time, maybe find a classical music concert to go to in the evening.

She was bitterly disappointed. The stay at the hotel had been a total disaster, Lillian reported. The girl had apparently spent the entire week refusing to leave her bedroom, and Lillian said she'd had no choice but to send her back to school early.

If anything, as the months passed, the adolescent girl became even more unruly. Charlotte could see that Lillian did her best to cover up her worries about her daughter by immersing herself in business, choosing to work full-time instead of the previous two days a week as a non-executive director of the Saunders Publishing Group. It was clear that she needed to be occupied rather than stay at home and dwell on the inadequacies in her life for which she knew that she herself was mainly to blame.

*

In 1972, for Charlotte's forty-sixth birthday, Lillian suggested that they should make an evening of it. She had somehow managed to obtain tickets for the newest show in town. *Jesus Christ Superstar* had just come over from Broadway and had its première in London's West End. Lillian had also reserved a table afterwards at J Sheekey, the renowned fish and seafood restaurant in nearby Leicester Square.

After the show, which she'd thoroughly enjoyed, Charlotte ate lobster for the first time. A bottle of vintage champagne was already embedded in an ice bucket when they arrived at their table. Lillian, as always, had considered everything. It was a wonderful birthday treat, and Charlotte thought that her friend had rarely seemed so relaxed. That evening, there was only a passing mention of Elizabeth.

A few days later, however, everything changed. Lillian was summoned to the boarding school by Elizabeth's house-mistress. It appeared that the now sixteen-year-old girl had been caught smoking marijuana in the grounds with a boy from a nearby public school. Charlotte, sharing her friend's concern, offered to go with Lillian to the school in Buckinghamshire. However, the other woman said that she preferred to go alone.

After Lillian had given assurances regarding Elizabeth's future conduct, the wayward teenager got off with a warning. It was made abundantly clear, however, that any repeat would lead to the girl's automatic expulsion. There would be no second chance.

For a while, Elizabeth buckled down and even achieved creditable results in her O-level exams. The improvement was to be short-lived, unfortunately. She had developed a strong feeling for the same boy and had no qualms about flouting the school rules whenever the opportunity arose to sneak away and spend time with him.

Both pupils were asked to leave their respective schools after being found at the local railway station. The young couple had planned, it transpired, to elope to Gretna Green. The boy was an accomplished musician and the couple intended to form a band together.

Lillian was at the end of her tether. Elizabeth announced that she had no intention of living with her mother in St John's Wood, and only agreed to attend a crammer to take her A levels on the condition that she could rent a flat of her own. Lillian realised that if she didn't want to become completely estranged from her daughter, she had no choice but to agree.

It took only two days to find the one-bedroom property in Earls Court, west London. Elizabeth moved in the same week. Her mother had guaranteed the rent and given her a monthly allowance. In return, Elizabeth had reluctantly enrolled in a tutorial college.

Charlotte, meanwhile, was encountering her own difficulties. The headmistress of the school at which she taught had retired and been replaced by a much younger woman. The latter had her own ideas about how the school should be run and considered that the teaching methods being employed were stale; to her mind, many of the staff had proved unable to adapt to the 1970s.

Charlotte was one of the first to be told that she was being dispensed with.

Her health was not good. Each winter her chest gave her further problems, resulting in frequent visits to the doctor's surgery and endless courses of antibiotics. Her savings had dwindled over the years, and being reliant on the school for the major part of her income, she didn't know how she was going to get by. Thank goodness she had taken Bernard's advice and had purchased her flat when she had the chance. Her mortgage had been paid off – but that still left all the bills.

On one occasion when she had been up all night worrying, she had finally managed to fall asleep, only to be awoken by the sound of the telephone ringing. Groggily, she made her way to the hall.

The hoarse, panicked voice at the end of the line belonged to Lillian. She said that a young man had just rung her from a phone box informing her that Elizabeth had been taken ill. Refusing to give his name, he stammered that he had waited with her until the ambulance arrived, and that she'd been taken to the nearby Hammersmith Hospital.

Lillian's first thought had been to call her old friend to ask whether Charlotte would accompany her; she couldn't face going to the hospital alone. Dismissing her own troubles, Charlotte dressed quickly and waited outside in the still-dark street for Lillian to collect her. A few minutes later, they were sat next to each other in the back seat of a black cab on their way to the hospital.

The distraught woman clutched hold of Charlotte's hand and began to sob silently.

'I'm sure she's being well looked after,' Charlotte said gently, doing her best to comfort her friend. 'Please try not to worry.'

'But don't you see, it's all my fault,' Lillian wept. 'If I had insisted that she lived at home, I could have watched over her.'

'I doubt that. You mustn't blame yourself. She is at a very difficult age, and we both know that Elizabeth is a head-strong young lady.'

'I'm afraid that's something she gets from me, rather than her father,' Lillian remarked sadly.

It was beginning to get light when the taxi pulled up outside the hospital. Lillian paid the driver and the two women hurried off, following the directions to the Accident & Emergency Department, where they assumed Elizabeth had been admitted. The waiting area was quieter than usual. They approached the nurse on duty, a grey-haired woman with an implacable expression sitting writing behind a desk.

'Excuse me, please could you tell me where I can find my daughter, Elizabeth Saunders?' Lillian asked. 'I'm her mother.'

'One minute, please,' the nurse answered sharply. There was a short pause while she finished writing up her notes. 'Right, what did you say the patient's name was?'

'Elizabeth Saunders,' Lillian repeated.

The nurse ran her finger down the clipboard of recent admittances. 'There's no one of that name here, I'm afraid.'

'There must be some mistake,' Charlotte interjected. 'She was brought in early this morning as an emergency.'

'There was a young girl a few hours ago, but she had no identification. Poor thing was white as a sheet. Lovely ginger hair, if I'm not mistaken.'

'That's my daughter!' Lillian cried out. 'Please, can you tell me if she is all right?'

'Can't be certain with a drugs overdose,' the woman said, disapproval showing on her face.

Lillian's mouth fell open. 'I don't understand. Why

would she do such a thing?'

'You'd be surprised what young people get up to these days,' the nurse said grimly.

Charlotte offered her arm as support, realising that Lillian had assumed Elizabeth had tried to commit suicide. She herself was more conversant with the drug culture that had become widespread in London since the 1960s. Her neighbours in the same house regularly smoked pot.

Even when she was caught at school, Lillian hadn't truly grasped that her daughter had been experimenting with drugs. It was obvious that the girl had progressed to more dangerous substances.

'She's in the Intensive Care Unit,' the nurse informed them after checking the records. 'Go to the end of the corridor and take the lift to the first floor.'

Appearing haggard in the harsh hospital lighting, the two friends walked as fast as they could across the linoleum floor to find the lost young woman whom they both loved so very deeply.

29

Elizabeth remained in a coma for three days. When she eventually stirred, she was in a private room in the hospital with her mother at her bedside. Lillian had spent the whole period keeping vigil until Elizabeth was strong enough to be moved from the Intensive Care Unit. Ignoring her own exhaustion, she was just thankful to have her daughter back.

The circumstances that had very nearly culminated in her death had shaken Elizabeth deeply, and she confessed that she had allowed her boyfriend to inject her with heroin. Some part of Lillian was greatly relieved that it had, at least, not been attempted suicide.

A week later, Lillian took her daughter home. Elizabeth moved into the flat overlooking Regent's Park without any resistance. Lillian resigned her position at the company so that she could look after her daughter. As she said, it was time that she became a proper mother.

Charlotte had returned home as soon as the doctors had confirmed that the young woman's condition was stable. However, her relief that Elizabeth was expected to make a full recovery was soon replaced by feelings of insecurity concerning her own future.

Over the coming months, she saw little of Lillian beyond the occasional invitation for tea at the flat in St

John's Wood. Elizabeth was still recuperating. She spent most of the time in baggy jeans and a sweater, curled up on the sofa glancing through a music magazine or else watching the television. The piano, taking up prime position in the living room, remained untouched. When she mentioned this to Lillian, the woman replied simply that Elizabeth would play when she was ready. In short, the young woman of twenty bore little resemblance to the high-spirited child whom Charlotte had first encountered eight years previously.

The change in her mother was even more profound. Lillian now doted on her daughter to such an extent that Charlotte had to bite her lip in case she spoke out about her smothering the girl.

For Elizabeth's twenty-first birthday, Lillian arranged a three-week tour of America. She said that she wanted to show her daughter some of the places she had visited with the girl's father on their honeymoon.

Charlotte, barely able to hide her disappointment that she was again being excluded, had to settle for presenting Elizabeth with a gift of leather-bound musical encyclopedias, which she had had engraved with her name.

Charlotte glanced at the elderly dog at the end of the bed. His breathing had become more laboured by the day. After the removal of the malignant growth on his back, the vet had only given the boxer a few weeks to live. Although she couldn't bear to see Hunter suffer, Charlotte didn't have the heart to put him down. He had been her cherished companion for so long.

She picked up the letter on the bedside table, wondering

if she had been too hasty in dismissing the offer from the estate agents on behalf of one of their clients. Twenty-five thousand pounds was a lot of money. Even after she had purchased a new property in a less sought-after location, there should still be enough left over to live on quite comfortably. She really had no choice but to sell.

Careful not to disturb the sleeping dog, Charlotte got out of bed with renewed resolve. She had made her decision. After breakfast, she would register with all the agents in the area to help her find a smaller flat. Her own flat had sold quickly, and in accordance with the terms of the sale, she would have to vacate the place that had been her home for so many years within a matter of eight weeks.

As those weeks slipped by, she became more and more frantic. None of the viewings had proven fruitful. What if she couldn't find anything suitable by the completion date?

Then late one afternoon when she arrived home from a visit to the dentist, she found Hunter lying on his side next to a pool of vomit. He had died while she had been out. With tears in her eyes, she wrapped his once-powerful frame in an old towel and called the vet to come and dispose of the body.

The next day, she telephoned Lillian and asked whether her offer for Charlotte to live with her was still open. Shortly after their return from America, Lillian had told her over lunch that Elizabeth had announced that she had no intention of completing her studies. The visit to Los Angeles had apparently left a great impression upon the young woman. She said that she wanted to work in the music industry and if necessary, she would happily move to America.

Desperate not to lose her daughter again, Lillian had made use of her extensive contacts to find her a job in London. Her persistence paid off. Elizabeth was offered a position as Personal Assistant to the Marketing Director of EMI, one of the industry's premier music publishers, and she quickly made herself indispensable. After six months, the girl was earning enough money to support herself, living on her own and told her mother she wanted to move out.

Lillian realised that she had to let go. Being in a position to help her daughter financially, when Elizabeth found a one-bedroom flat in a pretty Victorian square in nearby Primrose Hill, Lillian purchased it for her. A month later, almost two years to the day after she had nearly died, Elizabeth moved out from her mother's home in St John's Wood.

Charlotte put down the phone and looked at the half-full tea chests scattered haphazardly around her flat. The realisation that it was her last day here filled her with nostalgia. She hoped that living with Lillian would work out.

Her friend had told her that she could have the guest bedroom and her own bathroom for as long as she wanted. Lillian had even arranged storage for her paintings and artists' implements and anything else that Charlotte decided to bring with her in a flat on her floor that was in need of refurbishment and had been empty for some time. Apparently, the owners lived elsewhere and the managing agents of the block had agreed to its use on a short-term basis, so the items could be stored there. What Lillian withheld from Charlotte was that it actually belonged to her. She had purchased the flat for Elizabeth when the house in Maida Vale was sold. She had only kept it in the hope that Elizabeth would eventually agree to live there, but now that her daughter was settled in Primrose Hill, Lillian planned to put it to good use.

One early-June morning, nine months after she had left Gladys Road, Charlotte woke up and cast her eyes around the spacious spare bedroom in Lillian's apartment. It had taken less time to adjust than she had imagined. The months had gone by so quickly – it felt as if she had been on an extended holiday. Lillian hadn't let her pay for anything, and even though Lillian had shown herself to be an accomplished cook, she much preferred eating out in any number of restaurants that were within a short walking distance of the flat.

When Elizabeth wasn't working late, she would join the two of them for dinner. The conversation invariably centred around her work. She had been promoted again, and with her own clients to look after, had been given another raise in salary. Elizabeth was always so secretive about her private life but recently, she exuded a radiance that indicated she had found happiness.

Charlotte stretched out across the king-sized double bed and sighed with pleasure, and some guilt. She had become a little too comfortable, she decided, and had imposed on her friend's hospitality long enough. It was time to find a home of her own. After breakfast, she would inform Lillian of her decision.

Charlotte got out of bed, put on her robe and slippers and made her way along the corridor to the kitchen. She found Lillian already dressed, sitting at the table, reading the morning paper. By her expression, she appeared particularly pleased with herself.

'Good morning, Charlotte dear,' she beamed. 'I trust you slept well?'

'Yes, thank you,' Charlotte replied, curious as to the reason for her friend's good mood.

'The percolator should still be hot, and the brioches are just out of the oven,' Lillian said, pointing to the breadbasket on the table.

'Thank you, that's very kind. Look, I've been meaning to talk to you,' Charlotte said, pouring herself a cup of coffee.

'I can guess what it is,' Lillian replied intuitively, 'but first, I have some good news that I want to share with you. Come and sit down.'

Cheated of her chance to have her say, Charlotte took her position at the other end of the table.

'So, what is it?' she asked, taking a bite out of her deliciously warm brioche.

'Elizabeth called me this morning. She told me that she's getting engaged.'

'I suspected something was going on,' Charlotte answered. She was thrilled.

'His name is Anthony and he's a lawyer,' Lillian revealed proudly.

'Has she known him long?' Charlotte asked. 'It just seems so sudden.'

'Charlotte, you sound like the mother!' Lillian laughed happily. 'They've known each other for a few months, so I hear. You know her friend Laura? Well, Anthony is Laura's older brother.'

'That's wonderful news.' Overcome with emotion, Charlotte took a handkerchief out of her pocket and wiped her moist eyes. She had always feared that Elizabeth, by immersing herself in her career in a way that reminded Charlotte of herself as a younger woman, Elizabeth might forfeit the chance of achieving happiness.

'Naturally I'm going to be needing your help with all the arrangements,' Lillian said, not wanting her friend to feel excluded again. 'I know it's usual these days for both sets of parents to consult together. But to avoid any confrontation, I've suggested that Anthony's mother and father can organise the engagement party and I'll take care of the wedding.'

'When will it be?' Charlotte asked.

'There's a party at the McCrearys' house a week on Saturday. If the church has got an opening, the wedding will take place at the beginning of November. I've made a tentative reservation for the River Room at the Savoy for the reception and dinner.'

'So, is he a Catholic?' Charlotte enquired.

'No, they're High Church actually,' Lillian admitted. 'Not that it's of any consequence. Donald was brought up a Protestant, but neither of us had any interest in religion.'

'But wasn't that confusing for Elizabeth when she was growing up?'

'Well, of course she knew that she is Jewish, because in Judaism, the child takes after the mother.'

There was a moment of silence. Charlotte had never before considered whether Lillian was Jewish: the subject had never come up in conversation. Then, out of the blue, she recalled Elizabeth telling her about the discovery of the old suitcase and the letters from forty years ago that had belonged to her mother. Charlotte calculated that, being five years younger than her, Lillian could have only been a child of eight when she was sent away. She wondered now whether the suitcase and its contents were connected with that.

Lillian put down her newspaper, got up from the table and went to sit next to her friend.

'Now - what was it that you wanted to talk to me about?' she asked warmly.

30

Elizabeth was married at a packed St Mary Abbots Church in Kensington on a bright Sunday afternoon. The arrangements for the wedding had started immediately after the announcement of the engagement, five months earlier. Putting her own plans on hold, Charlotte helped organise all the minutiae that Lillian insisted were attended to, in order to ensure the perfect occasion. Both families and their three hundred guests were not disappointed. The next morning, the newly married couple left for their honeymoon in the Caribbean.

A few days later, while Charlotte was in the dining room helping sort out and list the large number of wedding gifts, Lillian appeared holding a small bunch of keys.

'Leave that till later,' she said excitedly. 'There's something I would like to show you.'

Together, the friends left the apartment and proceeded along the communal corridor, stopping outside a glossy front door.

'Who lives here?' Charlotte asked. Her first thought was that it must be a new neighbour; someone had just moved in and they were coming to introduce themselves.

But as Lillian herself let them into the empty flat that still smelled of fresh paint, Charlotte stood completely still, a look of confusion on her face.

'What are we doing here? I don't understand.'

'Come with me,' Lillian said, leading the way.

They entered a bright living room. Charlotte saw that her storage boxes had been stacked in a neat pile. Her easel had been placed in an alcove by the fireplace and there were paintings resting upright on the newly laid carpet against the ivory-coloured walls.

'Obviously, it looks a bit bare without curtains and furniture,' Lillian declared, showing her friend around the property. 'This is the second bedroom, which you could easily use as your studio.' She pointed to the large window that let in an abundance of light. 'And here, next door, is the main bedroom. Look! There's more than enough room for a double bed. It's already got fitted wardrobes and so you'll have plenty of room for all your clothes.'

'It's wonderful, Lillian, but I shan't possibly be able to afford it,' Charlotte replied, unable to disguise her embarrassment.

'Wait! You haven't seen the kitchen yet.'

Charlotte walked hesitantly across the tiled floor to the range of traditional light oak units. She opened the door of the tall fridge-freezer and then peered inside the sparkling new double oven.

'It looks as if it's never been used,' she whispered, running her hand along the smooth marble work surfaces.

'The rent is only one hundred and fifty pounds a month. What do you think?' Lillian took her hand and said gently: 'Will you agree to give it a try?'

Charlotte embraced her. She was lost for words.

'And if you want me to come and help you choose the rest of the furniture, the winter sales are starting shortly,' Lillian smiled.

The two women left the newly refurbished flat with

distinctly different thoughts. Charlotte was relieved that she would have her own place and would no longer have to impose on her friend's generosity. Above all, she would be next door to the woman who had become like a sister. It had been a long time - ever since Bernard, in fact - since anyone had treated her with such kindness.

Lillian herself was delighted to have found a way to repay the woman with whom she had developed such a close relationship. Naturally she'd asked Elizabeth's permission to allow Charlotte to reside in her property at a subsidised rent; although she needn't have bothered. Elizabeth had given her consent immediately.

Within a few days, Charlotte had moved into her new home. Apart from her paintings, most of which were still under wraps, the curtains had been fitted and the furniture she had chosen in the sale at Heal's in Tottenham Court Road had been delivered and was in place. Charlotte couldn't believe her good fortune. Most of the items had been substantially reduced. It was the first time that Lillian had allowed her to spend her own money and dip into the proceeds from the sale of the flat in West Hampstead. She had even gone to the trouble of organising the tenancy agreement. In her haste to sign the contract, Charlotte hadn't spotted that the landlord E.R. McCreary, to whom she had already made her first monthly payment, was actually Elizabeth.

It was time to look to the future. Charlotte had been aware for a while now that she needed to go back to work. By a lucky chance, the local newspaper contained an advertisement from an Arts Centre in Hampstead requiring an experienced teacher for its Monday and Thursday evening classes. She reached for the telephone on the table beside her and dialled the number. After arranging an interview with the Principal the following afternoon, she spent the evening typing out her CV on her old portable typewriter.

The next day, Charlotte took the bus two miles northwards along the Finchley Road to Hampstead, jumped off and stood looking at her destination, a substantial red-brick Victorian building that appeared badly in need of repair.

Charlotte presented her details to a pixie-like silver-haired woman wearing black stockings and a hand-knitted multi-coloured cardigan. It was explained to her that the classes were an experiment aimed specifically at its senior members, many of whom had never painted before. The pay was seventy pounds a week and the courses were to run initially for eight weeks. There were a few other applicants to see, and Miss Brown would be informed of their decision by the end of the week.

A few days later, she received a telephone call offering her the position.

The first thing Charlotte did was to go and tell Lillian the good news. Apprehensive about whether there would be sufficient numbers to make the project a success, she even asked her friend if she would consider enrolling just to lend her support.

She needn't have worried. The take-up was immediate. Charlotte's classes were full and her pupils responsive to her teaching methods. It was as if she had provided these older men and women with a final chance to learn a new skill and they were determined to make the most of the opportunity. Several were so enthusiastic that they asked Charlotte if she would add an extra lesson to the week.

She soon realised that for many of these senior citizens, her classes were their only chance to go out at night and socialise with others of the same age.

Charlotte's contract was renewed, this time for a whole year. Word had spread and she was now teaching privately again most evenings. Although she liked the routine and was now earning enough money to live on and pay her rent, she was seeing less of her friend. After a miscarriage, Elizabeth had eventually given birth to a baby boy, Freddie Donald McCreary, and Lillian spent every spare moment with her new grandson. She said that she was determined to make up for the lack of attention Elizabeth had suffered as a child.

It was now, however, at Elizabeth's instigation as much as her mother's that Charlotte was routinely invited to all their celebrations. One Christmas she agreed to accompany them all to the same hotel on the coast that Lillian had taken Elizabeth to during the school holidays. The two women were the nearest thing to having a family of her own, and she was always made most welcome and would willingly babysit to give Elizabeth a break. It was at these times, however, that Charlotte reflected on her own lonely life, the part that the war had played in it, and the choices she had made.

The years continued to pass, bringing with them the changes and challenges of life in a capital city. One evening in the mid-1990s, after she arrived back from her classes, Charlotte decided to go along the corridor and pay her friend a visit. Leaving her flat, she was surprised to find Lillian returning from a night out. She was accompanied by a sprightly-looking older man with thick-rimmed glasses.

'Charlotte, what a nice surprise,' Lillian said affectionately. 'Do come and join us for coffee. By the way, let me introduce you. This is Allen.' She opened the door and let her guests into her flat. 'Sit down and make yourselves comfortable. I'll be with you shortly.' She went ahead, switching on the lights.

Allen and Charlotte passed into the living room and sat down on leather armchairs that were placed around an octagonal Chinese coffee table. Charlotte looked admiringly at the green inlaid top. She was certain that she hadn't seen it there before.

'Beautiful piece, isn't it?' the white-haired man commented in a broad American accent. 'We bought it at auction.'

'Yes, it is magnificent,' Charlotte agreed. Noticing that he had emphasised the word *we*, she wondered why Lillian had never mentioned him before.

'Lillian and I have been seeing quite a lot of each other recently,' the American said assertively. It was as if he were staking his claim on the woman in the kitchen, warning Charlotte off.

Lillian had never hidden the fact that she had a wide circle of acquaintances, but her apparent closeness with this stranger came as a surprise. Charlotte knew it was wrong but she couldn't help taking an instant dislike to the man in the black and white check sports jacket sitting a few feet away and looking so pleased with himself.

Just then, Lillian appeared with a trolley of coffee and biscuits.

'Here she is, the beautiful lady of the house!' A schoolboy grin appeared across his suntanned face.

'I do hope you've been getting to know each other?' Lillian commented. She placed the refreshments on the table and sat down on the sofa opposite her guests. 'Allen was an actor in Hollywood,' she disclosed, giving Charlotte a look as if she were seeking her approval.

'Oh, it was only a couple movies in the forties when I came out of the forces,' Allen said with unconvincing humility.

'So, what brought you to England?' Charlotte asked politely.

'The last film was shot in London. I came here and fell in love with the place.'

'More likely your leading lady,' Lillian muttered under her breath.

'Now that's not fair, honey,' the man protested, happy that he was the centre of attention. 'Anyway, Charlotte, I decided to settle here. There were no more decent acting parts, so I went into the antiques business.'

'Allen has a shop in Mayfair,' Lillian explained.

'It pays the bills and keeps me out of trouble,' he said, looking fondly at her.

'That's where we met,' Lillian said. 'I was on the lookout for a few things when I bought this flat, and I came across Allen's Antiques in Mount Street.'

'So that must have been . . .' Charlotte started to say. She was curious to establish exactly how long the relationship had been going on.

'June 1970, to be precise,' the American butted in. 'Twenty-six years – but who's counting?'

'And we've been friends ever since.' Lillian beamed at her male companion.

'Wouldn't have left it at that, if it had been down to me,'

the man sniggered.

'Allen, please.' Lillian looked a little annoyed.

'Now, honey, you know I don't mean anything by it. I'm just foolin' around.'

There was a moment of uncomfortable silence.

'So, Charlotte, Lillian here tells me that you're an artist. I sure would like to see your work some time,' the man said, deftly changing the subject.

'Actually, I'm a teacher,' Charlotte corrected him. 'I've not painted in a long, long time.'

'Charlotte's just being modest,' Lillian said. 'She's really very accomplished.'

'It's still early, I'm sure this young lady wouldn't object to showing us what she's got hidden away,' the man persisted.

'Well, so long as you don't mind that the place is in a bit of a mess,' Charlotte answered. She suspected that the American was used to getting his own way.

After they had finished their coffee, the three of them got up and went along the corridor to Charlotte's flat.

'You've kept it marvellously well,' Lillian noted. She gazed around at the place that she had originally helped to furnish. Sensitive to her friend's predicament, she wanted to appear as supportive as possible. 'And the paintings make so much difference.'

'The others are still in here,' Charlotte said. She led her two visitors to the spare room at the end of the hall.

'May I take a look?' Allen asked.

'Please, help yourself.' Charlotte pointed to several paintings stacked against the wall.

The two women went to sit down in the other room and continued with their conversation. Suddenly, an enthusiastic shout reverberated through the flat. They rushed back to the small room to discover what had caught the American's attention. They found him standing in the hallway, staring at *Blight,* the painting by Daniel Petrovitch which had been placed on top of a tall chest of drawers.

'This is somethin' else!' he exclaimed. 'Where did you lay your hands on this fella?'

Charlotte felt a lump in her throat as she once again saw the gaunt faces staring out at her. 'I had it on the wall of my old flat,' she said. 'I really must put it up again.'

'I don't think I've ever seen it before,' Lillian said slowly. How she hadn't noticed it previously, she couldn't think. 'The look of despair on such young faces is really quite disturbing,' she added, deeply moved. Her expression had changed and she seemed to be in the grip of a powerful memory.

'Allen, I'm feeling quite tired,' she said then. 'I think we should be going.'

'I'm just coming,' he replied, looking surprised and rather put out, not picking up on her change of mood.

'Thank you for showing your work to Allen,' Lillian said, turning to her friend. 'Please don't trouble yourself – we can let ourselves out.'

As they left, the American gave the painting that had captivated him a final look.

'It was good meeting you, Charlotte,' he said, as he stepped out into the hall. 'If you ever consider selling that painting, remember I saw it first.' He chuckled and walked away.

Charlotte shuddered. The man was brash and clearly insensitive. How Lillian could ever say she had anything in common with him was beyond her. All she could think of was that the American must be after her money.

31

It was September 1996, and the beginning of a new course. Charlotte was late. She hurried through the arched door of the austere-looking building, pelted to the end of the poorly lit passageway and then went down the stairs to the lower-ground floor. Breathless, she entered the stark, windowless space that had been designated for her evening classes, and there, mingling amongst several of her pupils, was Lillian.

'I hope you don't mind,' Lillian said, going up to greet her friend. 'I finally decided to come along. The girl in the office said that she thought it would be all right and I've paid for the course.'

'You are v-very welcome,' Charlotte stammered, surprised by her unexpected appearance.

'About the other night,' Lillian said quietly, taking her friend aside. 'I'm sorry. You must have thought me terribly rude, rushing off like that. Allen said that I had behaved badly.'

'I just assumed that you suddenly felt unwell.' Charlotte had wondered afterwards about Lillian's strange reaction to the Daniel Petrovitch painting. But then, hadn't it also had a profound effect on her too in the past?

'So you're not upset with me?'

'No, of course not,' Charlotte smiled, clutching her friend's hand.

'I used to draw a lot when I was a child,' Lillian confided. 'I know it's been a long time, but for some reason I want to start again.' She didn't divulge that, after returning to her flat and bidding good night to Allen, she had been unable to sleep. She just couldn't get the images in the Daniel Petrovitch painting out of her mind. And something deep inside was compelling her to find a way of keeping them alive.

'Good evening, everyone,' Charlotte called out from the front. 'It's good to see so many familiar faces back again. For those who are attending for the first time, my name is Charlotte Brown and I shall be helping you develop your artistic skills. If you haven't painted before, please don't worry; it's never too late to start.'

Laughter rang out around the room.

'The project for this course is your first truly evocative memory. As before, I want you to first sketch out your subject to scale. This may take two or three sessions, so don't hurry. The important thing is to get it right. Then when you're satisfied with the detail, you can start applying paint to canvas. I can see that most of you have come equipped with your drawing materials. There are some additional pads and pencils for those who have forgotten,' she added, specifically searching out Lillian, who had taken a position at the back of the room.

But Lillian had spent the morning trawling the centre of London for a full range of art supplies. Settling down and starting to focus, she began to sketch the scene of nearly sixty years ago – an event that had changed the entire course of her life. The train station in Vienna, covered in snow. Tearful parents forced to watch behind tall metal gates as their children, identified only by numbers tied around their necks and carrying small leather suitcases, proceeded uncertainly onto the frozen platform.

Her last glimpse of her mother and father as the grimy train, billowing smoke, puffed slowly away. Finally, the fair young German guard in grey uniform who, to punish her for falling asleep and missing the roll call, had maliciously torn up the only photographs of her family that she possessed.

By the third week, most of the pupils had completed their sketches. Charlotte then demonstrated the technique of transferring their drawings by tracing the outline of their images on to a bare canvas. She found herself paying particular attention to Lillian's subject. The painting showed that even without any formal training, her friend had an uncanny ability. Her style, albeit simple, conveyed a poignancy that she had only ever seen in more experienced artists. Lilian had told Charlotte about the torn-up photographs. There was something haunting about the man and woman's weeping faces as they gazed at a young girl on the train: they or the subject seemed familiar. Then, when Charlotte saw the sign for Westbahnhof, Vienna's railway station, she recalled the conversation with Elizabeth about the letters she had found with Austrian stamps on the envelopes, in the old suitcase in the attic.

Charlotte tried talking to Lillian about her painting, hoping that she would open up to her about the child on the train. Was it Lillian herself? But her friend wouldn't elaborate. All she would say was that, as a child, she had lived with her family outside of London, and that both her parents had died many years ago. It never occurred to Charlotte that her friend had been forced to flee to

England when the war started.

As the last week of the ten-week course arrived, most of the class's paintings were nearly complete.

Charlotte noticed that her friend was looking unusually perturbed, wiping her brush and frowning.

'Do you need help with something?' she asked, standing a few feet away from the canvas.

'It's the guard. I can see his face in my mind, but the detail is still not right,' Lillian fretted.

'Try and describe him to me,' Charlotte suggested.

'He had a wide jaw and deep-set blue eyes. The nose is wrong here. It was actually very short, turned up at the tip.'

'You've given him fair hair – is that right?' Charlotte asked, focusing intently on the canvas.

'Yes, I'm sure he was fair,' Lillian nodded.

'And his complexion, was it smooth? Was he clean-shaven?'

'Yes, it was completely smooth. How did you know?' Lillian asked.

Charlotte's brother Hans had the same features as the guard Lillian had described to her. Shock sent her into a trance-like state.

'There's something missing,' she murmured to herself. 'He had a scar on his left temple.'

'I'm sorry, what did you say?' Lillian asked, looking curiously at her.

'I was just wondering whether he had any other distinctive features, like a scar or birth-mark?' Charlotte said nervously. She needed to know whether it really was Hans. Before being sent to Russia, he had been stationed in Vienna. She remembered how, when he was home on leave, he would drink too much and then gloat about the number of Jews he had herded onto trains, and sent on their way to internment camps.

'It's possible, but I'm afraid I don't remember. I was only a child,' Lillian replied with a shrug.

But Charlotte knew, with every part of her, that it was *him*. Her own brother. It was he who had destroyed those precious photographs, just as he had been complicit in destroying precious lives.

Inside her, something broke.

Without any explanation to the class, Charlotte snatched up her belongings and rushed out of the basement studio, needing to get far, far away from the image of the guard's face that would haunt her for the rest of her days. The contrast of the cold night entering her lungs caused her to wheeze as she braved the torrential rain on the two-mile walk back to St John's Wood.

By the time Charlotte got home, she had decided what she was going to do. After changing out of the sopping wet clothes into her dressing gown, she took her suitcase from the spare room then went into her bedroom, emptied the wardrobe and began to pack. In the morning, she would go to the bank and withdraw just enough money to give notice on the flat and purchase a ticket to Switzerland. There, she would retire to the mountains and lead a quiet life. She still had most of the money on deposit from the sale of the flat in West Hampstead. It would be more than enough to live on. Once she was settled, she would close her account in London and request that the bank transfer the balance.

Charlotte looked around at her comfortable surroundings and felt a momentary pang. She had enjoyed a settled life but now it had come to an end, and in a most abrupt way.

Just before she got into bed, she paused. She knew that she couldn't leave without saying something to Lillian. Her friend deserved to know the truth. She went over to the sideboard, took out a sheet of headed notepaper from her stationery drawer and sat down at the dining-room table. Before she could begin writing, however, there was a ring on the doorbell. For a second, she was tempted to go and see who it was, but then changed her mind. She didn't hear it ring a second time.

Charlotte wrote:

My dear Lillian,

What must you have thought of me rushing away without any form of explanation? The truth is that I felt ashamed. The painting that you have been working on so diligently over the past weeks and which so explicitly depicts your traumatic experience has caused me to question certain aspects of my past that I hoped would remain hidden.

We have been friends for thirty years, ever since our first meeting on that long-ago cruise. During that time, you have become the sister I never had. You have been my family.

I'm afraid that what I'm about to reveal will prove that our friendship was built on a false pretence. The person to whom you have always shown such kindness is not who she claims to be. My real name is Eva Schlessinger. I was born in Berlin in 1926 and moved to Switzerland after the war. There I took Swiss nationality, which was afforded to me since my mother was born in that country. I also changed my identity, which I was at liberty to do, and since I intended to move to England, I chose an English name. I became

Charlotte Brown.

There have been a few occasions over the years that have reminded me of my past, but nothing that left a lasting impression - until today, when I quizzed you about the guard on the train.

That young man who destroyed the only record that you would have of your parents could well have been my brother, Hans. He was doing the same job as a guard, and his similarity to the fellow in the painting is unmistakable.

I don't know whether you will be able to find a way to forgive me for my deceit. That's for you alone to decide. I shall, however, have to live with the guilt of doing so little when I was part of a world that brought devastation to so many.

I shall be moving abroad as soon as possible.

Knowing you, Lillian, has made my life richer.

With all my love, Eva

P.S. Please find enclosed two months' rent to terminate my tenancy. I should be most grateful if you could forward it to the landlord.

Charlotte folded the letter with the cheque and wrote Lillian's name on the front of the envelope. She planned to put it through her letterbox before she left.

In bed, Charlotte slept fitfully. She dreamed that she was playing in the street outside her home in Berlin. It was snowing heavily. She was in the middle, being pulled by the hand in different directions by a boy and young girl. One hand was held by Lillian and the other by David Goldstein. The children's faces were dirty and their clothes were torn. Tears were running down their cheeks.

'We don't know where our parents are. There's nowhere for us to go. Please let us come and live with you!' they cried.

Just then, there was the crunching sound of heavy boots walking through the snow. In the distance, she saw her brother Hans marching angrily towards her.

'Eva, you know you've been forbidden to have anything to do with filthy Jews! Now go home or you'll be late for supper!' he ordered.

He then grabbed hold of the two other children and slapped them viciously across the head with the outside of his leather-gloved hand, sending them sprawling into the gutter.

Charlotte ran up the steps into the apartment building. She didn't look back.

She woke exhausted, quickly got dressed and went around the corner to the High Street for breakfast, while she waited for the bank and travel agent to open. An hour later, she returned home with her plane ticket to Zurich and a brown envelope containing fifteen hundred pounds.

Just as she turned the corner into Prince Albert Road, a youth in a balaclava and black windcheater jacket pushed her against some railings. He placed his arm against her throat so she couldn't move and ran his other hand down the outside of her coat and over her pockets. Not finding any valuable jewellery or an expensive watch, he yanked the bag from Charlotte's trembling hand and scurried away.

Unharmed, but in a considerable state of shock, Charlotte rested against the railings while her heartbeat slowed and she was able to decide what to do next. The police station – that was it. A crime had been committed and she needed to report it.

It was three in the afternoon by the time Charlotte had finished making her statement at the police station. The officer in charge gave her no grounds for optimism that she would recover her belongings. Feeling dejected, the plans she had made in disarray, she went slowly back to the home she thought she had vacated.

32

While Charlotte was being interviewed at the police station, Lillian got out of her daughter Elizabeth's car and was walking up to the main entrance of the apartment building when she suddenly noticed a woman's handbag lying tossed in the flowerbeds. Certain that it hadn't been there when she went out, Lillian stepped onto the grass verge and picked it up. She recognised the bag: it belonged to Charlotte. Taking it with her, she went up to her flat and waited for her friend to return.

Charlotte let herself into her flat with the spare keys that she retrieved from the porter's desk and made herself a strong cup of tea. Her head was much clearer now, and the decision she had made last night now seemed rash and unwise.

She had spent her whole life running away whenever she was confronted with anything unpleasant. Wasn't *that* the message contained in the dreams that had plagued her since the end of the war? She felt profoundly ashamed. It was time to admit to herself who she really was and, more importantly, to face Lillian in person.

Charlotte unpacked her suitcase and then proceeded resolutely to her friend's flat at the end of the corridor.

'The door is open,' Lillian called out, hearing a distinctive knock.

Charlotte passed through the hall to the living room. There was Lillian poised in front of her easel, dressed in a stained blue smock and working on the same painting that had caused Charlotte to react so dramatically the previous day.

'Do you recognise this?' Lillian said, directing her gaze at the handbag on the chair next to her.

'Where did you find it?' Charlotte gasped.

'I'm afraid there's nothing in there other than a rather damp letter. I thought I'd let the bag dry out first and then give it a thorough cleaning.'

Charlotte was stunned. She'd forgotten all about the letter. She wished she had never written it. Since it had been addressed to Lillian, her friend must have read it and now knew everything.

'Lillian, please allow me to explain,' she began hoarsely.

'There, that's about the best I can do,' Lillian murmured, looking intently at her painting. 'What do you think?' She put down her paintbrush and gestured to Charlotte to come and have a look.

'The letter was meant for you,' Charlotte said, paying more attention to the envelope jutting out of her handbag.

'And no doubt you assumed that what you were going to tell me would make a difference to our friendship? My guess is that because you think you recognised the guard in my painting, you have now convinced yourself that you're responsible for what happened sixty years ago.'

'But the separation from your parents – I was part of that world which caused it to happen,' Charlotte lamented.

'What, just because you came from Germany?' Lillian said.

'You knew?' Charlotte gaped. She was now certain that

her friend had read the letter.

Lillian took her time replying. She could see that Charlotte was distressed and she didn't want to add to her anguish.

'Come and sit down,' she said calmly, removing her smock and wiping her hands on a clean cloth.

The two women moved over to the sofa in the middle of the room.

'Do you remember many years ago, when we met for tea at that place on the canal?' Lillian asked. 'It was just after Elizabeth had gone off to boarding school.'

'Yes, I think so,' Charlotte replied hesitantly.

'If you recall, you became extremely upset. I couldn't establish at the time what it was that I might have said. It was only when I went in person to pay for Elizabeth's last set of treatments that it fell into place.'

Charlotte was only half-listening. Since Lillian already knew everything, she was convinced that it was the end of their friendship.

'Dr Weber mentioned that I had apparently called to speak to him about Elizabeth. He said that when he picked up the phone, the other person had mysteriously disappeared. I then recalled seeing the strange look on your face when I mentioned that he was Elizabeth's psychiatrist. It was as if I had reminded you of something from the past.'

'It was just the shock about Elizabeth going away to school,' Charlotte lied. 'After all, we were extremely close. I loved her.' She again felt herself becoming tense.

'Yes, of course. I know that is true. Dr Weber informed me that Elizabeth had talked about you regularly, to the extent that he worked out that Elizabeth's Charlotte Brown was the same one he knew too. That was when I deduced that it must have been you who made the call.'

Charlotte flushed. She felt highly embarrassed that she had resorted to such a childish prank.

'You must have had your reasons, Charlotte. Anyway, it was only after he expressed an interest in Elizabeth's relationship with you that he informed me that you knew each other.'

'What did he say?' Charlotte whispered. She dreaded what was coming next.

'Just that he had been a friend of your father's in Berlin.'

Charlotte fell silent. At least Johann had been sufficiently discreet not to mention their affair. Strangely, she found that a weight had been lifted from her shoulders. However, she still didn't know how Lillian could be so forgiving.

'Actually, I count myself as one of the lucky ones,' Lillian added, after a brief pause.

'How can you possibly say that, with everything that you had to endure?'

'I was given another chance, one denied to the majority of other children,' Lillian said quietly.

Charlotte could now see that everything had fallen into place. The Daniel Petrovitch painting had been the catalyst. She turned around and stared at the still-wet canvas. It was Lillian's attempt to come to terms with the traumatic experience she had suffered.

'I was taken in and given a loving home,' Lillian continued. 'I even inherited a younger brother that I would never otherwise have had.' It had been years since she had thought of Myra and Stanley Shaw. Now for the second time in less than twenty-four hours, she found herself reliving her experience as a child of the Kindertransport.

'It was extremely fortunate that my foster-parents could afford to send me to private school.' She remembered her first day at St Margaret's Girls' School and her smart brown uniform. The small Austrian girl, who spoke such little English that she had to be given extra tuition to bring her up to the required standard, soon settled in and made friends. Despite the wrench of being sent away from her parents, she had fond memories of her school years in England.

'And then you went to university?' Charlotte prompted.

'No. Unfortunately, my foster-father suffered with bad health and I was needed to help in the family business.'

'But you said they had a son?'

'Yes, Norman. He wasn't cut out for the commercial world. He was extremely artistic and wanted to be on the stage.'

'What happened to him?' Charlotte asked curiously, wondering why they had never had this conversation before.

'Mr Shaw couldn't accept that he had a son who would never live up to his expectations. Norman was forced to join the Army. His father said it would help make a man of him. He was a sweet boy,' Lillian sighed.

'And are you still in contact with him?'

'Norman died, shortly after you and I met. He had moved to Australia with his male partner and became a well-known television personality. Unfortunately, he had a heart attack during a live performance. Poor Norman. All he ever wanted was his father's approval.'

'So, when did you meet Donald?' Charlotte asked.

'After Mr Shaw passed away, the business closed down and I went to work for my foster-mother's brother. The family dealt in furs and I was put on the export side, where I could make use of my languages. You see, I had learned French and Spanish at school.'

'And of course, you knew German?' Charlotte added.

'I hadn't spoken it for years. Strangely, that's the language I found the most difficult. I was spending most of my time doing translations when it occurred to me to start up my own business doing the same thing. There seemed to be a need for it.'

'But wouldn't that have required a great deal of capital?' Charlotte asked. It was now clear that the drive that had enabled Lillian to make such a success in business must have started to show itself all those years ago.

'I had some savings and the fur business helped me with some paid work.' Lillian shrugged. 'I found a room above a newsagent's in Bloomsbury – it only cost a few pounds a week. One morning, this tall, very handsome man strolled in off the street. He wanted to know whether I could oblige him with some translations that he required for the following day.'

'So, what happened?'

'I did as he requested. He must have been happy with my work because soon I was getting all his business.'

Charlotte waited, and then she said gently: 'Your parents – did you ever see them again?'

'Their letters suddenly stopped in 1941. I found out later that they were deported from Vienna to Poland. They didn't survive the concentration camp.' Lillian smiled sadly. 'It's odd, I still have a vague recollection of our house in the Ringstrasse. When I first came to England, I used to dream about my mother, who was a concert pianist. I would spend hours just sitting and listening to her play.'

'So that's where Elizabeth gets her musical ability,' Charlotte murmured.

Lillian nodded, but was clearly still immersed in her thoughts of the past.

'I don't suppose the house is there any more,' she mused, 'not that I have ever had any desire to go back.'

'And your father?'

'His family was extremely wealthy. They owned property in Vienna, or so my Uncle Theodore told me.'

'You didn't mention that you had an uncle,' Charlotte said.

'Theo was my mother's older brother. He was a reporter on an Austrian daily newspaper and he was very well connected. It was really due to him that I managed to escape to England. He could see what was happening and he begged my parents to leave Vienna while they still had the chance. But my father wouldn't hear of it.'

'Did Theo survive?' Charlotte asked.

'I never found out. I just remember him telling me that England was a wonderful place and that he wished he was coming with me. He and my mother were very close. I doubt he would have been prepared to leave her.'

Charlotte found herself so caught up in the tragic demise of Lillian's family that for a moment, she was unable to speak.

'So now that we know everything about each other, there's no need for this,' Lillian said, snapping out of her contemplative mood. She reached over, plucked up the letter on the chair next to her and tore it into small pieces.

Charlotte saw that there wasn't any point in delving further into the past. She would, however, have to come to terms with the knowledge that the guard in her dearest friend's painting was almost certainly her brother.

'Now I think that a celebration might be in order, don't you?' Lillian pronounced. 'It just so happens there's a bottle of champagne in the fridge.' She got up from the sofa and headed off towards the kitchen.

Relieved that she had made the right decision in staying, Charlotte began browsing through the copy of *The Times* on the coffee table. Her attention was suddenly caught by a headline: *Aristocrat Settles Out of Court Action for Missing Art*

The article went on to say: *Viscount Chesterfield, 62, one of the wealthiest landowners in England, has agreed an undisclosed sum to settle a case against himself and society banker R.P. Meredith.*

Trying to recall where she had heard the names before, Charlotte carried on reading.

The action was brought by lawyers representing several Jewish families who claimed that their art collections had been plundered by the Nazis. An Interpol investigation thirty-eight years ago had focused on some of the same works of art that were displayed in the former Muller Gallery in Mayfair. However, the case was dismissed for lack of sufficient evidence against its then owners.

The episode of Susana's mysterious disappearance and the ensuing police investigation came flooding back to Charlotte. Of course! Rupert Meredith. He was Bernard's trusted banker, who for his own gains had had no qualms about thrusting a knife in his back. She had no doubt that it was he who had caused Bernard Morris's death. She remembered wondering at the time whether people with influence like Rupert Meredith were beyond the law.

Charlotte now pursued the rest of the story with

an uncharacteristic desire for vengeance. The article continued: *New evidence arose when a painting of three nudes by Rubens was discovered, due to a tip from an anonymous source, hanging in the boardroom of Meredith's Bank in London.*

When asked whether they had considered that justice had been done, the lawyers for the families responded that the settlement, which is estimated to have run into millions of pounds, was sparse compensation for their loss, since by far the major part of the theft had yet to be traced.

A spokesman for Viscount Chesterfield said that the Earl had willingly co-operated with the investigation and had offered full transparency of his dealings with Meredith's. He was pleased to have been able to help in correcting a gross injustice.

Meredith's were unavailable to comment.

Charlotte shut her eyes and put the paper down.

'You must have been miles away,' Lillian remarked. She was holding out a glass of champagne to her friend.

'I didn't hear you come back,' Charlotte answered, still thinking about the newspaper article.

'I read about that this morning,' Lillian said, glancing at the open page. 'The tragedy is that after the cost of a three-year investigation, especially with what lawyers charge, I'd be surprised if the victims got very much at the end of it.'

Charlotte knew there were bound to be other claimants without the means to effect any restitution of the items that had been stolen from them. The injustice struck her deeply. Her mind turned to David Goldstein. She wondered if he had succeeded in his efforts to trace his works of art, recalling his expression when the postcards that he was grasping matched the items being auctioned.

He had relied on her to help him - and she had let him down.

Turning to the woman next to her, Charlotte took a sip of champagne, saying with all her heart: 'Thank you for being such a special friend.'

'Actually, there's another piece of news I'd like to share with you,' Lillian announced, her face lighting up.

The elderly solicitor smiled and put his mobile phone back in his dressing-gown pocket. He was satisfied with his fee but more importantly, he had eventually discredited the man he had detested, Rupert Meredith. As far as he was concerned, the bloated reptile could rot at his villa in Barbados, so long as he never had to set eyes on him again.

One simple phone call was all it took to the Jewish organisation in Frankfurt. David Goldstein had responded immediately and had boarded the next flight to London. It hadn't taken the Jew long to trace the owners of the remainder of the collection. This was the case for which he, James Robson, had been waiting so patiently and for so long, in order to exact his revenge. Like everything else in life, timing, he had learned, was everything.

He looked out of the bedroom window of his Mayfair home. Bertie Chesterfield wasn't such a bad sort for an upper-class English twat. At least he kept his word. 'Get that bastard Meredith off my back and you can name your price,' he had said.

James Robson had always liked the house, ever since that first time when he was invited to Bernard Morris's dinner party. Susana was never aware that she only had a lease on the place, nor of the fact that the Chesterfield Estate had granted it to her.

James Robson exhaled a contented sigh. Stepping agilely out of his robe, he climbed into the king-sized double bed, next to the smiling young girl who was waiting for him.

33

Charlotte opened the hand-delivered envelope that had been put through her letterbox. It was the refund from the travel agent for her abortive journey to Switzerland. Fortunately, she had been able to inform them in time for them to cancel the stolen ticket.

The events of the last twenty-four hours had taken their toll – after all, she was nearly seventy by now, not a young woman. The article in the newspaper kept going over and over in her mind. What about all those others who couldn't afford the cost of challenging the authorities about Nazi confiscation and theft of their artworks? How would they ever recover what was rightfully theirs?

Suddenly it struck her. Switzerland – the family money in Zurich! Could this be her chance to finally make up for what she had offered to do all those years ago?

Charlotte looked at her watch: 6.30 p.m. The travel agent would be closed by now. Her mission would have to wait until the morning.

Charlotte then went in search of David Goldstein's business card. The trouble was, she didn't know where to start looking. The card had probably been left in the old flat at Gladys Road or somewhere in Lillian's spare room – or had simply been thrown away. None of her efforts proved fruitful. Then, just as she was about to give up the search, something made her go up to the Daniel Petrovitch painting that stood on top of the tall chest of drawers in the spare room. Running her fingers around the edges of the canvas, Charlotte felt something. Wedged in its back, covered in dust, was David Goldstein's card. She must have placed it there for safekeeping, subconsciously making a connection.

The next morning, Charlotte booked herself on a morning flight to Switzerland; she would carry on by plane to Frankfurt the same evening. She then telephoned and made an appointment at her bank in Zurich. Herr Grossman, she was informed, had been retired for many years but Herr Klauser, the present manager, would be available to see her at two o'clock, just after lunch.

Leaving the same discreet premises in the Bahnhofstrasse that she had last visited forty years ago, Charlotte put the bank draft carefully away in her handbag and hailed a taxi back to the airport. The manager had been an exact replica of Herr Grossman, down to the same navy-blue suit and impeccable white starched shirt, and like his predecessor, he exhibited the same reserve when she told him of her desire to withdraw her entire balance and close her account. The amount had grown over the years to the considerable sum of just over twenty million Swiss francs.

Charlotte arrived in Frankfurt on that mild autumn evening just after eight o'clock. It was the first time she'd been back to Germany in over half a century. She looked in bewilderment at the dramatic skyscrapers and high-rise buildings on the horizon as she approached the outskirts of the city. It resembled more closely Lillian's photographs of New York than the Germany she recalled from her youth.

The travel agent had booked her into a functional business hotel, located in the centre of town, for her one-night stay.

The next morning, she departed early with directions to an office situated in the fashionable Westend district of the city. Standing outside the imposing nineteenth-century villa with the faded business card clasped tightly in her hand, Charlotte started to worry about how she would be received. Perhaps David wouldn't remember her after such a long time. Worse, he might have taken umbrage because she had let him down. That was the reason she had decided to turn up without making an appointment.

Gathering her courage, she went up a few stone steps to the beautifully restored building and rang the bell. On announcing her name, the door opened automatically. Entering into what felt like a drawing room in a private house, she approached a smartly dressed young woman, sat working behind an expensive oak desk.

'Good morning, my name is Charlotte Brown,' she said in her perfect German. 'I don't have an appointment but I was wondering whether it would be possible to see David Goldstein. It concerns a matter of very great importance.'

The young woman tapped the name she had been given into her computer. After a few seconds, she looked up at the visitor and said, 'I'm sorry, Frau Brown; there is no one of that name at Weil Richter.'

'But I have his business card! There must be some mistake,' Charlotte insisted.

'Well, he may have worked here at one time, but certainly not in the five years that I've been here,' the secretary replied curtly.

Charlotte was completely deflated. She had taken it for granted that David would be here. She had even expected him to look exactly the same. How could she have been so foolish, expecting time to have stood still?

'Excuse me, Frau Brown,' the secretary said, trying to attract the attention of the despondent-looking elderly woman, 'perhaps you would care to take a seat while I make further enquiries. There may be one or two of the older staff here who remember your David Goldstein. I will send out an email.'

Charlotte made her way over to the reception area and lowered herself wearily into a stylish leather armchair.

Ten minutes passed by, then the phone rang. The receptionist scribbled down the details she had just been given and, in a complete change of mood, she hastened across the room to Charlotte.

'Frau Brown, it appears you are in luck,' she smiled. She tore off a sheet from her firm's note-pad and passed it to the visitor. 'Here's the address. It's in the old Jewish district. Take the Westend subway to *Börneplatz* and I'm almost certain that the street you are looking for will be in a turning off the square.'

'Thank you! Thank you so much!' Charlotte cried out. She shot up and kissed the young girl on both cheeks. 'Please extend my gratitude to the colleague who provided you with the information,' she said before being let out of the luxurious offices.

It didn't take long to follow the instructions she'd been given; her destination proved to be a street teeming with sightseers. Many of them were gathered in front of a long concrete wall. They were looking at the rows of bricks which protruded all the way along. Charlotte went up closer and saw that each carried an inscription. She was at the memorial to Frankfurt's Jewish community, for those who had perished in the holocaust.

Deeply moved, she walked to the end of the road and found the address. David Goldstein's company was listed on the fifth floor of a drab office building that seemed out of keeping with the rest of the area.

Charlotte rang the intercom. It was answered by a man's gruff voice. 'Yes?'

'Good morning. My name is Charlotte Brown.'

'What do you want?' he growled.

'I should like to see Herr Goldstein.'

'And he's expecting you?'

'No – I mean, I can explain . . .'

The line went dead.

Charlotte wondered whether she should try a second time. Maybe there was some mistake and she'd been given the wrong information. Again, she began to harbour misgivings about coming to Germany.

Just as she made to walk away, another gentler voice came on the intercom.

'This is David Goldstein. You said that you wanted to see me, but I don't know a Charlotte Brown. Perhaps you have mistaken me for somebody else. I'm sorry that you have had a wasted journey.'

Charlotte knew that she had to think quickly before he put the phone down. There wouldn't be a second chance. If she tried again, he would probably assume that she was deranged and call the police. *Say something!* she urged herself.

'Herr Goldstein,' she said hurriedly, 'it was many years ago. You came to London trying to trace your family's art collection. We met at the auction at Brockets.'

'All that may be true, but I'm afraid it still doesn't prove that you are who you say you are.'

Charlotte was becoming desperate. There had to be something that she could say. Suddenly, she saw the face of the woman sitting by the lake at the sanatorium. That was it!

'I also remember telling you that I had had the pleasure of getting to know your mother in Davos, at the Blauberger sanatorium.'

There was a moment of silence.

'Can you tell me her name?' came the response. The man's voice was so quiet, it could hardly be heard.

'Her name was Margot. Your mother's name was Margot,' Charlotte repeated.

At that very instant, the door opened.

Charlotte took the lift to the top floor. Standing waiting for her was a chubby grey-haired man.

'I'm David Goldstein,' he announced. 'You had better come in.'

Charlotte was led into a cheaply carpeted area that had been sectioned off by glass partitions to make several small, nondescript offices.

'Please sit down.' David Goldstein gestured towards a solitary chair in front of his cluttered desk. 'I must apologise for the interrogation. Security is a big problem in Frankfurt. The memorial has been vandalised more than once. Even now, there are gangs in the city who don't want *us* here. We're only a charitable trust and yet racial graffiti regularly gets daubed on our walls. We have to be very careful.'

'I understand,' Charlotte replied, clearing her throat, but she didn't. How could it be, that there was still animosity towards the Jews, so long after the end of the war, and when they had suffered so much?

'So you say that we've met before?' he said thoughtfully. 'To be honest, I remember going to London many years ago, but . . .'

'Surely you remember coming to my flat? We had dinner before your train went back to Germany,' Charlotte said anxiously.

'And that's when you told me that you had met my mother?'

Charlotte nodded. She had trouble reconciling herself to the fact that this was the same sensitive young man whom she had wanted to hold in her arms when she told him how much his mother had loved him.

She peered at the photo-frame on the edge of the desk. It was David with two young children. All three had the same face of the woman who had befriended her such a long time ago at the lake.

'How did you find me?' he asked, noticing his visitor's interest in the photograph.

Charlotte fumbled for the old business card, which she produced from her bag.

'You gave me this,' she replied, handing it to David. 'I promised to try and help you,' she added quietly.

'I left Weil Richter well over twenty years ago. I'm surprised there was anyone still there who remembers me.'

'I didn't expect to find you . . .'

'What, you mean in a place like this?' David interjected. 'It's not very grand but I'm afraid it's all we can afford. I've actually been in London quite often,' he went on.

'For your charity?' Charlotte asked.

'A case was recently settled in our favour. We were able to recover a large amount of our beneficiaries' property.

Although after all the legal costs, the compensation was not as much as we would have wished for.'

Charlotte recalled Lillian making the same comment about that article she had read in *The Times*. Surely it could only have been a coincidence? She was tempted to ask David Goldstein whether it was the same case that she had read about. But he appeared distant, as if he still didn't completely believe her story.

'Frau Brown, I don't know how you think we can help you,' he said briskly.

'I needed to see you again,' Charlotte answered. 'To make up for a great injustice.'

'So you say. But I'm afraid that you are here under a misapprehension. You see, we work exclusively on recovering property stolen from the Jewish community. Any personal injustice that you say I may have suffered is quite incidental.'

'But surely you still want to find . . .'

'Frau Brown, I'm really short of time,' the man said, glancing at his watch. He then got up from behind his desk, indicating that their meeting was over.

'David, don't you remember the postcards – the photographs?'

The man's expression became more pensive and he returned to his chair.

'You brought them with you to London,' Charlotte reminded him. Knowing that she still had a lot to do to convince him, she became agitated. 'I was sitting in the same row at the auction. I quite clearly recall being captivated by Monet's use of colours that so brilliantly depicted the time of day. Then there were the Degas ballerinas and the Cezanne landscape. You said that they matched identically with the pieces being sold, that they belonged to your family.'

David Goldstein stood up and, taking out a small bunch of keys from his trouser pocket, he went over to an old iron floor-safe, tucked away in the corner of the office. He opened the heavy door and withdrew a beige folder. Returning to his desk, he took out the photographs that he had shown to Charlotte forty years previously. Methodically, he went through them, looking at each one, until he stopped at the three that Charlotte had described.

'So it really is you,' he said, his voice filled with emotion.

Charlotte, finding it impossible to hold back her own tears, delved into her handbag for a handkerchief.

'Yes, David, it's me,' she said, her voice shaking. 'Have I really changed that much?'

'I just needed to be sure,' he answered softly. 'When I didn't hear from you, I assumed that you hadn't been successful, and that we came up against the same problem.'

'I could have done more, but I was going through a difficult time. The truth is that I was only concerned with saving my job.'

'And I had become so obsessed with wanting to see justice done. That's when I gave up being an accountant. I went out on my own and started Goldstein Claims. The fact that I also happened to be a victim was no longer my main motivation. A few years ago, a London firm of solicitors contacted me. They told me that they were in possession of certain information that I might find of use.'

'But how was that possible?' Charlotte breathed.

'They probably got my name from the Interpol investigation that I instigated years ago. It made the press, which is how they managed to track me down.'

Charlotte thought about it. She now understood that the investigation into the Muller Gallery had been as a result of David Goldstein's visit to London.

'The newspapers at the time made a big thing of it,' he continued. 'I remember the headline: *Stolen Jewish Art Finds Its Way to London Auction House*. But after a while, it went quiet. It was as if all the people we were relying on to come forward, suddenly changed their mind.'

Charlotte would never forget that she herself had been placed under suspicion, and how the threat that she would be sent to prison had caused her to have a breakdown.

'Anyway, a man named James Robson mentioned that he could lead us to recover a substantial collection of art that had ended up in London. I have to say that he sounded quite ancient on the phone. At first, I thought it was a hoax.'

Charlotte gasped at hearing the name of her old solicitor. She couldn't have imagined that he was still alive.

'So what did you do?' she asked, eager to know what happened next.

'He may have been old but he was alert enough to negotiate a heavy contingency fee for himself. We had to agree, otherwise we could never have afforded to bring the action. After nearly three years, we reached a settlement last week.' It was clear by David Goldstein's expression that he was disappointed by the outcome.

'I assume it wasn't what you expected?' Charlotte said.

'The other side were people of very considerable means. They made it abundantly clear that unless we agreed to their offer, they would be prepared to let the case drag on indefinitely.'

'So they were blackmailing you,' Charlotte said angrily.

'Yes, indirectly. They knew that eventually we would run out of money.'

Charlotte recalled being in a similar situation. It was when she learned how Bernard had lost his business. Again, James Robson was involved. Hadn't he also convinced her that he had got the best possible deal for his client? What she had learned from bitter experience, was that the man only ever thought of himself.

But having established that it was David's organisation that had brought the case in London, she was certain that he was in need of a great deal more money to continue his work.

'David, I should like to make a donation to your charitable trust,' Charlotte said. She passed across the envelope containing the banker's draft that had been made out in his name.

'It's kind of you, but it's really not necessary,' the grey-haired man replied. He seemed genuinely embarrassed by the unexpected gesture.

'And now I should be leaving.' Charlotte began doing up the buttons of her coat. 'My plane leaves for London at five, and I still have to go to the hotel and collect my luggage. And I haven't even asked you about *your* family,' she said, glancing again at the photograph on the desk.

'I'm a widower. My wife died shortly after our daughter was born,' David Goldstein replied.

'I'm so sorry. It must have been very difficult for you.'

'You could say that. Then starting up on my own with no regular income was also hard.'

'How did you manage?' Again, Charlotte could feel herself overcome with emotion.

'With a number of different nannies. In the circumstances, the children grew up fairly well-adjusted. Margot, named after her grandmother, is a dancer – also like her grandmother - and Gustav, named after my father, is training to be a pilot.'

'Forgive me for prying, David, but you were still young. Weren't you tempted to get married again?'

'There were others but Marthe was the love of my life. I was always making comparisons. It would never have worked.' David sighed. 'And how about you?' he asked.

'There was one person in particular. He was a lovely man,' Charlotte said, remembering Bernard Morris.

'What happened?' David asked.

'I was foolish and never appreciated how much he loved me. Nor did I realise how much I loved him in return.'

'Can't I persuade you to let me take you to lunch, even though it is a bit late?' David said unexpectedly. 'After all, if I remember correctly, it *is* my turn.'

'I really can't,' Charlotte smiled regretfully.

'Well, at least allow me to call you a taxi.'

'David, if you don't mind, I'd prefer to walk.'

'An independent woman. I like that,' he grinned, looking young again.

'And a little too old for you, I'm afraid,' she riposted. Then she got up, saying, 'This time, if you let me, I will remain in contact. My address is inside the envelope.'

'In that case, you had better take one of these.' With a flourish, he produced a new business card from his wallet.

They both laughed.

David politely accompanied his visitor to the lift. When she was out of sight, he returned to his office, picked up the envelope and put it in the drawer of his desk without opening it.

Charlotte left the building and followed the same route back to the Börneplatz. When she arrived at the monument, she paused and walked slowly past the inscriptions on the blocks, stopping when she reached the letter G. There, she found what she was looking for: the names of the Goldstein family. For a long while she stood, head bowed in respect.

Her thoughts now were not with David but with his mother Margot, whom she had known for too brief a time. Today, and at last, Charlotte hoped she had shown her contrition for the loss they had all suffered.

Epilogue

Two years later

Charlotte glanced at the large, carefully packaged item with the Frankfurt postmark that had been left in the storeroom behind the porter's desk. It had arrived at the block of flats in St John's Wood while she was out at her art class. What could it be?

At first, David had insisted on returning her donation. He rang and said that it was impossible for him to accept such a large sum, and for weeks he had refused to bank it. He finally agreed to utilise the funds to continue with his work bringing restitution to more Jewish victims identified by his charity.

After that, more than a year went by without any contact. Then, a few weeks ago, he had telephoned Charlotte with the news that he had finally recovered his own family's art collection from Argentina. According to the press reports, a group of wealthy individuals of German extraction had been involved in supplying stolen works of art to major auction houses in London and New York. They had then arranged to buy them back under a different name as laundered items.

'Charlotte, dear, aren't you curious to see what it is?'

Lillian asked, gazing at the package, which was now resting against the fireplace. She and Allen had dropped in for a quick visit and were keen for her to open it.

'It might be something valuable,' the American added. 'My hunch is that it's a painting.'

'Allen, darling, don't push Charlotte. She'll open it when she's ready.'

'Married for five minutes and she's already telling me what to do,' the smartly dressed man quipped.

'I wouldn't exactly call our second anniversary five minutes,' Lillian retorted sternly.

'I haven't missed it, have I?' Allen replied, looking horrified.

Lillian gave Charlotte a sideways glance as if to say that he was unlikely to forget again.

'I think you make an ideal couple,' Charlotte beamed. 'And so, might I add, do Elizabeth and Anthony.'

'I seem to have convinced everyone apart from my wife,' Allen said, winking at Charlotte, who had overcome her initial dislike and now accepted him.

'So, are you going to leave it unwrapped or are we going to see what's inside?' he added restlessly.

'All right, all right – I give in.' Charlotte got up from the sofa, went into the kitchen and returned carrying a knife with a retractable blade.

'Shall we let Allen do the honours? It'll make him feel useful,' Lillian said affectionately.

Charlotte handed the implement to the man, who began deftly and very, very carefully cutting away at the thick folds of packaging.

'I'll say one thing,' he commented to the two women watching him, 'whoever packed this little beauty knew what he was doing.' He handed an envelope that he found inside to Charlotte. She opened it and saw just one sentence on a card:

A single act of kindness can transform darkness into light.

And the ray of light that burst through the remaining layer of covering showed that they were in possession of something very special indeed. When it was finally unwrapped, the American lifted up the painting and placed it with awe on the marble mantelpiece.

Charlotte stood arm-in-arm with her dear friend Lillian, both mesmerised by the reflection of brightly coloured flowers floating on the still pond under a sky of unforgettable blue. It took them only a moment to register that they were staring at one of Monet's *Water Lilies*.

NADINE
John Steinberg

London 1974 - and Peter Greenberg is riding high. Thanks to his magic touch, every play he puts on in Theatreland is a hit and the money is rolling in. Then one day, everything changes. Greenberg falls head over heels in love.

The beautiful Paris-born dancer who catches his eye is Nadine - a major star in the making. Like Greenberg, the young dancer too is in love - but with someone else. The eternal triangle is complicated by the birth of a child, and by tragic secrets that go back before World War Two. Little by little, these secrets reveal themselves in a drama that out-performs anything on the West End stage or Broadway.

Nadine is a poignant story of unrequited love, a love that will one day be returned – and in a most unexpected way . . .

ISBN 978-1-912014-28-6   £9.99

Lightning Source UK Ltd.
Milton Keynes UK
UKHW040713211219
355800UK00001B/26/P